Abigail's Journey

The Catskills Saga, Volume 1

Jean Joachim and Michael Magness

Published by Moonlight Books, 2020.

Abigail's Journey
Copyright © 2020 Jean C. Joachim
Edited by Katherine Tate
Proofreader – Renee Waring
Cover design – Dawne Dominique

PUBLISHER
Moonlight Books

Dedication

To Karen Wenderoff and Larry Joachim

Thank you for your patience and support during the creation of this book, and for the ideas you so generously shared with us.

Chapter One

M *ay 1786*
"Pack up and get out, Chesney. I'm moving in."

No sooner were the words out of the scoundrel's mouth than George Chesney hit him square on the jaw. The man exploded in rage and landed two on George before bystanders pulled him away. Chesney had never been much for fighting to settle a dispute. However, when the welfare of his beloved family hung in the balance, he'd gladly trade fisticuffs with the devil himself.

Leaving the Danbury Inn, he wiped the blood off his nose. Tramping through town, he breathed deeply. The bell of the town crier stopped him.

"Seven o'clock and all is well."

He compressed his lips together as bitterness soured his mouth. It might be seven o'clock, but all was not well, not for the Chesney family. Old Luke Morton had gambled away the deed to their farm. He had been Morton's tenant, working the farm for the past ten years. He figured to own it outright in another five. Luke's one whiskey too many and his losing hand at cards smashed George's dream to bits.

Laughing in his face, the winner had dashed any hope of staying to farm the land. So, he'd lashed out at the man who'd threatened his future but had come out the worse for it in the end.

Fear spiked in George's chest, slowing his pace. For once, he dreaded returning home. Since he was late, his beautiful wife would have kept a plate of dinner aside for him. She'd be wondering where he was. How could he tell her Morton didn't own their farm anymore and they had to pack up and leave?

As he struggled to find words, his heartbeat sped up. Sweat poured off his forehead and soaked his shirt. He wiped his face with his sleeve and shivered in the chilly May wind under the cold light of a full moon. The sweet smell of freshly turned earth met his nose. Crops were already planted, but he'd not be around to harvest them. Where would they go? Farming was all he knew. How would he make a living and feed his family?

It didn't help that his face had swelled and the flesh around his eye throbbed. Gently, he fingered his nose and flinched in pain. He grew angry. It wasn't his fault Morton was an old, drunken fool.

Seemed like bad luck had dogged his steps lately. They'd lost a goat through a hole in the fence. Fox killed two chickens. He figured it was timing. He'd had the best fortune in the world to win lovely Abigail's hand. And the three wonderful children she'd given him had brought him much joy. Now he was thirty-six years old, maybe his luck had turned.

As he drew near to the little farmhouse he'd called home, emotion choked him. How could he tell his family they'd have to leave the life they loved—the only life they knew?

Smoke curled up from the chimney and the aroma of burning logs drifted his way. Yep, his son, Samuel, had remembered to bring in wood. He could almost taste his wife's fine stew and smell the freshly baked bread his daughter, Sarah, had put up in the afternoon.

George directed his gaze upward and uttered a prayer as he approached his home. He stopped halfway up the path to swallow hard and wipe his cheek. The wetness wasn't blood, but tears. He took a deep, shuddering breath. No nice way to break such bad news. They were losing their home—he'd come right out with it.

He pushed the door open.

"George! I'm so glad you're home. Where were you? We were worried."

Speech eluded him. He stood, solid, feet spread slightly, and reached for words that wouldn't come. His gaze hopped from his wife to each of his children in turn. They stopped what they were doing. She approached and put her hand on his arm.

The smile faded from her face. "You're bleeding. What happened? Are you all right?"

He shook his head. "No, I'm not. And nothing is going to be all right again for a very long time."

Her eyes widened. "What?"

"Sarah, put Lizzy to bed then come back. You and Sam are old enough to hear the truth." He ran his palm over his face then sighed, sinking into a chair. His wife picked up a dish towel, removed a plate from the warming oven and placed it on the table in front of him.

"Hungry?" She raised her gaze to his.

"Not really." But the aroma of the stew set his mouth to watering.

"Eat. Whatever it is will wait." She poured a cup of tea for him and one for herself.

"You deserve better," he mumbled, picking up his fork.

"Better?"

"Better than me."

"Hush, George Chesney! I don't know what happened today, but I married the finest man in all of Danbury. And don't you dare disagree with me." The fire in her eyes, and her high spirit turned her cheeks a becoming rosy shade.

"If you aren't the prettiest woman in all of Connecticut, I don't know who is." He leaned over to plant a gentle kiss on her lips then took her hand and raised it to his. "And you make the best stew in God's creation."

His daughter returned. She joined Samuel on a bench across from their parents. Sarah fiddled with her long hair, while Sam tried to twirl a penny on its end.

"What is it, Papa?" her young voice squeaked. The children raised their gazes to meet his.

He poured out the story. Shame filled him to admit he'd struck the first blow and yet had still come out the worse for the battle. When he finished, silence blanketed the room. The only sound was the scraping of his spoon against the plate as he finished the last drop of gravy.

"Don't worry. We'll be all right," she said.

"How, Mama? How?" The boy's eyes filled with fear.

"Your mother's right. We'll be all right. Go on to bed now. We need you to be ready to help at sunrise." He stood.

The children hugged him and left the room. When he turned around, Abigail fisted his shirt and pulled him toward her. Gently, she cleansed his face then brushed her fingers through his hair.

He drew her into his embrace. "I'm so sorry."

"Stop apologizing. It's not your fault."

"We'll manage."

"Yes. We will. "Get some rest. You look all in."

He trudged off to their room. "You coming?"

"As soon as I clean up a bit."

WHEN THE DOOR TO THEIR room closed and Abby was alone, she bit her lip. She made quick work of the last dish, dried it, and put it away. Picking up her shawl, she headed for the window, where she stared up at the moon.

Tears stung her eyes. Panic rose slowly in her chest.

"No! I will not lose faith." She wrapped the garment around her shoulders.

Startled by the sound of footsteps, she glanced over her shoulder. George came up behind her. She spun around to face him. Her gaze searched his sad, dark eyes. She saw pain and strength. Tears burst forth as she flung herself into his arms. He held her close, patting her and uttering soft words.

When she could speak, she stepped away. "How could this happen to us?"

"I don't know how, but what's done is done. We need to figure out what to do now."

"How much do we have saved?"

"Not enough to buy another farm." He sighed, lowering himself to a chair, then patted his thigh. She lowered herself onto his lap.

"Do you have an idea?"

"First, we need to sell everything we can. The farm equipment. Anything you don't need in the house. We can raise money and lighten our load. Moving will be easier if we don't have anything more than we need."

"True. I have a little money saved up from my sewing."

He put his hand on hers. "You keep it. You've earned it. Save it for fabric for new dresses for you and Sarah."

"We can't afford new dresses now."

"We'll see how much we can raise. Tomorrow, I'll go into town. Check with the newspaper. Maybe there's a small farm for sale or someone looking for a new tenant. And I'll ask them to put out a notice of our sale."

Pain shot through her. "We have to sell everything?"

"Yep." He yawned. "Come to bed."

They rose and entered the bedroom.

"As long as we're together, we'll be all right. I believe it to be true." She hugged him.

He cupped her cheek before slowly shedding his clothes and climbing into bed.

She stripped down to her shift and slipped in next to him. Exhaustion pulled at her but worry left her jittery. "You have always talked about farming. You love the soil."

"Even if we could find another farm, we couldn't afford it. Since the war, land in Connecticut has been going fast. Prices rising daily..."

"Do we have to leave Danbury?" She chewed her lip.

"I don't know."

"What about my sister? Can we ask her for help?"

"We can solve this on our own. I'll not go begging to Wolcotts." In the dim light from the moon, his jaw tightened.

"I know they'd help us. This wasn't your fault."

"No. The Wolcotts didn't want you to marry me. Maybe they were right."

"They were wrong." She snuggled closer, resting her head on his bare shoulder. He closed his arm about her. Before long, he snored softly. Exhaustion seeped deeper into her bones. She yawned twice, but still couldn't sleep. Fear kept her awake. She tossed and wrestled with the covers, waking her husband.

"What's wrong?" He rubbed his eyes and yawned.

"I don't want to leave Danbury." She sucked on her lower lip.

He took her in his arms, holding her to his chest. "Don't worry. I'll find a way. Trust me."

"I always have." She rested her palm on his bare skin and sighed.

He stroked her. The warmth of his body relaxed her. Sweating, he rolled over. His soft snore met her ears. Still she lay awake, staring at the ceiling. She recalled a long-ago conversation with her mother.

"George Chesney? Why would you want to marry him? He's a tenant farmer."

"He's a good man."

"So's the preacher, but you wouldn't want to be a preacher's wife, would you? The wife of a tenant farmer? Abigail, you're a Wolcott, meant for a better life."

"*I love him.*"

"*Pish tush. Marriage isn't about love. It's about a life. What kind of life will you have living on a farm? Your sister married a doctor. She lives in town, has a lovely home and a husband without dirt under his nails.*"

"*I'm going to marry him, Mother.*"

"*Foolish girl.*"

Had she been foolish? Seventeen happy years belied her mother's words.

I have to have faith. He has never let me down. He won't this time, either. Rolling onto her side, she watched her handsome husband. Slipping her arm around his waist, she snuggled up to his strong back, closed her eyes, and gave in to sleep.

GEORGE AND ABIGAIL awoke right before the sun. She prepared tea for their morning ritual of welcoming a new day together. They'd stand, side-by-side in the doorway, sipping hot tea and watching the sun rise. As he slid his arm around his wife's waist, pulling her closer, his brow furrowed.

"Breakfast, then morning chores." She rested against him.

"Then off to town." He lifted his cup.

When the last drop was gone, he kissed his wife and washed up. She woke the children with a gentle shake. Yawning, Sarah ambled into the kitchen to prepare the first meal of the day—bread, eggs, and milk.

"Sarah, you're a fine baker." George took the last bite of his first slice.

"What are we going to do?" Sam slathered butter on two pieces.

"You and your sister are going to do your chores. I'm going into town." He finished his milk, licked his lips, then rose from the table. "I hope to have good news when I return."

Abby raised her gaze to his.

"Don't fret. We'll be all right." He shrugged his jacket on and opened the door. "I don't know when I'll be back."

"We'll save dinner for you." She followed him to the door.

He leaned down to kiss her, ruffled little Lizzy's hair, smiled at Sarah, and strode off toward the barn. Within an hour, Sam joined him.

"I'll milk Sadie, Dad." Sam picked up a milking stool and approached one of their two cows.

"Good. I'll go to town." George patted the boy's shoulder. He had shot up in the last year or so and was almost as tall as his father.

George walked alone along the bumpy, dirt road to Danbury. What opportunity might he find in town? When he arrived, he beelined straight for the newspaper office. Nathanial Smith, the editor, greeted him.

"Morning, Nate."

"Heard about last night, George. Thought you might be stopping by."

George looked at the farms-for-sale advertisements but, as expected, all were too expensive. There were no tenant farms available. The only jobs listed in the newspaper were for apprentices. Those didn't pay enough to feed his family.

Discouraged, he wandered to the general store. Folks sometimes told the proprietor, John Ludlow, when they were selling their land.

"Sorry. Nothing today," said John. "Why don't you look at the post office notices? Sometimes, people put up land for sale signs there."

"Thanks, I will." He approached the counter in the store that served as the local post office. He had forgotten about the for sale and help wanted notices posted on a board next to the post office section until he set eyes on them.

For sale, fine cow. Two dollars silver

Cast iron pots and pans, cheap.

He found nothing and turned to go.

"George? George Chesney?"

He stopped. Glancing over his shoulder he spotted the postmaster behind the counter. "Hi, Cal."

"Got a letter for you. Arrived some days ago."

"Me? A letter?"

"Yep. Wait a moment." The postmaster returned a minute later, waving a worn square of paper. "Personal like."

"Thanks." He read his mother's address in the corner. He hadn't had a letter from her in ages. Easing himself down on a bench in the town square, he opened the missive.

Dear George,

It is with a heavy heart I write you this sad news. Last month, your father had an accident. Daniel Rhodes did what he could, but Papa passed on to the other world. I've tried to carry on, running the inn by myself. But I'm not doing too good. I need help. I know you love your farm, but if you and your family could come to Fitch's Eddy, I could use the help. I can offer you a half-partnership in the boarding house. Then you'll own it, too.

I hope you, Abigail, and the children are all well. Please write and tell me you'll save The Chesney Inn.

Your loving mother,

Martha

George's eyes watered. His father had been a good man. Sorrow gathered in his chest. Gone too soon. He never had a chance for a final farewell, and his father had never known his grandchildren. He blinked away tears, folded the letter, slipped it in his pocket, and sat back, absorbing the news.

Maybe this was the best way to save his family. At least he wouldn't be beholden to a Wolcott or anyone else. He'd never have to fear losing the land under his feet. Moving to Fitch's Eddy would be a huge upheaval in their lives. Abigail would have to leave her sister.

What did he know about running an inn? Nothing. But his mother would teach him. Hope sprang forth inside him where there had been none only a few minutes ago.

He pushed to his feet and hurried home. Picking up his pace, he'd make it in time for dinner. Could he get his wife to agree to travel far from Danbury and take a chance on a new life?

"We'd own half. My mother would help. Enough space for all of us. Maybe a garden, too? Maybe we could save up and buy a farm there?" As many benefits as he could cite, he couldn't ignore the negative aspects.

"No friends. No family except Ma. Do they have a school there? What if Ma and Abby don't get along? Will Sam and Sarah find new friends? Little Lizzy could be happy anywhere as long as she had her mother around."

He couldn't escape the one deciding factor, they had no other option. It was move to Fitch's Eddy or live in the woods on whatever they could catch. Maybe starve.

Abby was a reasonable woman. She knew they had little choice. Glancing at the sky, he uttered a prayer.

Rounding the final bend, he spotted his little house. Pain stabbed him for a moment at the thought of leaving it. They had been so happy here. His amazing wife, cozy little family, and a decent piece of land. Could any man want more?

ABBY STIRRED THE SOUP.

"You just did that, Ma." Sarah took the spoon out of her mother's hand. "You feelin' okay?"

"Fine. I'm fine." She wouldn't let on she was so far from fine she didn't think she'd ever remember how it felt to be fine.

George had gone to town to look for a cheap piece of land or a job. As time wore on, her nerves kicked up. Waiting and worrying upset her stomach. Preoccupied, she'd burned an onion but dumped it in the soup anyway. Chores got only half her attention.

She bit her lip. Unable to avoid the biggest question, the one most terrifying, she had to ask herself. What if he could find neither land nor job? Where would they go? What would they do?

Standing by the soup kettle, she looked around their house. Her gaze stopped on the pretty calico print curtains hanging in the window. She'd fashioned them out of a large tablecloth, discarded by a fancy woman in town. Abby had snatched the material up, washed it, and sewn the window coverings, brightening the room.

Her touches here and there had created a home. The small wooden figures of birds George and Sam had carved during the winter months perched proudly by the window. The china teapot handed down to her by her parents had been a touch of fancy when they took their tea.

This was her home. Surely, she'd lose it and have to move on, but to what? Something better? Or something much worse? Dread sent a shiver through her. She kept her thoughts to herself to avoid upsetting her children. By the expressions on their faces, they were wrestling with the same fears.

Where the devil was her husband? What was taking so long? Was it something good? Must be, or he'd have been home by now. Peering out the window, she spied his figure coming up the path. Grabbing her shawl, she yanked open the door and fairly flew down to meet him, her feet barely touching the ground.

"George! George!" she called and waved her arms.

She crashed into him, almost knocking him down. He steadied her in his embrace. Her gaze searched his face, but it was a mask.

"Well? Did you find a farm or a job?"

"We're leaving, Abby."

"Leaving the farm?"

"Leaving Danbury. In one week, we'll be hitched to a small wagon train and headed for Fitch's Eddy."

"Fitch's Eddy?"

He smoothed her hair with his palm. "Yes."

Tears gathered in her eyes as she tried to understand his words. "Why?"

He fished the worn letter from his pocket. "I didn't find a farm or a job, but I did get this."

She rushed through the letter then returned to the beginning to read it again, slowly.

"Your father?" She looked up.

His eyes misted. "Gone."

"I'm so sorry." She cupped his cheek.

"This misfortune may be our salvation." He rested his palm on her shoulder.

"We have to leave?"

He drew her to him, whispering as he held her. "I know it means leaving your sister. But my mother needs us, and we need her. We'll be half owners. No more tenants. No more beholden to strangers. Besides, running the place won't take as much time as the farm. You might have a spare moment to devote to your sewing."

She rested her head on his shoulder. "You always find the silver lining, don't you?"

"I try, honey, I try."

"I love you." She tightened her arms around him.

"I love you, too. At least we'll be together. And I'll be glad to see my mother again."

"You must miss her." She leaned away, her gaze connecting with his. "Tell me what we have to do tonight. After the children are in bed."

"I will."

Clinging to each other, they strolled toward home. Abby stuffed down her fears. She had a hundred questions. He would answer them all, he always did, and she recalled how he often used their intimate time together to quell her fears.

"What if your mother doesn't like me?"

"Who wouldn't like you?" His face broke into a warm grin.

Peering up into his dark eyes, she calmed. In their years together, he'd never let her down.

"You always know what to say, don't you? We start a new chapter of our life?" She raised her eyebrows.

He gave her waist a quick squeeze before opening the door. She stopped, grasping his forearm. He peered down at her. "Maybe the best chapter is yet to unfold."

Chapter Two

June - Moving day

"Sam, take the chest to the wagon. Sarah, bring Lizzy outside." George barked orders.

Abby stood in the doorway, her hands fisted, resting on her hips. "Could you come in for a minute?" she called to her husband.

He glanced up and strode toward the house. She stood aside to let him pass.

"What is it, dear? We've so much to do." He cupped her cheek.

She pointed to a wrapped package sitting in an open trunk. "What's that?"

"Oh, I'd forgotten." He bent down and picked up the package.

"Forgotten what?" She eased closer to stand next to him.

"It's a present I bought you."

"A present?"

"Open it."

She carefully untied the thin leather strap and pushed away the covering to reveal yards and yards of pure-white silk, folded neatly.

She sucked in air. "Oh, George! It's beautiful!" She wiped her hands on her apron before fingering the material. Sunlight streamed in through the window, making the fabric sparkle as if it had an inner light of its own. She ran her fingers lightly over the rich cloth.

"I thought you could make a dress for yourself. I saw it in the general store. A woman was buying it. And all I could think of was how beautiful you would look wearing a dress made from this fabric."

"That's the sweetest thing."

"It's special. Different. Just the way you are to me, my sweet." He pulled her close to kiss her.

She wrapped her arms around his neck.

The children had congregated by the front door, listening.

George broke, keeping his wife close and stroking her long honey gold hair. "It was supposed to be your Christmas present."

"This is too fine for a farmer's wife."

He smiled. "Perhaps it's good, then, that you won't be a farmer's wife for long. Soon, you'll be an innkeeper's wife."

"But surely we can't afford this?"

"I traded for it. I saw it at McIntire's General Store four months ago. It was expensive. But every time I went in there, I saw it. One day, Mac asked me if I'd like to have it."

She listened, mesmerized, along with the children.

"I asked him what he'd take for it. He said, since his wife was having another baby, they could use another goat."

"A goat? You gave him one of our goats?"

"Nelly had just given birth. I figured we could part with one."

"You gave him Nelly's baby?"

"No, I gave him Fanny."

"The one you said got away?" Her eyes widened.

He stared at his hands, his face coloring. "I know. I lied. I admit it. But it was for a good reason." At her gasp, he looked up. "I've never seen a finer silk on any lady, no matter how rich."

She trailed her fingertips over the fabric. "True."

"Nothing's too good for you, honey. Maybe there's enough for two dresses, even three, if one's very small?"

Smiling, she raised her gaze to his and cupped his cheek.

"It's June, but Merry Christmas, Abigail." He kissed her.

Emotion caught in her throat. She couldn't speak. She picked up the package as tenderly as if it were a newborn babe. She stroked it once and stopped. "My hands are dirty." She returned the fabric to the wrapper. "You're full of surprises."

"Forgiven?" He cocked an eyebrow.

"Forgive him, Mama!" Sarah said.

"It was for a good reason," Sam put in.

She laughed. "Forgiven. And thank you. It's beautiful!" She handed the present to Sarah. "Find a safe place for this in the wagon. Lizzy, go with your sister."

"Abigail?"

A female voice caught her ear, and she raised her gaze. Her sister, Clarissa, approached, in her hands, a small basket.

"I came to say goodbye."

Her words cut straight to her heart. And when Clarissa got close enough, Abby reached out. The sisters hugged.

"Oh, Clarissa. How can I leave my home in Danbury?"

They parted, each reaching in a pocket to produce a handkerchief. Her heart pounded.

"You can and you will, dear sister." Kindness in her eyes belied the harsh words.

"I'll miss you, Clarissa."

"And I you. But life goes on. We do what we must, even if we don't like it." But her sister didn't meet her gaze.

Abby smiled "You sound just like Papa."

Clarissa raised her chin and made eye contact. "I brought you this." She handed the basket to her.

Abby pushed the cloth aside. Inside lay a portion of dried meat, a dozen peppermint sticks, and a small box. She fingered the worn package. "What's this?"

"Open it! Mama gave me two before she passed. One of each grandmother. This one is of Papa's mother. You were her favorite."

Gently, Abby lifted the cover. Inside lay a beautiful cameo.

"I have Mama's mother." Clarissa touched the cameo pinned to her dress.

"It's beautiful. Yes, she was my favorite, too." She picked up the blue-and-white brooch.

"When you wear it, think of me." Her sister's eyes misted.

"I will. I will. Help me." She took the heirloom out of the box, and Clarissa pinned it on.

"There. Now you're one of us. A Wolcott. Still my family, even when you're far away."

Abby touched the pin. "Thank you so much. Yes, I will think of you. Always."

The women embraced. Tears slipped from Abby's eyes as she closed them. When they separated, Clarissa spoke first.

"Be safe. Take care. Always remember where you came from and know you'll always have a home with me in Danbury—should you ever need it. Godspeed."

She kissed her sister's cheek and touched her hand. Clarissa turned to leave. *Will I ever see her again?*

AFTER LOADING EVERY possible thing that would fit in the wagon, George and Sam hitched the team of oxen and began their journey.

"We're meeting up with the others at Round Hill Crossing." He took hold of the bridle and led the oxen to the rendezvous. The morning sun painted the sky pink and purple. He loosened the kerchief tied around his neck to soak up sweat.

"Gonna be a hot one, Dad?"

He glanced up, "I reckon so, son."

George kept his eye on the road ahead looking for the other wagons. Before long, he spied them in the distance and called over his shoulder to his wife. "There they are!" He pointed.

Sam waved to the strangers in the distance. As they drew closer, George made out two men and a woman. Maybe there were young'uns inside?

A man, who appeared to be in his twenties, jumped down from the wagon and raced to them, startling the oxen.

"Whoa, Spirit. Easy, Nellie." George placed a calming hand on the animal.

"Sorry, sorry. I'm Josiah Quint." He extended his hand. "You must be George Chesney?"

"I am. This is my son, Sam. My youngest is inside. The other womenfolk are right behind the wagon."

"Excellent. I'm traveling with my brother and his family. Up ahead." The dark-haired young man nodded.

"We're going all the way to Pennsylvania. Where are you headed?"

George offered a half smile to the enthusiastic Josiah. His excitement about the trip amused him. What did this youth know of hardship? He could teach him a thing or two about bad luck and hard times.

While his family had to take this trip, George had kept his worries about the perils of the journey to himself. Last thing he needed was to make his family more apprehensive. Regrets, tearful partings, and anger at being uprooted had soured Sarah and Sam's moods. Josiah's friendliness put a smile on Sam's face, which had worn a perpetual frown since he'd heard they were leaving.

The other man from the wagon ahead joined them.

"Jeremiah Quint." He offered his hand.

"George Chesney." They shook.

"I see you've met my brother?"

"Nice young man," George said.

"And he's strong. He'll help with the wagons."

"Fine." George glanced up. "Sun's rising fast. We'd best be underway. I'd like to get some distance in before the heat of the day."

"Right. Josiah, tether Mr. Chesney's oxen to the back of our wagon." Jeremiah climbed onto the front seat.

While the men worked, Abigail strolled to the wagon ahead. Sarah picked up Lizzy and followed her mother.

"I'm Abigail Chesney, George's wife." She stopped at the Quint wagon.

"Susanna Quint. Good to meet you. It's good to have another family along."

"Yes, indeed. This is Sarah and my youngest, Lizzy."

"My son and daughter are sleeping."

"Don't disturb them," Abby said, lowering her voice. She glanced at the men.

"Looks like we're ready to move on." She raised her hand in a brief wave to her husband and returned to the rear of the wagon. Still holding her little sister, Sarah joined her mother.

Jeremiah Quint stood up and signaled for them to proceed.

"Ready!" George called, urging his oxen forward. He glanced at Sam, pleased to see his son paying attention, keeping a sharp eye on his father. Sam was a quiet one, but he took in everything, picked up things fast and carried responsibility well for a boy his age. When he looked at him, George's heart swelled with pride. No finer lad lived in all of Connecticut.

Father and son kept the long tether line loose and guided the oxen as the wagon bumped and lurched along the rutted path toward their new life. Relieved at not making the trip alone and pleased to see two friendly strong men part of the group, he relaxed.

Of course, he couldn't keep Mother Nature at bay. Who knew what disasters lay ahead? But with the help of the other families, they'd make it through. He'd yet to meet those occupying the lead wagon. He followed the Quints but kept checking the terrain and the sun to make sure the two wagons didn't wander off in the wrong direction.

"WHO IS THAT MAN, MAMA?" Sarah asked.

"I don't know his name. He's from Mrs. Quint's wagon."

Sarah bowed her head, staring at the ground in front of her as she marched along behind. Lizzy peeked out from the rear of the wagon and waved.

"Buck up, Sarah. We have too long a distance to travel to be sad all the time. Maybe something good will be waiting for us in Fitch's Eddy."

"I don't think so."

Abby hugged her daughter. Then the two women struck a reasonable pace, staying a short distance behind the wagon. She hiked her skirt up on the sides, tucking it into her waistband to make walking easier. Sarah followed her mother's lead.

"When will we get there, Mama?" Sarah bent to pick a buttercup.

"I don't know." She held her hand to her forehead to shield her eyes from the sun.

"Why did we have to go?"

"Because Mr. Morton was stupid and lost our farm. Life will be better in Fitch's Eddy. You'll meet your grandmother. And we'll have our own place." She wiped her forehead with her sleeve.

"Our own house?"

"It belongs to Daddy's mother, but we'll have our own rooms."

"Good. What's Grandma like?" Sarah picked the leaves off the buttercups.

"I don't know. I've never met her. Please stop asking questions for a little bit." Abby's mind whirled with her own worries. She glanced at the sky. The sun was straight up, bearing down on them.

"I'm hot, Mama. Can we stop and rest?"

"Your father will pull up when he can. Yes, it is hot. You'll have to make do." Her head ached from the heat. She breathed in the dry smell of parched earth, much in need of rain.

When they had been traveling for three hours, they got the call to halt from the wagon ahead.

"Pull up!" Jeremiah Quint hollered.

"Pull up!" George echoed.

The wagon stopped, and Sarah and her mother sank to the ground in its shade. George joined them.

"Everyone all right?" He offered his hand to his wife.

"We need a rest." Abby stood up.

"We all do. There's a spring up ahead. We'll water the oxen..."

"And ourselves. Come, Sarah." She extended her hand. "Water."

Lizzy slept in the wagon while the rest of the Chesney family made their way to the spring. Susanna and her brood were already there. Her little boy, who Abby guessed to be about three, splashed in the water, dousing his sister, who screamed.

"Sam, fetch the goatskin sacks," Abby shouted.

The boy climbed into the wagon. She splashed cool water on her face, neck, and arms. Raising her skirt, she shed her shoes and waded knee deep in the spring. Sitting on the bank, she closed her eyes and sighed. Sarah did the same.

After Sam dropped off the sacks, he met up with his father and guided the oxen to the water. While the animals drank, the men doused themselves, dunking their heads in the stream and soaking their neckerchiefs completely before tying them back on.

George gazed at the sky. "Sun's moved west. We have a while before dark." The oxen lifted their heads. "Let's get on the trail. We can still make good time, Sam."

Abby and Sarah tied wet cotton scarves around their necks, shoved their feet into their shoes, and hauled full water bags to the wagon.

Lizzy sat up. "Water."

"Here, drink." Abby held up a goatskin bag to her child. When she was done, the wagon lurched forward. Lizzy fell on a bed of clothing and a straw mattress, giggling.

Conserving their energy, the Chesney family trudged on in silence. As the small wagon train pulled forward the only sound was the thump of the big wheels over rocks and earth rutted by rain. An occasional wail from the Quint wagon put a brief smile on Abby's face. Of course, the little boy would be teasing his sister, like Sam used to do to Sarah.

As the sun slowly dipped west, the wagon train slowed. Before the sun disappeared and the sky painted a picture of bright orange and pink, the men had to find food.

"Halt!" hollered Jeremiah Quint.

"Halt!" echoed George.

Abby uttered a prayer of thanks to have the day over. "We're making camp." she said to Sarah. "Get Lizzy. We need to gather firewood."

While Josiah and Sam took their muskets to the woods to hunt for dinner, George took the oxen to a stream. Abby, Sarah, and Lizzy gathered twigs and sticks for kindling.

In a clearing away from the wagons, the families sat around a small fire. They ate fresh caught rabbit, bread, dried fruit, and vegetables. Susanna cradled a sleepy little boy in her lap. Her daughter, who appeared to be about six, stayed close by her mother's side.

George sidled up to his wife. She scooted down the log she sat on, making room for him. They exchanged a loving glance before turning their attention to their family. After supper, Susanna started a round of "Yankee Doodle." Her melodious voice cheered Abby, who joined in. By the third time, Sarah and Sam knew the words and they sang, too.

Abby bedded Lizzy and Sarah down in the wagon for the night. Sam slid under the wagon, where he'd sleep next to his father and their musket. Abby joined George, watching the flames from the campfire light up his face. The Quint family had retired to their wagon.

"I'll refill these and be right back." George disappeared in the dark as he ambled toward the stream.

Sitting alone in the cool night air, Abby shook as a chill stole up her spine, but it wasn't from cold air—something or someone was nearby. A rustle in the brush caught her attention. Although she couldn't hear footfalls, a low snarl froze her to the spot. Too terrified to look, but afraid not to, she turned her head, slowly to the left.

Something crept through the darkness. She sensed it drawing closer.

"Don't move!" George warned, his voice low and urgent.

To stay as still as possible, she hugged her knees to her chest. Out of the corner of her eye, she spied a quick movement as something lunged toward her. She jumped at the sound of the shot. Something fell and lay still not five feet from her. He reloaded and shot again.

George appeared out of the darkness, holding the gun. "You all right?"

Still filled with fear, all she could do was nod. He sat next to her, wrapping her in his embrace. "Mountain lion."

She dared to glance at the shadowed figure lying still on the ground.

"I got him."

"Thank God!" Trembling, she clung to her husband. He stroked her back.

"It's okay now, sweetheart. Guess we'd better get to bed." He rose, gripping the musket.

She stood on shaky legs, her knees like jelly. He gripped her around the waist and half carried her to the wagon. She flung her arms around his neck and buried her face in his chest.

"You're still scared?"

"I am."

"I'll be right under the wagon. Sam, too. Don't worry. Nothing can harm you as long as we're here."

"I love you," she murmured

He chuckled. "I love you, too."

He lifted her and set her inside. She leaned out to give him a long, grateful kiss.

Grinning, he whispered, "Maybe another mountain lion will come along tomorrow night?"

She gave his shoulder a playful shove. "George Chesney. You don't need a mountain lion to get a kiss from me."

"Is that so? Well..." He leaned in and stole another one before she could object.

She giggled. "Good night. Thank you for saving me."

"Good night, my sweet Abigail."

Chapter Three

A *week later...*
"I reckon in three more days we'll get to Cold Spring."
Jeremiah spoke with the faintest twinge of hope in his voice.

George glanced up at the sky. "Weather's held pretty good up until now. But it looks like it might be changing."

He furrowed his brow as he gazed at thickening clouds, each one darker than the one before.

"Rain coming. You can smell it in the air." Josiah joined the two men.

A lowing sound from the oxen captured their attention. "Even they know it." George took a swig of water from a goatskin bag.

"How long do you think we have before it breaks?" Josiah asked.

The men examined the sky one more time.

"Maybe an hour?" Jeremiah answered.

"Maybe less. Best be moving along." George turned toward the oxen.

"Josiah, scout out a clearing where we can make camp until this blows over."

The young man ran ahead.

"Best prepare the women," Jeremiah muttered.

The wagon train arrived at the clearing as scattered raindrops fell. The family piled into the wagon to wait out the storm.

A sudden sharp crack of thunder broke through the low hum of voices, making the children jump. Lizzy burst into tears and crawled into her mother's lap. Sarah snuggled closer, too. Sam glued himself to his father.

The gentle rainfall soon became an angry, pelting sheet of water. Though the front flap was down, wind blew wetness inside the open section of the wagon. Despite it being June, the Chesney family huddled together, shivering.

"Papa tell us a story. Please," Sarah begged.

"Your mother is a better storyteller. Abby?"

His gaze connected with hers, pleading for her to provide a distraction for their children.

"Well, have you heard about Balboa, the boy who cried wolf?"

The children shook their heads.

"I'll tell you his story."

Within minutes, she had their full attention. While the storm raged outside, the Chesney family, wrapped in blankets, sat quietly, listening as Abigail wove the tale. She'd even captivated their father. She loved how he became like one of the children, hanging on her every word.

When she finished, Sarah piped up. "Tell another one, Mama."

As the weather still hadn't cleared, she launched into one about a fox. By the time she finished, the storm had passed and only the sound of crickets filled the air. All the Chesneys settled down for the night in the wagon, because the ground was too muddy.

The children slipped into slumber quickly. George cupped his wife's cheek and kissed her.

"Well done. I didn't know you knew so many stories," he whispered.

"A woman has to have some mystery left for her husband." She shot him a mischievous grin.

He chuckled softly. "You've mystery enough for three husbands."

"But one is all I need. Goodnight, darling." She cuddled into his embrace.

"Goodnight, honey." He pulled the blanket up over them.

Abby shifted, trying to get comfortable in the small space. The cry of a coyote broke the silence, the howl sending a spike of fear through her. Small, but fierce, coyotes were known to attack even humans if the critters were hungry enough.

After her encounter with the mountain lion, she feared the creatures who hunted in the dark of night. The hoot of an owl startled her. Lying next to her husband brought comfort. She clung to him, trying to shut her eyes, but afraid something would sneak up and jump in the wagon.

She talked softly to herself, to rid her mind of useless fear, but it didn't work. She spent the next hour lying awake, listening to the night sounds, and wondering what other threatening aspects of nature would they have to contend with?

Although her mind knew it was fruitless, her heart yearned for the safety of their old home. Having a roof over her head during a storm and being able to shut the door to the dangers outside had made her feel safe. Security had been ripped out of her life. Uncertainty—which frightened her most of all—took its place.

In his sleep, George slid his arm over her waist. Thank God for her husband. He'd protect her with his life, if necessary. Abby sighed. Thankful she had him to stand between herself and adversity, she snuggled closer, his body heat warming her.

He didn't appear to be afraid. He forged ahead like a man with a mission. His steadfast determination buoyed her spirits, fueled her energy to continue. He slept quietly with her on one side and his gun on the other. Knowing he was armed, calmed her and she drifted off to sleep.

IN THE MORNING, AS he took Nellie down to the stream for water, his children approached.

"How much longer?" Sarah asked, her footsteps matching his.

"We'll be at the river in three days. Then we'll have a day of rest."

"Why?"

"Because the flat boat can only take one wagon across at a time. It might take a whole day or more to get all three wagons on the other side." George nodded at Sarah. "Get Lizzy ready."

"Yes, Papa." Sarah returned to the wagon.

Sam helped his father yoke the oxen again. The men flanked the beasts.

"Ho!" Jeremiah Quint hollered.

George returned the call and got the oxen moving. Pulling the wagon through the mud created by the storm was slow going. He turned to wave to his wife and daughter. He had feared Sarah and Lizzy weren't strong enough to make the trip, but so far, they had fared well. His fine wife had borne up, too. Used to tending the house, the chickens, and the goats, she'd never been thrust out into the wild before.

He considered himself a lucky man to have a wife who didn't complain. He'd heard stories from other men in Danbury of wives who did nothing but carry on about how terrible their lives were morning, noon, and night. Not Abigail. He reckoned she'd have good reason to complain now, and he thanked God she had kept her worries to herself. Lord knew, he had enough of his own.

"Nice shooting, Papa." Sam glanced at his father.

"What?" He faced his son.

"The big cat. You got him quick."

"Didn't have much time before he'd be on your mother."

"How much longer to Fitch's Eddy?" Sam kept his hand on Nellie's harness.

"Maybe two more weeks. We'll be at the river soon. Then we can rest a bit."

"What's Fitch's Eddy like?"

"I don't know, son. Never been there." He rested his hand on Spirit's back.

The cool morning breeze following the rain turned warmer by afternoon. Welcome clouds obscured the sun, He glanced up often to see if the weather would hold for the time being. He pulled at the kerchief around his neck, using it to wipe the sweat off his face. Maybe this wasn't a good time of year to be making this trip?

Could be worse. He could be pushing against the snow and freezing cold of winter. Every so often, he'd glance at the horizon in case a twister came their way. So far, their luck held.

After three hours, the wagon train stopped for water and a brief rest. The men took the oxen to the nearest watering hole. As the big beasts drank, George picked up a strange sound. He gripped his musket, aiming it at the woods behind him.

"What's that?" Sam asked.

"Dunno. I'll find out." With his gun cocked and ready, he approached the forest. He couldn't tell if it was a howl from a coyote he heard. He stole closer, treading as quietly as he could. Leaves rustled. Something shifted in the brush. He took aim.

Out popped a good-sized brown-and-white dog. The creature cowered in front of him, whimpering. George shouldered his musket and stared.

"Sam!" he called.

The boy ran up to his father. "What is it?"

"I'll be damned. It's a plain ole dog."

The creature turned sad eyes on the men. So skinny his ribs were showing, he got down and crawled toward them. Sam approached the critter.

"Careful, Sam! He's hungry and scared. He might bite you."

Sam extended his hand. The dog sniffed it thoroughly then licked it. "He's friendly. Can we keep him, Papa?"

George laughed. "Always the soft heart. Let's see if he'll follow us to the wagon. We can spare some food for him."

Sam reached in his pocket. "I've got something." He held out a piece of dried meat to the dog, who came close enough to snatch it from his hand and wolf it down.

"He's afraid of you, Sam. Go slow." George stood a few feet away and watched his son make friends with the animal. Timid at first, the creature responded to Sam's offering and his soft voice. Within minutes, he was close enough for Sam to pet him. The dog wagged his tail.

"Can we keep him? Please?"

George shook his head and chuckled. "Let's get him to the wagon and see what your mother says."

They tramped through high grass and weeds on their way back. The dog followed along.

"Well, what?" Abby asked, her hands on her hips.

"A dog, Mama. He likes me. Can we keep him?" Sam's eyes pleaded his case.

The canine sat in front of her, wagging his tail and raising soulful eyes to hers. Sarah stepped forward and little Lizzy reached out from her stance in the wagon.

Sarah knelt in front of the dog. "He's pretty. Can we keep him?"

George put his arm around Abby's shoulders. "He's pretty smart. Cottoned to Sam right off."

"You, too?" She cast a jaundiced eye on her husband.

"Once he puts on a few pounds, he'll be a mighty fine animal."

"Oh, please, Mama. Please!" Sam pleaded.

"I suppose your heart will break if I say "no." She threw her hands in the air, shook her head, and laughed. "You win. But how will we feed him? We barely have enough for our family."

"I'll give him some of my supper," Sam said.

"Me, too," Sarah chimed in.

"Me!" Lizzy added.

"Best give him a bit of our meat and cheese now, Sam. Poor creature will have to walk with the rest of us."

"He'll help guard at night, too." George bent to scratch the dog behind the ears.

"You won't be sorry, Mama. I'll take care of him." Sam beamed.

"He's gonna need a name." She looked squarely at her son.

Sam shrugged.

"Lucky," Sarah said.

She turned to her daughter. "Why Lucky?"

"Because he sure was lucky to find us."

"Lucky it is. Sam, get the poor thing some food."

"Come on, Lucky," Sam called, leading the way to the back of the wagon. The dog took to his name as if he'd had it all his life.

"After you feed him, he needs a bath. Take him down to the stream, Sam."

George planted a kiss on Abby's cheek. "Thank you."

She smiled. "You knew I'd say 'yes', didn't you?"

He chuckled. She shook her head and tucked a goatskin bag under her arm, then picked her way through the tall grass and weeds down to the watering hole. George returned to the oxen, who munched tender grass on the path.

When Sam took up his position next to Nellie, George raised his arm, to signal the Quints they were ready. Jeremiah called out, and the wagon train lurched forward.

Josiah ran to the rear and fell in step with the Chesneys.

"Heard you got a dog."

"News travels fast. He's Sam's now." George pointed.

Josiah scooted around the oxen and joined Sam on the other side.

"Kinda scrawny, ain't he?" Josiah eyed the animal.

"Maybe now. But he'll be lookin' fine in a few days. Once he gets some food in his belly, regular like. You'll see. He'll be the finest dog in all of Fitch's Eddy."

George chuckled to himself. *Our boy sure doesn't lack confidence, does he?* He was grateful for anything that put a smile on his son's face. Looked like the Chesneys were as lucky to find the dog as he had been to come upon them.

THEY ARRIVED AT THE river about midday. The flatboat, weighed down with cargo, flowed slowly across the Hudson, bobbing slightly with the river's current. Abby and the girls plopped down in the shade, fanning themselves and drinking water.

"Might use this time to do some hunting, Sam." George wiped sweat from his brow.

Josiah ambled along to the Chesney wagon.

Sam got the musket and slung a small bag of water over his shoulder. "You coming?" he asked Josiah. "Not you, Lucky. You stay and guard the womenfolk."

The dog whimpered.

"I said stay, and I mean it." Sam raised his voice. The dog cowered.

"He's a hunting dog, Sam. Looks like a hound," Josiah offered. "Bring him."

"You sure?" Sam cast a doubtful eye.

"I know a hunting dog when I see one. Come on— What's his name?"

"Lucky."

"Come on, Lucky. Find us some deer, boy." Josiah ran ahead. The dog turned toward Sam.

"It's okay, boy. You can come. But you'd better rustle up some deer, 'cause I'm mighty hungry. And I bet you are, too." Sam followed Josiah's trail. Lucky put his nose to the ground and loped along at Sam's side.

George took the oxen down to the water. Once they'd had their fill and he'd refilled the goatskin water bags, he joined the women. They sat under some trees where they could see the river. By then, the flatboat was halfway across.

"Probably take them a couple of hours to come back. I doubt we'll be crossing before morning." He sat cross-legged next to his wife.

"Mama, I'm gonna take Lizzy down to the river for a bath."

"Go ahead."

Happy to have some time alone with his wife, he inched closer. She picked a blade of grass and tucked a few stray strands of hair into her bun. He slid his hand over hers.

"You all right?" he asked.

"Been better." Her gaze searched the sky.

"What's wrong?"

"It's hard not to have a home. A roof. Safety. A place to make meals. I miss Sarah's bread." She gave a half-smile.

"I know, honey. It's not for much longer."

"How long will it take?"

"Depends on the weather. If it's clear, we can go a far piece in a week. But if it rains and we have to stop, it'll take longer. Once we get to Fitch's Eddy, you'll see. It'll be like we've been there forever."

"About the boarding house..."

"Something wrong?"

"It's still not ours, is it?" She shaded her eyes with her hand.

"Farm wasn't ours, either."

"Felt like ours, though." She stared across the river.

"It did. Anywhere you're at will be home for me." He lifted her chin and kissed her.

She touched his cheek.

He cleared his throat and dropped his gaze to his hands which fumbled with a dandelion. "There's a little clearing not far from the wagon. Do you think? I mean, do you suppose tonight?"

"Why George Chesney! Are you trying to sneak off for private time with your wife?" She shot him a mischievous look.

"You always see through me."

"One of the things I like about you. You're honest and direct. Always have been."

"Not much for lying or making up pretty words."

"Thank goodness. Yes, I would like to meet you at the clearing when the children are in bed."

"Excellent." A bit of lust glowed in his eyes. He brought her hand to his lips. Before they could utter more tender words, the sound of a gunshot interrupted them.

George sprang up, running towards the woods. Another shot stopped him in his tracks. He glanced over his shoulder to see Abby on her feet, her hand to her mouth. Before he could make his way into the thicket, a cry halted him.

"Yeee haaaa!" Josiah came out first. "Mr. Chesney, Mr. Chesney, come quick."

"What happened?" George's stomach lurched.

"We got 'em. Two of 'em."

"Two of what?"

"Deer. The hound dog sniffed 'em right out, chased 'em toward us. Sam and I took aim. We've got venison for dinner!"

Lucky bounded out of the woods as if the dog knew he'd been a star. A ways behind him came Sam, dragging a doe by the hoof.

"There's another in the woods, Papa."

"Well done, son! Does the other one belong to Josiah?"

"Yes, but it's pretty big."

Jeremiah wandered over to see what had happened. Together the four men brought both deer out of the woods and cut them up. The women prepared the fire and found sturdy sticks. They set up a spit. Now they'd have fresh meat for the next few days, too.

Susanna worked alongside Abby while Sarah amused Lizzy. Lucky beamed a doggish grin at the praise heaped on him.

"Guess our luck has changed with Lucky in our camp."

"Can Lucky get the first piece, Mama?"

She nodded.

Sam tossed a cooked chunk to the hungry canine, who gobbled it up.

As night fell, the flat boat pulled into shore with a load from the other side. They'd be ready to leave first thing in the morning. Susanna put her children to bed then retired. Jeremiah joined her. George grabbed Abby's attention and raised his eyebrows. She hustled Lizzy and Sarah off to bed.

"But I'm not tired," Sam said.

"You need to be rested for tomorrow." She tucked their plates in the wagon.

"I'm wide awake."

"You can take Lucky under the wagon with you."

"I can?"

"If you go now."

"Sure thing. Thanks, Mama. Come on, boy." Sam trotted over to the wagon. Lucky loped along after him.

George approached. With the sun setting and the children taken care of, his wife was finally free for the night. He offered her his arm.

"Would you like to take a stroll and see a nice little clearing not far from here?" He wore a sly smile.

Abby clutched his arm and burst out laughing. "Yes. There you go, trying to be subtle."

"Can't fool you, can I?"

"Never can and never will. Come on. I'm hankering for a little private time myself."

She gave him a gentle tug, and he scooped her up in his arms and carried her over to the clearing, laying her down on a soft bed of grass surrounded by shrubs. Looming over her, he kissed her long and slow. She stretched her arms out and joined her hands behind his neck.

"I do love you. You're an amazing man."

"And you're a wonderful woman. I love you with all my heart and soul."

Uttering sweet endearments, the husband made love to his wife with tenderness and passion.

Chapter Four

Second week of June

S Abby was surprised the flatbed boat could hold their wagon and the oxen, too. The morning was cloudy and cool. But by the time they were loaded on, the sun had peeked out from behind a cloud to warm their journey.

Lucky barked and barked at the men wielding the poles and at the river. He trotted from fore to aft and back again, howling and growling. His noise startled the oxen. Nellie and Spirit lowed and stamped. Abby feared they'd upset the boat and everyone would slide into the river.

"Lucky's scared. He's pacing and staring at the water." Sweat broke out on Sam's forehead.

"Hold him, Sam. Calm him down. Poor thing." She stood by her husband's side. "Are Nellie and Spirit going to bolt?"

"In a minute or two, they'll be fine. If Lucky quiets, they will as well." He faced upriver. "Water's beautiful. Makes me thirsty just looking at it," he mused.

"It's hot. Can I go for a swim? I'll take Lucky. I bet he can swim." Sam sat cross-legged with one arm draped around his dog.

"Let's see what the other side looks like. We're the first wagon to ford the river. We have to wait for the others, so maybe there'll be time." He shielded his eyes with his hand as he peered across the Hudson.

Abby slipped her arm through her husband's, closed her fingers over his forearm, and spoke quietly. "There were days I didn't think we'd make it this far."

The boat rocked gently along with the river's current. She turned her head to watch the men manning the poles, pushing, and guiding the vessel across the water.

"It's a miracle we don't all fall in." She tightened her grip.

"Don't borrow trouble, honey. These men do this all the time. We're safe. Trust me."

"Oh, I trust you. Just not sure about those men with the poles."

He laughed and slung his arm over her shoulders, pulling her to him.

"The Hudson is a peaceful river," one of the men said. "Can't say the same for the Delaware."

"No, we won't be crossing the Delaware. Fitch's Eddy is right up against it, I hear. But on this side."

"Good." Abby smiled. She leaned against her husband.

The boat lumbered along, taking its time pushing against the river to get to the other side. Sarah sat next to her brother. Lizzy curled up and fell asleep in her big sister's lap. Sam kept his arm around Lucky.

"Papa, can Lucky swim?"

"He can. He's a hound. They hunt and retrieve. He'll jump into a pond to fish out a duck you shot."

Ashamed at not appreciating how much luck they'd had, she said a silent prayer for her three healthy children. The farm had produced a decent living—at least they'd never left the table hungry or passed a winter without a warm coat. She had been content with their simple life.

Despite the never-ending work, at the end of the day, the Chesney family got along. The one time she'd bragged about it, her mother had put her right straight away.

"No one ever promised you happiness, Abigail. Be satisfied to have a roof over your head, a man who's a good provider and doesn't beat you. And children who obey. You ask too much. Expect too much. Love. What a silly notion!"

She hadn't listened to her mother—thank the Lord. Tucking herself into George's embrace every night was a reward she cherished.

A breeze kicked up, cooling her as she watched one shoreline disappear and the other draw near. Resting her head on her husband's shoulder, she stood, swaying with the gentle rocking of the boat. What would come next?

Her peaceful moment came to an abrupt end when the boat neared the dock. The men on board bustled about, grabbing thick ropes and tossing them ashore. Some men jumped off onto the wooden dock, pulled the boat in, and secured it.

The oxen lowed, their eyes widened with fear.

"Sam! Mind Nellie," George ordered as he grabbed hold of Spirit's harness. Lucky barked but followed the boy.

"Sarah, Lizzy, come here." Abby gathered her daughters near and eased away from the wagon. After the men tied up the lines, grabbed the leads, and led the frightened oxen to solid land, she breathed a sigh of relief. They'd made it. Another miracle to be grateful for. She let out a breath and smiled at her daughters.

Happy to be the last off the boat, she stood quietly in the corner, holding hands with her girls.

"I loved the boat, Mama. Maybe I'll be a sailor when I grow up."

"You're almost grown now, Sarah. Stay on dry land. It's safer."

Lizzy clung to Sarah's leg as they waited for the wagon to be unloaded. The boat would return for the next one, probably the Quints. Having more rest would do them all good, especially George. While he didn't say much, the deep lines between his eyes and around his mouth had eased up since they had embarked on their journey.

The family, including Lucky, had traveled without trouble. The adventure had lifted their spirits. As the heavy wagon wheels bumped along the gangplank to dry land, the boat jumped. No longer weighed down with such a heavy load, it bobbed and swayed. The womenfolk lost their footing, tumbling in a heap one on top of the other. Unhurt, Sarah and Lizzy sprang up. Sarah offered Abigail a hand.

"I guess a sail on a river is full of surprises." She brushed herself off, reclaimed her dignity and joined the men on shore.

WITH ALMOST HALF THEIR journey behind them, George embarked on the path to Fitch's Eddy with a light heart. Proud of his family for weathering the arduous trek with little complaint, he'd welcomed a chance for them to rest and play while the other wagons came across the Hudson.

Sam and Lucky romped by the shore and played in the water. Under the blanket of darkness, the Chesney women folk bathed in the river. Sitting around the campfire, they finished most of the venison. Lucky gnawed on a bone while the family snuggled together and listened to Abby telling "The Fox and the Grapes" story from Aesop.

After the story was finished, it was time for sleep. Huddled in the wagon, the women bedded down for the night. The men and Lucky slept underneath. George laid the musket between him and his son.

The next morning, with all three wagons ready, they set out to make up for lost time. George glanced at the overcast sky. Puffy white clouds occasionally hid the sun, but didn't threaten rain, like the dark ones. With Sam next to Nellie and George walking alongside Spirit, they continued.

Every day, Sam and Lucky combed the woods, looking for game. The dog added to their success in finding food, often by chasing ducks out of hiding. The Chesney boy became a crack shot, hitting ducks on the wing. Then Lucky would leap into the pond or lake and swim out to retrieve the fallen fowl.

Slowly they whittled down their supply of potatoes and dried vegetables and fruit. They trudged on for another week without incident. Then the weather turned against them.

A crack of thunder woke George and disturbed the oxen. It was before sunrise when he looked up. Since he couldn't see stars, he figured clouds must have rolled in. He slid out, pushed to his feet, and took a deep breath. He smelled rain in the air.

"Sam, get up! Get up!"

Not bothering to wake the women, he sent his sleepy son ahead to alert the other wagons. If they got moving, they might be able to get ahead of the storm. He took his place next to Spirit and put his hand on the creature's back.

"Whoa, boy. Take it easy."

Sam returned. "They're starting."

"Ho!" came the cry from Jeremiah Quint.

"Take Nellie," he said.

Sam took his position, and the two men got the oxen moving. The wagon jerked and bumped up and down over a rut in the path. Abby's head appeared out of the front.

"Rain's coming!" he hollered to his wife.

She pulled back inside. Within minutes, she and Sarah appeared at the front of the wagon. No time now to stop and let them down. He figured even a bouncy ride was better than walking. The three wagons plodded up and down the small, green hills of New York state.

The rich, dense forests and verdant fields held the promise of fertile land. Good land meant prosperous towns and villages along the way. Hope grew in his chest. Perhaps Fitch's Eddy was one of those towns?

The storm kept coming, cracking thunder at their heels. After each one, Lucky would bark, and the oxen would low in response. Tension gathered in George's shoulders. Could they beat the storm nipping at their heels? Should they stop, break camp, and wait it out? With his free hand, he rubbed his neck. Josiah ran to the rear and fell in step with George.

"When the storm hits, are we going to keep going or make camp?"

"I'll ask my brother." He ran ahead.

George and Sam kept the oxen at a steady pace. They needed to push farther. Since the team had rested for two days, they should be able to keep going, no matter what. In short order, Josiah returned.

"Jeremiah said we should keep going. Unless the rain gets so bad we can't see or hold our footing."

George welcomed the wisdom of another man. He glanced at Sam who shot back a questioning look.

"Keep going!" he hollered over the wind whipping around them, eating their words.

Josiah returned to his family. Dirt blew in George's face and eyes. The oxen appeared unaffected. Lucky trotted along beside Sam.

As they pushed on, the rumble of thunder increased in frequency and volume. Finally, a sprinkling of rain blew across his face. Moving faster, he urged the oxen on, hoping they'd pick up their pace. They had to beat the storm, or at least find a copse of trees for protection.

His gaze searched for shelter, a dense cluster of trees, shrubs, or even a cave, but found none. *Keep going, keep going* he said to himself. The women jostled and jumped with the rise and fall of the wagon wheels. He could barely see them. He hoped the uneven movements of the wagon didn't knock them to the floor. The air fell heavy with the smell of rain.

Spirit looked at George with fear in his eyes.

"You smell it too, don't you, old boy?" He patted the creature.

A deep-throated lowing answered him. He kept moving. It had been three hours now and his legs wearied at the rapid pace.

In an instant, tiny, misting raindrops morphed to larger ones. Huge heavy rain pelted his shoulders and pounded on the brim of his hat. The storm was upon them. Josiah returned.

"Jeremiah said we should keep going until the rain blinds us. If we can't see, we'll stop."

"Right."

Josiah returned to the wagon ahead.

The heavens opened up and buckets of rain poured down. The water beat on the brim of his hat and ran in rivulets down his neck. Sam was drenched in seconds. The men kept putting one foot in front of the other — slow but steady.

The next crack of thunder was so loud, George jumped. The oxen bolted, moving as fast as they could, knocking him onto the pathway. His hat flew off. Nellie ripped the harness from Sam's hand and took off, keeping pace with Spirit. The wagon raced after them, bumping and jumping into the air over rocks and banging down into holes.

The team was so strong, they ripped the reins attached to the Quint wagon right off. They raced around to the right of the Quints as another sharp crack of thunder shook the Earth.

George pushed up, his feet sliding out from under him. Rainwater cascaded down a hill on his right turning the dirt beneath him into slippery mud. Getting his bearings, he shielded his eyes from the heavy downpour as he raced after his team. Gazing to the right, he spotted a stream up ahead. He swallowed hard. Before long, it would be a raging waterway. He needed to get the oxen in place and make it past the stream fast.

Sarah kneeled by the rear of the runaway wagon. George ran past her, gaining on the team. At the stream, the team slid to a halt. He grabbed Spirit's harness as Josiah ran up.

"Jeremiah says we should stop and wait out the rain. We're going to pull up over there." The young man pointed. Sam caught up and the two men got on either side of the oxen and directed them over the stream to join the others.

George settled the wagon under some trees, trying to keep the oxen as protected as possible. He hitched them to a large tree and climbed into the wagon, Sam followed.

"You're soaked. Here. Both of you. Change into dry clothing." Abigail handed garments to the men.

The storm raged for three more hours. The women broke out some of their dried food and the family huddled together under blankets to stave off the chilliness brought on by cold rain and wind. An hour after the thunder stopped, the oxen settled down.

Darkness blanketed the small wagon train. The Chesney family snuggled together to sleep. The children drifted off. Restless, George sat up. His brow furrowed as he contemplated what they might find in the morning. He stared into the blackness of night. *How deep will the mud be? Will Nellie and Spirit be able to keep their footing? Will we have to lay over for another day?*

His wife rolled over. "What's the matter?" She closed her hand over his shoulder.

"I should have foreseen Nellie and Spirit charging off like they did. I should have had control, calmed them. Guided them. What if they had run over a hill? You might have been killed. All of you." He clenched his jaw.

"But they didn't. And we're all right. Don't worry. The force of the storm was unexpected."

"No, it wasn't. I knew it would happen. I was waiting for it. But I wasn't prepared. I'll be prepared next time."

"Good. Come lie down. Sleep. You need the rest."

She was right. George was plum exhausted. He joined her but didn't stop thinking, figuring out what he could do should a similar storm hit them again. Once he had the solution, he closed his eyes and fell to snoring softly.

IN THE MORNING, THE oxen were wide-eyed again. George studied the sky. Josiah joined the Chesneys.

"Jeremiah said this storm isn't over yet. We'd best get moving before we have to stop."

George and Sam took the harnesses while Sarah and Abby climbed down to walk. Looking ahead, he spied an embankment on the right. The ground dropped off on the left of the pathway. Glancing down, he saw a steep decline to a forest. The muddy road was slippery underfoot. The oxen slid once or twice.

The wind picked up. He motioned to his wife.

"Best get Sarah in the wagon. You, too. Things don't look good." Unwilling to spill his true fears, he gestured. Abby helped Sarah into the wagon then returned to her husband.

"I'll stay with you."

"Suit yourself. But be careful."

"I will."

The look of concern on her face confirmed his fear he'd never fool her. She knew him too well. He turned his attention to Spirit and Nellie. He and Sam needed to keep them on the path, which had narrowed. One false step, and they'd slide down the hill into the woods and certain death. He glanced up. The clouds had darkened, some were almost an eerie greenish shade. They swirled dangerously. Could there be a twister rip through here? He swallowed hard, his throat dry.

As the wind increased, Abby refastened her hair. The wind flapped the sides of his pants as if they were wings as he hurried along. *We have to get past the embankment before the rest of this storm hits us.* Then he felt it, the air chilled, a sure sign something bad loomed ahead.

"In the wagon, Abby. Now!" He hollered. But she didn't move. Stubborn and loyal, a bad combination when he needed her to obey orders. She marched behind him.

The sky darkened. He turned around. Was that a funnel cloud heading their way? Before he could ponder further, a burst of rain shot out of the sky, pelting them. Hail joined the rain, then it all became water. Sheet after sheet fell, obscuring vision.

They had come abreast of the embankment on the right. He didn't know where to look first. They kept going, and when they were almost past it, the already muddy earth loosened more. Looking to his right, he saw it start to slide.

"Abby! Look out! Sam!"

She looked up in time and ran out of the way. Sam stopped, dropping Nellie's harness and running to safety. But it was too late for George. He and the oxen were in the thick of it. As the terrified animals lowed and pulled, He saw them falter. He leaped up on Spirit's back and made his way to the heavy wooden pin fastening the team to the wagon.

If the beasts slid down the hill on the left, they'd take the wagon and his children with them. He had to save them. The only way was to disconnect the oxen —sacrifice his team to save Sarah and Lizzy. He crawled up the wet beast then across the narrow and slippery wood to the pin.

He pulled, but the pin didn't budge. It was stuck! His heart leaped into his throat. He had to get it out before the wagon with his daughters in it tumbled over the edge. Mustering every ounce of strength he had, he yanked on the pin again and again. On the fourth try, it flew up, out of his hands and was blown down the hill. The force of the motion knocked him back on the animal. The wood connecting the wagon to the team stayed still. The wagon balanced precariously on the path, while the oxen continued to slide.

As he rolled over and attempted to dismount, the embankment gave way. A huge wave of mud, sod, and small trees hit the oxen. Their knees buckled. The force of the beasts moving ripped him from the wood, which tore his flesh as it slid through his fingers. He gripped their harness to keep from falling beneath their feet and getting trampled. He looked up— his gaze connecting with his wife's as the landslide carried him away over the edge with Nellie and Spirit, leaving the wagon safely on the bluff.

Abby screamed. "George!" She reached out, but he was too far away. Sam clung to the wagon and watched as his father and the two oxen slipped over the side. Running to the edge, she screamed again. George reached out. He hollered, "I'll always love you," as he fell down, down, down.

Josiah rushed up behind Abby and grabbed her arms, pulling her back before the Earth gave way and she followed her husband. Right before the mudslide engulfed the animals and George with them, he heard her scream his name.

The thick mud carried the animals and George over the edge. The oxen tumbled over and over again, trapping him beneath them. They crushed him as they rolled, then slid all the way down, disappearing in the underbrush under the trees.

Chapter Five

itch's Eddy— Last week of June

F Caleb Tanner, blacksmith, rose with the sun. He shoved his sandy-colored hair out of his eyes and swung his legs over the side of the bed. As he did every morning, he gazed at the drawing of his wife, Emily, setting on his nightstand.

Caleb had lost her and his daughter during childbirth. It had been four years, but the wound to his heart had not yet healed. Every night he missed her soft roundness in his bed and every morning he missed her cheerful greeting and excellent breakfast.

When word came a year ago to Caleb's father from his friend, the Fitch's Eddy blacksmith, that he needed an apprentice, Jeb Tanner sent his son. Caleb made the journey to Fitch's Eddy from Connecticut. Six months later, the old blacksmith passed away, leaving the shop to his apprentice.

He lived in a small cabin set about a hundred yards behind the smithy shop. He smiled at Emily's image and pulled on pants and a muslin shirt. After washing up, he checked his small chicken coop and found two eggs, freshly laid.

After stoking the fire in the fireplace, he added another log. He didn't need a roaring fire because it was summertime and he'd be off to the shop after breakfast anyway. As the eggs simmered in a hot, cast iron pan, he heated a thick piece of bread quickly over the fire, then buttered it. He added jam and sat down to a hearty meal.

He wolfed down the food, noting to himself that Martha Chesney made the best bread in town. He'd traded a couple of cast iron pans for a loaf of her fresh bread once a week for three months. He finished eating, cleaned up his utensils, and strode the short distance to the shop.

A well-built, strong man, he easily hauled a large bag of coal to the forge. He had several orders to complete for the Fitch family. As impatient as he was wealthy, Elijah Fitch wanted new pans for his kitchen and new tools for his farm. And he wanted them yesterday.

Caleb donned the cowskin apron his mother had made him, and manned the bellows, hoping to get the forge to the proper temperature quickly. While the fire grew, he set out his tools.

"Morning, Caleb," said a singsong female voice.

Caleb grimaced. It was Charity, Reverend Ebenezer Bloodgoode's daughter. Despite her father's standing in the community, she'd become known as the town flirt. She'd set her cap on marrying Caleb—according to town gossip. No matter how many times he told her he wasn't fixin' to marry again, she kept coming around, like an annoying mosquito, intent on getting some of his blood.

"Busy today, Charity. Best to go on home." He examined his tools with extra care, hoping she'd leave.

"You always say that. You and them tools." She huffed. "I've got my new hat on."

Caleb glanced up momentarily. "Very nice. Now run along. Don't want the dust and soot in this place to muss up such a pretty bonnet."

"Oh, my goodness!" She scurried out the door as fast as a mouse fleeing a cat.

Caleb chuckled. Nothing like the threat of soot to get rid of an unwanted female. He'd picked up a few things in addition to blacksmithing from the old man who'd owned the place. Caleb worked hard and stayed to himself, mostly. He saved his money in a can under his front porch. In such a small town, everyone knew everyone else's business, but not his. He didn't drink at the Black Dog Saloon and preferred a home-cooked meal by Martha Chesney at Chesney Inn, instead of saloon fare, for his Sunday dinner.

He didn't jaw with the locals or hang around Rhodes' General Store, either. When asked about his background, he answered in clipped sentences with only basic information. Townsfolk knew he wasn't married, but they didn't know the particulars.

When asked, "Why is a handsome man like you not married, Caleb?" by the likes of Charity Bloodgoode or the other town busybodies, he'd shrug. Sometimes he'd say, "I prefer my own company." Or "Haven't met her yet." And then he'd leave fast, before a second question could be posed.

After working hard on pans for Mr. Fitch, Caleb put the cast iron in the quenching bucket and hurried to the general store. He needed mending supplies for the shirt he'd torn on a branch in the woods when foraging for kindling. When he was leaving, Old Zeke, warming the chair in front of the store, as usual, stopped him.

"There's a mite bit of gossip 'bout you goin' around town." He set his rheumy eyes on Caleb.

"Oh?"

"Yep. Man your age without a wife? Someone said you had one and killed her. Came here to escape the law. Folks are suspicious. Is it true?"

Caleb frowned. "Let those flappin' their jaws keep their stupid ideas to themselves."

"So you ain't runnin' from the law?"

"What do you think?" Caleb spat out and strode away, returning to the easy solitude of his shop.

Today he had to return to Rhodes' to pick up oatmeal. He attempted to brush by Zeke, who grabbed his sleeve. "What's your hurry?"

"Got things to do."

"I hear Martha's expecting her family. Any day now."

"Yeah?"

"Her son, his wife and kids."

"So?"

"Thought you'd like to know. Maybe they need some horseshoes or something.'"

"If they do, I'm sure they can find me. Excuse me." Caleb snatched the bit of sleeve in Old Zeke's wizened hand away and entered the store.

As he returned to his shop he thought about the news. *Good for Martha.* Since John had died, the older woman had struggled to run her inn without him. Caleb had volunteered to do odd jobs from time to time, and she'd appreciated it by placing a small bag of muffins on his stoop. He liked Martha. She had guts, worked hard, and didn't gossip or complain.

A woman like her, but younger, might tempt Caleb out of his celibate existence and convince him to try marriage one more time.

THE SOUND OF WAGON wheels bumping along the ruts and depressions of Main Street caught Caleb's attention. He finished his task, then faced the street. Leaning against the door frame of his shop, he watched a small wagon train pull up in front.

A young man approached him and offered his hand.

"Josiah Quint. We be looking for Chesney Inn."

"Caleb Tanner. Right down the street." Caleb pointed. "About six houses down. On the right. You'll see the sign. You looking for lodging?"

"No, sir. We're looking for Mrs. Chesney. I've got her family in the wagon, over there." Josiah gestured.

"Her son and his family? I heard she'd sent for them."

Josiah shook his head and trained his gaze to the ground. "No, sir. There was an accident. Tragic. George Chesney was killed."

Caleb sucked in air.

"Thank you for your help. I'll be getting along." Josiah returned to the wagon, spoke to the man driving and boarded the second one. The travelers' wagons jostled their way down the uneven path, and over the grooves from spring rain. Caleb stood with his hands on his hips and watched as they stopped. The commotion brought Martha Chesney hurrying out of the inn.

Caleb frowned. Since she'd lost her husband, Martha'd had a hard time. She needed her family around her. He heard a loud wail. Martha put her hand out to lean on the wagon and covered her eyes. He rushed down the street and stopped in front of her.

"Oh, Caleb. He's gone. The Lord has taken my George, too. What am I going to do?" Martha's tear-soaked eyes met his. His gut roiled. He knew all about loss. His heart hurt for her.

"You'd better sit down, Martha." He took her arm. She leaned against him as he escorted her to a chair in the front parlor. She sank down like a balloon losing its air. Not knowing what to do, he fetched a glass of water from the kitchen, then joined the men outside to see if he could help.

The wagons pulled up and stopped. Men and women alit. A little girl came running ahead, stopping abruptly in front of Caleb. She blinked, staring straight up at him.

For a moment, he couldn't breathe. She had blonde curly hair and eyes the size of Wedgewood blue saucers. Her smile rivaled the sun for brilliance. If his beloved daughter had lived, he figured she'd be about the same age as the pretty little angel before him. He crouched down to meet her eye-to-eye.

"How old are you, little girl?"

Before she could answer, a plump woman addressed him. "Step away, mister. You got no call to address this child. She ain't yours. Move away. Leave her alone."

He blinked at the woman and took three steps back. If this was Mrs. George Chesney, poor Martha had another unpleasant surprise coming.

"No harm meant," he said, giving a nod.

She stuck her nose in the air, grabbed the child's hand, and huffed off. But the little girl looked over her shoulder at Caleb and smiled.

"I'm five," she said before the disagreeable woman yanked her away.

Five... same age as mine would've been. Her sweet expression touched his heart, melting his pain. He turned to Josiah.

"I didn't mean the child any harm. For a woman who just lost her husband, Mrs. Chesney sure has some temper." Caleb shook his head.

"Her? Oh, she's not Mrs. Chesney. She's my sister-in-law, Susanna Quint. She's helping Mrs. Chesney tend to her children. That's Lizzy Chesney. Mrs. Chesney, Abigail, is in that there wagon. She couldn't walk. Plum tuckered out. Excuse me." Josiah pointed.

The news intrigued Caleb. Now he wanted to see the widow Chesney, mother of such a beautiful, charming child. He stepped aside, near the second wagon where he could get a good look at the Chesney family. Josiah reached up and clasped a slender woman by the waist. He lifted her as if she weighed no more than a leaf and set her down on the dirt road. She grasped the wagon for a moment, steadying herself.

A young man joined her. She rested one arm around his shoulders, using him for support. The woman must have been the widow Chesney for her whole being was tinged with sadness, from her crumpled dress, to the limpness of her arms. Fronds of her honey-colored hair, sprang from the loose bun gathered at the nape of her long, graceful neck, turned gold in the sunlight,.

Her slender figure was clad in a dark brown ankle-length skirt and white muslin top. Mud stains on her sleeves and the hem of her skirt bespoke of hard times. Her face was delicate but pale, and haggard. She mumbled something to the boy, pointed and then covered her eyes with her hand. He half carried her.

Caleb identified immediately with her anguish. He recognized the signs of mourning. Sweat broke out on his brow and his stomach churned as he recalled the day his wife died. He wanted to reach out to Mrs. Chesney, share some words of comfort and wisdom about accepting loss— as if he had any! But she was a stranger and mired in grief, so he stepped back to study her.

Despite her stricken countenance, her beauty shone through. He noticed how handsome she was, or would be, when she tidied up and got accustomed to grief. He guessed underneath the heavy weight of sorrow, Mrs. Chesney had a delicate beauty like none he'd seen before in Fitch's Eddy.

As she took tentative steps toward the inn, Abigail's light brown eyes, clouded with pain, lit on his only for a second. Her sad expression spoke of grief too immense for words. Caleb knew the signs and identified with her immediately. Only a few years ago he had been in the exact same place.

He wanted to take her in his arms and comfort her but hung back— uncomfortable with the depth of his feelings. He fought to control his emotions as he watched her climb slowly up the two steps to the inn, as if each movement brought her pain.

A handsome dark-haired boy, a lovely blonde girl, and little Lizzy surrounded Mrs. Chesney. How glorious to have such a beautiful family. Caleb had been left alone with his sorrow, but Mrs. Chesney would have her children to bring her comfort. How he longed to have a family of his own. Drawn to the Chesney family, Caleb approached soundlessly, remaining in the background.

When she stopped at the door, Josiah rushed up. "The chest is still inside. I'll get it next," he said.

Clutching her son's hand, she gave him a weak smile. "Thank you."

Boldly, Caleb stepped forward and addressed the strange woman. "Caleb Tanner, Mrs. Chesney. I'm a friend of Martha's. Can I be of service?"

Josiah spoke up. "Could you help me with the chest? It's a might heavy."

Caleb nodded. "Of course."

Mrs. Chesney spoke in a wispy voice. "Thank you. Abigail Chesney. These are my children, Sam, Sarah, and Lizzy."

"Pleasure to meet you. I'm so sorry for your loss." Caleb gave a short bow.

"Thank you." She lowered her head for a moment, hiding full eyes. Holding hands with her two eldest, their mother and Lizzy went inside.

For the first time, Caleb had met someone who could understand his feelings of loss at the passing of his wife and child. The revelation left him dazed, speechless. When he comprehended the kinship he felt could not be returned, he swallowed hard. He'd have to continue struggling with his feelings as alone as the last leaf of autumn before the chill of winter sets in. Although he lived at peace with his sorrow most of the time, she had only begun her journey into widowhood. He knew there lay a rocky road ahead that she could not avoid.

GRAPPLING WITH THE reality of his death, Abigail couldn't quite believe her husband was gone. Still in shock, fear gripped her. How could she go on without George?

Only this morning, she awoke expecting to see him—figuring the horrific scene of his demise had only been a bad dream. How could she face each day without her dear partner? How long would it take her to accept the truth?

She approached her mother-in-law, slumped in a wing chair in the parlor.

"Sarah, go to the kitchen and put up water for tea." Abby stood silently by, waiting for Martha to recover her senses.

She looked up. "Oh, my. You must be Abigail?" Martha pushed to her feet and took Abby's hand between both of hers. "Oh, my dear. I'm so, so sorry George is gone. He was such a dear boy."

"I can hardly believe it," Abigail admitted.

Martha sighed. "Me, too. But I am grateful you have come. The inn needs you. I need you. And you have such fine children."

"They are my comfort."

"Yes. And will be mine as well. There's so much to do here. I hope you don't mind a bit of work."

"I'm sure it will be easier than the farm. My daughter, Sarah, has put water on for tea. Come." Abby put her arm around her mother-in-law's shoulders.

The door opened and Caleb entered, holding the chest from the wagon. The two women watched as he carried it with ease, as if it were a simple bag of fruit.

"Martha, where should I put this?"

"Let's get you settled, Abigail. First room on the left at the top of the stairs, Caleb."

"Thank you," Abby muttered, staring at him with unseeing eyes.

"Come. Let me take you to your rooms." Martha took hold of Abby's hand and they followed Caleb to the second floor. "This is for the ladies. I have a small room off the foyer for Sam. Come, my boy."

While Martha took Sam downstairs, Caleb faced Abby.

He placed the chest at the foot of the bed. "May I ask you a question?"

"Yes?"

"How old is the little one?"

"Lizzy? She's five." Abby clasped her hands together.

"I see. Thank you."

"Why?" She quirked an eyebrow.

"No reason. She's sweet."

"Yes. Thank you for helping."

"I help Martha with chores from time to time. She rewards me with her fine bread."

She struggled to smile.

He blurted out, "I'm so sorry for your loss. I lost my wife and child. It's hard. I'm so very sorry." He gave a quick nod and left the inn. She stared after him, barely able to comprehend his words.

She joined Martha and the children in the dining room. Her mother-in-law had laid out a meal for the Chesneys and the Quints, consisting of meat, potatoes, squash, fruit, bread, and milk.

Hunger gripped Abby. She sat between Sam and Sarah and filled her belly.

Martha took a seat across from her. "When you get settled, would you tell me what happened to my son?" she asked quietly. "My sweet George. Gone before his time," muttered the older woman, wringing her hands. "Did he get a decent burial?"

Abby chewed a bite of bread and shook her head. After she swallowed, she spoke. "We couldn't."

"He's lying out there? Oh my. Oh dear." Martha covered her mouth. She drew her brows together. Her eyes wetted, and her voice grew raspy. "He must be laid to rest next to his father."

Jeremiah Quint interrupted. "Mrs. Chesney, Josiah and I could take a few days to go back for him. And we can gather some of the belongings you had to leave behind in the wagon."

"Would you?" Martha's eyes lit up.

"We will. But we need one more man. Not to go into details. I don't want to upset you. But we need three men to do the job."

Martha's eye's teared. "Oh my goodness. No, no. Please don't tell me."

"Do you know where we could get a third?" Josiah asked, tearing off a piece of bread.

Silence lingered for a moment.

"Yes. Yes, I do," Martha announced. "I'm sure Caleb Tanner would help. I'll write out a message. Sam, would you please take it to the blacksmith shop?"

"He's a blacksmith?" Abby asked, cutting off a piece of meat.

"He is. Come Sam."

Martha and the boy headed to the front room.

A half hour later, Caleb joined them in the dining room. Martha set a plate of food before him.

"Mighty kind of you, Martha. Sure. I'd be glad to help." He turned to Josiah. "When do you plan to leave?"

"First thing in the morning. Do you have a wagon?" He cut off a piece of meat.

"I do. How far is it, do you reckon?"

"Maybe one day."

"He almost made it." Martha sounded wistful. Abby patted her on the shoulder.

"I want to go, too," Lizzy piped up.

Abby's mouth fell open. "Elizabeth Chesney, you will stay right here with me. No children allowed on this trip."

"Not even me?" Sam asked.

She put her hand on his arm. "No, dear. I'm afraid not. Best for you to stay here with us. We'll need you. You're the man of the family now."

Josiah, Jeremiah, and Caleb finished their meal, discussed details of the trip, then the men left the dining room.

Abigail climbed the stairs to her own room and lay down. She tried to get the picture of her husband falling down the hill out of her mind. But when she closed her eyes, she relived every moment. Jerking awake, she sat up, panting and sweating. Would the memory leave her when they buried him? Would a funeral make his death real? Exhaustion claimed her. She slid into dreamless, restorative sleep.

Chapter Six

C aleb prepared a quick morning meal then waited in the shop for the Quint brothers. Shortly after sunup, the three men climbed on his wagon and headed east. Old Nick, Caleb's horse pulled the heavy load without complaint.

The Quints didn't have any difficulty locating the exact spot where George and the oxen went over. The three men gingerly inched their way down the still-slippery slope to the bottom. After they had secured George's remains in the wagon and filled the rest of the space with Chesney possessions, the three men turned toward Fitch's Eddy. As they rumbled along the uneven path, Caleb spoke.

"Where are you all headed?"

Jeremiah carried on about their journey to Ohio and the farm he planned to buy and run. Josiah was oddly quiet. Caleb figured maybe the younger Quint wasn't quite so keen on the idea of farming in the middle of nowhere.

"Josiah? What say you to farming in Ohio?"

"Don't know. I'll make up my mind when I get there."

Jeremiah laughed. "My little brother didn't want to leave Danbury. I'm thinking it wasn't the city so much as the warm smile from one Prudence Brent."

Josiah's face turned red.

"Did you know George Chesney well?" Caleb asked.

"Long enough to know he was a good man," Josiah said.

"Aye. He was," Jeremiah chimed in.

He must have been a fine man, indeed, to have such a beautiful wife for so many years.

They returned to Fitch's Eddy early the next morning. Martha and Abigail came to meet them. The Quints alit from the wagon.

"Let's unload the things we got from the wagon first," Jeremiah said.

Martha held out a bushel basket and Josiah dropped the smaller items in.

"Oh, my cameo!" Abby clutched the item to her chest. "And George's uniform. He fought in the war." She turned to her mother-in-law.

"Fine. Let's bury him in it then."

Someone standing behind her cleared his throat. Abby turned. Sam stood quietly. She watched his loving gaze sweep over the uniform.

"Oh, wait." She stared at Sam. "This is precious. George talked about the war from time to time. Always with pride of being on the winning side. Sometimes he'd share stories with Sam."

"You knew?" Sam's eyebrows shot up.

"Your father and I didn't have secrets." A small light shone in her eyes for a moment. She faced Martha. "I think he would like his son to have his uniform. Sam? You'll take good care of it?" She handed the garments to the boy.

"I will. Yes, indeed. I will."

"Martha?" she asked.

"Fine idea. Okay, Sam. That makes it official. You're the Chesney man to be reckoned with now."

"Thank you." Sam hugged his mother.

When they finished unloading the wagon, the bushel basket was full.

"Sam, take it inside. Put it in your room, please," Abby said.

"Let's take him right to the cemetery." Martha climbed up on the wagon, followed by Abby. "We can come back for the children."

Caleb helped Martha into the space next to him. He extended his hand to Abby, who took it. Hers was warm and soft.

Jeremiah removed his hat. "We're mighty sorry for your loss, Mrs. Chesney, Abigail. George was a fine man and a good neighbor."

"Dinner is laid for you and your family in the dining room, Mr. Quint. I thank you from the bottom of my heart," Martha said.

"Thank you, ma'am." Jeremiah and the brothers turned toward the inn.

Caleb slapped the reins gently against his horse's back, and Nick walked leisurely toward the town burial grounds.

Once they arrived, Caleb and one of the grave diggers transferred the remains of George Chesney to a wood coffin. The blacksmith had thought by never marrying, he'd never have to be in a cemetery again except for when he was laid to rest. The atmosphere chilled him to the core. He stole peeks of Abigail's stricken face, and his heart melted.

The Reverend Bloodgoode escorted the children in his wagon. He took over, organizing everything. Martha insisted on looking at her son's face. But Abigail refused and kept the children away.

"I want to remember him the way he was," she replied to the Reverend.

"Very well, Mrs. Chesney. As you wish."

Though he wasn't needed, Caleb stayed out of respect. He couldn't see stealing away, although the pain and sadness in the air was almost palpable. Wasn't his presence the least he could do for Martha, who had taken good care of him when he was new in town or fell ill? When it was over, he'd take them to the inn. Standing in the background his hands joined in front of him, he observed the Chesney family.

Lizzy clung to her mother's skirt while Sarah cried. Sam, attempting to appear strong, couldn't hide the tears on his cheeks. Abby eased her arms around Sarah and Sam's shoulders, drawing her children nearer.

Her grief-stricken face reminded him this was only the beginning. She'd soon discover she'd be waking up to sorrow every day. Pity filled his heart for the woman who would live with a ghost instead of a flesh and blood man. The specter of grief would replace the hearty image of her beloved husband and would haunt her the rest of her days.

After the service, he paid his respects to the family. When she extended her hand, he took it with both of his.

"I pray for comfort for you and your children." He released her hand, then made his way to his wagon, shadowed by the ghost of his wife at his every step.

THERE WAS NO TIME FOR grieving while running the inn. With housekeeping chores in the morning and meals to attend to, Abigail and her children were too busy to be sad. Sarah helped tidy the guest rooms, make the beds, and do the laundry. Sam chopped wood, and, with Lucky by his side, hunted for game. Even little Lizzy worked –she fed the chickens and gathered eggs.

Abigail worked in the kitchen with Martha. They cooked and baked every morning to serve the diners who stayed at the inn, as well as some single town folk who were regulars. She figured they served at least a dozen people at every meal.

Sunday night, after the children were put to bed, Martha retrieved a bottle of whiskey from the pantry. She poured two small glasses and sat down with her daughter-in-law at the spacious kitchen table.

"Here. John always kept a bottle. For emergencies. I reckon after what we've been through, we need this." Martha took a sip. She made a face as the harsh liquid burned her throat.

Abby hesitated. She'd never tasted liquor before. She raised the glass to her nose and sniffed.

"Go on. It'll do you good," Martha said.

The first sip tasted bitter on her tongue. She coughed and choked down the brown liquid. It burned her insides.

Trying to catch her breath, she stared at Martha. "What is this?"

"Something to take the sting away. A little bit." Martha twisted the gold band on her finger.

"You must miss John." Abby let the whiskey settle in her stomach before tasting more.

"I do. So much. He was a good man. I'm sorry you never met him. And now, my son." Two tears ran down her mother-in-law's cheeks.

Abby took her hand. "I still can't believe it. My George." She shook her head.

"He was a wonderful boy. Smart. Hard working."

"Oh, yes," she said.

Martha faced her. "And he loved you very much. He wrote to me before the wedding."

Abby covered her face with her hands, then lowered her head, sobbing.

Martha stroked her hair. "Cry for him. He was a good man taken too soon."

She sat up, wiping her face with her fingers. "I can't believe he's gone. I expect him to come around the corner any time."

"I know, my dear. I know. But now you must go on. You have children to raise. And we have an inn to run. I thank God you have arrived."

"We'll do what we can."

"Remember, the inn will continue on, no matter the weather or insects or anything. It's not like farming. We won't have those problems."

"How have you been running the place since John died?" She sat back.

"I made a deal with one of Elijah Fitch's tenant farmers. I hired his two daughters to help tidy up the rooms and do laundry. In return he gives me eggs, milk, and vegetables. He doesn't charge me much for beef, either."

"Smart." Her gaze connected with Martha's.

"John put aside a little money he had left after selling our farm in Danbury and buying the inn. He repaired a lot himself before we opened. He kept a few silver coins in a small can tucked away in the chicken coop. Thank God."

"Half the inn now belongs to your family. It's handed down to Sam, as the law dictates. Next time the lawyer comes to town, we'll make it official. I'm sure your son will let you be in charge of his share."

"Thank you. Yes, he will. He's cut from the same cloth as his father, a good man." She clasped Martha's hands. "By the way, I sew, too. I've been teaching Sarah, but it's been slow. There's so little free time on the farm."

"Can you mend?" Martha raised her eyebrows.

"Mend and make dresses."

"Excellent. It'll bring in extra money."

"I need to keep busy. Idle time makes me miss George."

Martha smiled. "Oh, I'll keep you plenty busy."

She smiled.

"He was right to marry you. You're a Godsend. Together, we'll get this place up on its feet." Martha leaned her elbows on the table.

The women choked down the last of the whisky in their glasses. Martha replaced the bottle and approached her daughter-in-law. "We're family. Whatever is mine is yours, too."

They hugged, and each retired to their own room for the night.

"WE NEED MOLASSES. ABBY, head on over to Rhodes' General Store, will you?" Martha tucked a coin in her hand. "Get the large size."

"Sure thing." She walked down the street, passing a modest house on each side, and the blacksmith shop. Fitch's Eddy was much smaller than Danbury, why hardly a smattering of homes! Danbury had many, some quite grand, and shops, too.

There was a town square, though so much smaller than the one in Danbury. Unable to take in anything about the town when she'd arrived, now she stared at the buildings, one at each corner of the square. The blacksmith shop, the Congregational Church, the school, and Rhodes' General Store. In the center stood a flagpole with the new American flag flying. The pole was surrounded by bushes and lovely flowers. Pinks, purples, and pure white blooms lifted her spirits. What did George always say? *Celebrate in summer, fall harvest comes fast.*

This year, she wouldn't be working in the fields for fall harvest. Although she'd not miss the long, backbreaking days gathering vegetables and fruit, she did enjoy being outside in the sunshine with her husband. Her eyes misted. Those days were over. She had no idea what to expect when fall rounded the bend. Thank goodness she had her children and Martha. With a shake of her head, she broke from her reverie and returned to her errand.

The Rhodes' General Store had a big glass window in the front. She took a passing glance, wondering if the items on display were for sale. Her eyes stopped at a lovely cameo, in a prominent place in the window. Her fingers trembled as she set them at the base of her neck, her thoughts turning to her sister. Her cameo, pinned proudly next to the neckline of her drab dress, comforted her. The one in the window may have been a touch bigger, but it wasn't nearly as beautiful.

As she pushed through the swinging door, a bell tinkled. A woman in a stylish dress stood at the counter, her voice raised. The woman behind the counter shifted her weight and wore a nervous grin.

"I'm sorry, Mrs. Fitch. I don't sew. I've told you before. I wish I could help you."

"When are you going to learn?"

Abigail approached the counter quietly. The attractive woman with blonde hair pulled up into a neat bun on the top of her head turned to peer at her. Abby tugged gently at her shabby skirt, knowing it wouldn't make her look more presentable. There simply hadn't been money for cloth to make new clothing. As long as the old garments fit and didn't have holes, they would have to do.

"Can you imagine? This woman, Virginia Rhodes, runs this shop and doesn't know how to sew? I have a terrible rip in my best gown. See?" The fancy woman held up a light blue silk dress, pointing out where the ruffle at the bottom had come apart from the dress.

"I see," she said.

"I'm Ann Fitch, wife of Elijah Fitch. I can't wear this dress like this. And it's pure silk. All the way from New York." Small, ice-blue eyes narrowed as they stared at her.

"I sew."

The woman's eyes widened. "You do? Who are you?"

"I'm Abigail Chesney, Martha Chesney's daughter-in-law."

The woman thrust the dress at her. "Here. Fix it. I need it by tomorrow night. We're having guests for dinner. Are you living at the inn?"

"Yes."

"I'll have my man pick it up tomorrow at two o'clock. I'll give you three shillings. See that it's ready." The woman flounced out of the store.

"Ain't she something?" Virginia Rhodes said under her breath, shaking her head.

"I need the work. I'm here to buy molasses, and, I guess, blue silk thread, if you have any."

"Come over here, Mrs. Chesney. Let's see what we have." Virginia walked to a cabinet at the side of the store and pulled out a drawer. "Well, well. Looks like we might have what you need right here." She picked up a spool of light blue thread.

"Perfect. I'll take it. And molasses, please."

"Sure thing. Right this way. Oh, and welcome to Fitch's Eddy. I'm so sorry about your husband."

"Thank you. Word travels fast."

"It does here, for sure. Now how much molasses did you need. We have jars in three different sizes."

She dug deep into her pocket for coins. "I don't have enough for the large jar of molasses. You'd better give me the small."

"Never you mind. We keep accounts for some people in town. Martha's credit is always good with us. I'll mark it down in the ledger." Mrs. Rhodes pulled a book with lined paper out from under the counter. She marked something on the page, then closed it.

"Thank you. I'll pay you when Mrs. Fitch pays me."

"Martha fixing to make some of her molasses cookies?" The woman tucked the jar into the leather bag.

"I don't know."

"Her cookies are famous around here. I keep telling her to make some for the store. We could get a good price. But she never takes me up on it. Says her boarders come there for the cookies and then take rooms and eat meals. Says she makes a lot more on a boarder than she could get from selling cookies in my store."

"Makes sense." Abigail turned to leave.

"Wait." Mrs. Rhodes grabbed her arm. "I can get you some sewing work if you're interested. Seamstress we had left for Ohio two weeks ago Thursday."

"Thanks. I'd appreciate it."

"Maybe you'd sew for me for free if I got you some paying customers."

"We'll see." She hurried out the door. Goodness, people in Fitch's Eddy were direct, weren't they? Still, she grinned in anticipation of the money she'd be getting from the stuck-up Mrs. Fitch. Guess when a town was named after your husband's family you got a right to be high and mighty. She frowned. Nobody had a right to be like Ann Fitch.

With a quick shake of her head, she cleared out the negative thought. As long as the woman paid her, she didn't care whether she was nice or not. They needed money to make repairs and buy supplies, and she was happy to contribute, even such a small sum.

Chapter Seven

M*id-July — one month after George Chesney's burial*
Martha Chesney hated to put the "closed" sign in the window of the inn's dining room. But on this Sunday, Reverend Bloodgoode was having a special service in honor of her son. She gathered her family.

"I don't close the inn. Even on Christmas, I keep the dining room open. But today is special. Put on your best clothes. There will be a service in honor of your father. We must attend." Martha stopped to wipe her eyes.

"I could be out hunting, Grandma." Sam leaned over to scratch Lucky behind the ears.

"Any other Sunday, Sam, and I'd agree. Not today."

"Let's get ready," Abby said, pushing to her feet.

When they were dressed in their worn, but clean best, they gathered as a group and marched over to the church. Spruced up, Abigail looked beautiful. Martha smiled at her daughter-in-law, by far the prettiest woman in town. At least by Martha's standards. *My son had good taste. Plucked himself the most handsome apple from the tree.*

The Reverend Ebenezer Bloodgoode stood at the door, greeting parishioners as they entered. When the Chesney clan arrived, the front pew was empty. Five rows behind were filled. The Reverend gestured to the front of the church.

"Mrs. Chesney," he greeted Martha. "Please seat your family in the front row."

Martha made her way down the aisle. The children followed. Abby was the last. The reverend extended his hand. Martha turned to watch as the clergyman held Abby's hand a mite too long.

Caleb rushed up, stopping right before he collided with the reverend.

"Be on time next time, Tanner," he barked.

Martha watched Caleb's gaze light on the reverend's hand joined with Abby's. The blacksmith frowned. With Ebenezer's attention diverted, she snatched her hand back and hurried forward to join Martha.

The two women exchanged glances. *So it's like that, is it? No way is the reverend getting his hooks into her.* Martha set her lips into a thin line. Caleb joined them. He offered his arm to Martha.

"Mrs. Chesney, may I escort you?"

"Thank you." Even though it was the hottest day in July, she took his arm for the short walk to the first pew. Whispering piqued Martha's attention. She turned and found Charity Bloodgoode and her sister, Catherine, with their heads together.

"She doesn't have mourning clothes."

"Too poor to have more..."

Martha shot a fierce look at the girls. Catherine stopped in mid-sentence. Caleb patted Martha's hand, then stepped aside. He took a seat several rows behind.

"We are here today to honor George Chesney, beloved son of Martha, loving husband of Abigail, and doting father of Samuel, Sarah, and Elizabeth," Ebenezer began.

Martha opened a fan she'd tucked into a purse. *The old windbag's gonna make it hotter in here than it already is.* She fanned herself as discreetly as possible.

After the service, before most of the folks returned home, Martha made an announcement.

"For those who'd like to pay their respects, personal like, we have tea and some cakes at the inn. Please join us." She took Abby's hand before Ebenezer could and hurried home. The children followed.

Once they arrived, the women rushed about, setting up the small cakes, plates, and cups for tea. Martha's closest friends gathered in the dining room, sipping the brew and chatting. She kept her eye on her daughter-in-law. It didn't take the reverend long to approach her. Side-tracked by the conversation of her two dearest friends, Martha couldn't break away to interrupt Ebenezer.

SHE KEPT A KEEN EYE on Reverend Bloodgoode, because she didn't trust him, especially around her daughter-in-law.

"Mrs. Chesney, let me express my deepest sorrow at your loss." The reverend inched closer.

"Thank you." Abby picked up a small sponge cake.

"I hope you will come to me to pray for your husband's entry into Heaven. I do hold private services for those who are grieving." His eyes lit up.

Before she could reply, Caleb butted in.

"Excuse me, Mrs. Chesney, could I speak with you a moment in private? It's about Sam."

"Of course, of course. Please excuse me, Reverend. Oh, and thank you for the offer, but I prefer to grieve alone." Hustled away before he could reply, she accompanied Caleb to a quiet corner. Martha's loud laugh caught Abby's attention. Martha grinned, then hid her face behind her fan.

She had kept her granddaughter, Sarah by her side. The girl's red-rimmed eyes and sorrowful expression touched the older woman. *Such a tender age to lose her father.* The girl fidgeted with the ruffle at her wrist and cast her gaze to the ground. *She needs something to do.*

"Sarah, dear, would you bring out more little cakes, and put the kettle on for more tea?" Martha patted her granddaughter's hand.

"But the platter is almost full."

"There's another one in the cupboard next to the sink. You can fill it."

"Of course, Grandma." The girl shot her a grateful smile.

"Thank you, dear." She watched Sarah wend her way through the crowd.

"She's a beauty, that one," Virginia Rhodes said.

"Yes, she is. She'll be setting male hearts aflutter before long."

"How old is she?" Virginia added sugar to her tea.

"Only fifteen. We'll have to keep her under lock and key until she's of age."

"Like we've done with our Becky. She's with me at the store all day."

"Wise, very wise, Virginia." Martha picked up another cake and took a bite. "She's a fine baker already." Martha finished her sweet.

"Then the men will surely be flocking."

She laughed with her friend. Virginia hugged her, then left the inn. Martha perused the remaining crowd. She and John had made many friends since their arrival. She turned her gaze to Sam. *Just sixteen, but the weight of the world's on his shoulders. A handsome lad with brown hair and eyes, like his father. He'll grow into the responsibility of being the head of his family. He's quick, learns fast. George would be proud.*

When she thought about how proud John would have been of such fine grandchildren, sadness filled her. Little Lizzy ran into the room, looking for her sister. *Oh the poor child. She'll never remember her father.* Martha's eyes wetted as she watched the youngster cling to Sarah's waist.

As Martha had predicted, the folks crowding the dining room finished off all the cakes on both platters and two more pots of tea. When the food was gone, they shuffled out, stopping to pay their respects to the Chesney women.

When the last well-wisher had departed, the family sat down to a cold supper.

"I saw you in conversation with Caleb. What did he want?" Martha refreshed her tea.

"We talked about Sam becoming his apprentice one or two days a week."

"Me?" Sam raised his eyebrows.

"It would be good for you to learn a trade." She buttered a piece of bread and handed it to Lizzy.

"I'm not sure, Mama."

"Maybe only one day a week? He'd pay you something. Not much, but at least it's something."

"I need him here at the inn. But I suppose one day a week would be all right." Martha gazed over her cup at her new family. What a joyous turn of unfortunate events, to have them here. Although the loss of her son was a heavy blow, she welcomed his family. Her worries about the inn could be put to rest. But what about her daughter-in-law? She was too young to be a widow. Maybe there might be a new worry brewing for her, like a cup of strong tea?

CALEB RETURNED TO HIS modest home behind his shop. He put together a small plate of cold food and set the kettle on the fire. He needed a strong cup of tea. Unable to resist the delectable cakes at the Chesney Inn, his appetite for food had been satisfied, but his yearning for a family had grown.

While waiting for the water to boil, Caleb thought about Abigail Chesney. Twice he'd watched Reverend Bloodgoode get too close to her. The man was a renowned lecher. With her doe eyes, she appeared like an innocent lamb to Ebenezer's wolf. Anger at the reverend's sneaky ways filled Caleb's chest.

Of course, he had no right to intervene or assume even a friendship with her, but he owed it to his friend, Martha, to protect her daughter-in-law. He shook his head as he laughed out loud. It was one thing to lie to the world, but a big mistake to lie to oneself. No, he wasn't being altruistic or unduly chivalrous. The beautiful woman drew him as if she'd cast a spell.

Having been closed off to women for so long, he surprised himself. He'd hardly exchanged more than a few sentences with the woman—and those mostly pertained to her son. Still, there was something about her, something soft and warm, yet strong. In some ways, she reminded him of his beloved Emily.

He'd made up his mind to accept a celibate life—and had lived alone for several years. He had his work and a friend or two in town—though most shunned him as a man of mystery. Convinced there would never be another woman he could love with such devotion as his dear wife, he'd given up searching. He'd be damned if he'd settle. Unmarried was better than being chained to a shrew or a greedy manipulator.

He didn't expect to have feelings for any woman. Then he'd met Abigail. Her pain, her sorrow, so evident in her eyes, and the way she carried herself touched him. He recognized her grief because it mirrored his own. He wanted to reach out, to be a friend, a sympathetic ear, but he couldn't figure out how to do it without being inappropriate and causing tongues to wag. There was already enough gossip in Fitch's Eddy—especially about him.

Though he chose not to drag her into the sights of the nastiest people in town, his constraint didn't stop his heart from feeling. Oh, how wonderful it would be to have a sweet woman to talk to again, one who understood his grief! In time, would it be possible with the young Mrs. Chesney?

Although he didn't need an apprentice, he'd broached the idea to rescue her from old Ebenezer. Of course, he could use some help and it provided a legitimate reason to talk to her. Her enthusiasm to have Sam take the job, even though it only paid a pittance, gave Caleb hope. Though he knew nothing of Sam, every boy could benefit from learning smithing, a useful trade.

Caleb made a reasonable living, enough to put food on his table, clothes on his back, and a fire going in his shop. He could easily spare a shilling a day for Sam. With the boy around, Caleb could learn more about her. He'd have to feign indifference, so Sam wouldn't catch on, but he could do it. Because she was a recent widow, Caleb would keep a respectful distance, even though he was smitten. Best to keep the boy in the dark, too.

The dozen or so times he'd seen her, his pulse had kicked up a notch and a smile had played at his lips. But he must put what was decent before his own desires. He'd tipped his hat and exchanged a pleasant greeting.

"Morning, Mrs. Chesney. Fine day, isn't it?"

"Morning, Mr. Tanner. Yes, it is."

He understood her heart hurt and needed to heal. Caleb was a patient man. He had waited years to meet her, certainly, he could wait a while longer.

The whistling kettle called to him. He prepared tea and settled onto a stool in his small garden. Blooming wildflowers gave it a colorful, fragrant, summery air. As he breathed deep of the sweet scents of Lily of the Valley and Heliotrope, A gruff voice interrupted him.

"I know what you're doing."

Caleb turned to face Ebenezer Bloodgoode.

"What?"

"I know what you're doing. You have the basest of desires regarding Mrs. Chesney."

"Martha and I have been friends since I first got here." He deliberately put on an appearance of misunderstanding.

"Poppycock! I don't mean the old lady. I mean her daughter-in-law."

"Oh, Mrs. Abigail Chesney? No, Reverend, you're wrong. You're the one with base desires. Stay away from her. Keep your hands off her."

"Oh? Or what? What will you do about it?"

Caleb rose to fist the man's shirt. "You'll be sorry. Trust my words."

Ebenezer pushed the blacksmith away. "I'm offering her spiritual guidance, is all."

"Rubbish. Stay away from her. I'm warning you."

Trembling slightly, Ebenezer put his nose in the air and turned toward the street. He left without another word.

A grin tugged Caleb's lips upward. He'd frightened the old man. Good. The reverend had two daughters, Charity, who was twenty-one, and Catherine, eighteen. Though he told people his wife had died, word around town was she ran off with another man. Caleb chuckled. Who wouldn't bolt tied to the old windbag?

He sipped his tea and wondered if the reverend would follow Caleb's advice. Maybe he'd have to teach him a lesson the hard way. His lips compressed into a frown. Even though he was one of the biggest and strongest men in town, Caleb didn't like to fight. But he'd not let old Bloodgoode take advantage of Abby. Not as long as there was breath in his body.

CALEB TIED HIS LEATHER apron behind him and stoked the fire in his shop. Someone clearing their voice interrupted him. He turned. Sam Chesney stood, his hands in his pockets, gazing at the floor.

"Oh, Sam! Welcome. Come in, come in." Caleb ushered the boy inside.

"It's hot in here."

"Yes. Hot in summer, but welcome in January. Here, put this apron on. We always wear these in the shop, so we don't get our clothes dirty or burned."

Sam eyed the garment. "What do you do?"

"I make things." Caleb took down one of his hammers.

"Make things?" Sam put the apron down.

"Yes. Tools, pots and pans. Horseshoes. Nails."

Sam glanced at the rack of instruments Caleb used in his work. He picked up a hammer. As soon as he realized he had soot on his hands, he hung it up.

"I'm sorry about your father." Caleb handed the boy the apron again.

After slipping the apron over his head, Sam gave one nod, but his expression didn't change.

"It's dirty work, isn't it?" Sam rubbed his hands together.

"Yes. Sometimes." Caleb fed oxygen to the fire with a bellows.

"Hunting is much easier." He wiped the rest on the apron.

"Are you a hunter?"

"I am. I have a dog, Lucky. He goes with me and finds rabbits and ducks. Deer, too."

Caleb spoke. "You don't want to be here, do you?"

Color rose to Sam's cheeks. "I didn't say so."

"You don't have to." Caleb filled the quenching bucket at the water pump.

"My mother wants me to learn a trade."

"And this is a fine one. But if you don't want to do it, I won't keep you. I'll give you your money for showing up and you can be on your way." Caleb spoke over his shoulder.

"I can't. My mother will be mad."

"I wouldn't want to make her angry. She's had enough heartache, don't you think?" Caleb stroked his rough cheek.

"What's it to you?" Sam spread his feet and fisted his hands on his hips.

"What?" Caleb stopped what he was doing and faced Sam.

"Are you liking my mother? I saw you at church and at the inn."

"I was talking to her about you at the inn." Caleb faced away from the boy.

"I got eyes. I'm no fool." Sam took a step closer.

"Never said you were." Caleb prayed the heat in his face would fade fast.

"Don't think you can step into my father's shoes. He was a great man. He fought in the war. I bet you didn't even go. Just stayed home making shoes for horses." Sam's lip curled in a sneer.

Caleb bristled. "I was in the artillery. Where I learned about blacksmithing and how important it is. And I have a few medals to prove it."

Slightly mollified, Sam quieted and shoved his hands back in his pockets.

"No one could ever step into your father's shoes. I simply wanted to help a widow and her family. You don't want the job? Don't need it? Fine. Run along home then." Caleb cringed inside because his words were not the whole truth. He reached into his pocket and found a coin. He offered it to the boy.

"Fine." Sam took the shilling and left as quietly as he had arrived. Caleb sat down on a bench and rubbed the back of his neck. The boy was a handful. But if pretty Abigail Chesney wanted him to be a blacksmith, like it or not, Caleb would teach him. He bolted up and ran after the boy.

"Sam! Sam!"

The young man stopped.

"Come back. Your mother wants you to learn blacksmithing, then I think we should honor her wishes. Let's start again."

The boy nodded, though his attitude hadn't changed.

Caleb scratched his cheek and handed the boy the apron. "Put it on!" His voice was a little gruffer than intended.

The boy jumped but did as he was told.

Sad, angry, and hostile, the perceptive Sam had pegged Caleb already. Perhaps he would present more of a challenge than a stubborn horse or a client who wouldn't pay?

Caleb sighed. He'd been looking for a way to do something for her. He figured teaching her boy and serving as a stand-in kind of father might be the answer. He swallowed. Sam would be difficult to win over. Was Caleb up to the task?

He approached the boy and put his hand on his shoulder. Sam pulled away, but Caleb grabbed him again.

"If this is going to work, we have to get along. It's too dangerous in here if we aren't speaking or respecting each other. Truce?" Caleb held up his hand.

"Truce," Sam replied.

Caleb let out a breath and launched into an explanation of how a blacksmith does what he does. He hoped the boy's mother would appreciate his effort and understand Caleb only wanted to help her family, not harm it.

THOUGH GEORGE HAD BEEN gone a little over a month, to Abby, it seemed like forever. Long nights alone in bed, she yearned for the comfort of his body next to hers, the feel of his bare chest under her fingers, and the soft sensuousness of his lips. Restless, she often tossed and turned, as the memory of his demise played over and over again in her dreams.

Sometimes, she'd steal away from the house to go for a walk or sit behind the shed and cry. Martha found her there from time-to-time and offered comfort and a clean handkerchief.

"Someday, you'll remember only the good. The vision of his death will fade from your mind and you'll rejoice to have had the time you did with him," Martha said.

"Is it the same for you with John?"

"Not yet. But every month, I feel his love in my heart. And missing him gets easier."

She didn't quite believe it.

"Once you get fixed in Fitch's Eddy, life will get better. Now everything is new, and he isn't here to help you. So, it's hard. But the sooner you get out and meet folks here, the better your life will be." Martha hugged her and returned to the kitchen.

Following Martha's advice, she filled her days by learning her way around town. She figured out who to talk to and who to only show a polite expression then move on.

Unlike Danbury, Fitch's Eddy was small. She drifted easily from the general store to the school to the blacksmith shop. Gone were the days of stopping at the Danbury dressmaker's window to drool over the latest outfit on display or dipping into their egg money to buy a newspaper. In Fitch's Eddy, she might be the only seamstress in town, and there was no local newspaper.

This little village seemed to have fallen off the map. The street, rough and muddy after a rain, reminded her how far they were from the sophistication of Danbury—where carriages outnumbered wagons, and women in fancy dresses, sporting parasols, strolled well-tended streets. She sighed and pushed memories of her hometown out of her mind. Fitch's Eddy was her new home, and the sooner she accepted it, the better.

No matter where she went, she ran into Caleb Tanner. Fortunately, he appeared almost magically, whenever she needed him. On the day the grand carriage of Elijah and Ann Fitch came to town, it nearly ran her over. A strong hand clamped over her upper arm and jerked her back from the vehicle trotting along as if it owned the street.

It was Caleb Tanner who'd pulled her to safety.

"Begging your pardon, Mrs. Chesney." His cheeks reddened as he tipped his hat and smiled.

"Thank you. You saved my life!"

"It was nothing."

"I'm beholden."

"Any neighbor would have done the same."

She appreciated his modesty, but knew darn well there were neighbors who would have preferred to push her in front of the vehicle rather than yank her to safety. Of course, there were nasty gossips in Danbury, but Abby had managed to avoid them. Fitch's Eddy was so small, she couldn't escape the wagging tongues.

"Jealous biddies! They're mad 'cause you're much prettier than they are. My son always did have an eye for a pretty girl," Martha had replied when Abby lamented.

Abby gave a half-bow to Mr. Tanner and made her way to Rhodes' General Store. Virginia Rhodes had been kind, passing along customers who needed mending. Ann Fitch even commissioned her to create an entire dress. Longer days of summer sunshine provided enough light for her to work into the evening on her sewing.

Since sewing generated a small income, Martha and Sarah took over more of the inn's tasks to free up Abigail for sewing. Her frequent trips to the general store for thread took her past the blacksmith shop. She'd slow down to gaze at the amazing array of tools, hung neatly on the wall.

Over supper, Sam regaled them with what he'd learned from Mr. Tanner. While Sarah didn't pay much mind, the facts about blacksmithing intrigued his mother. One day, Sam came home with a set of tiny utensils. A little knife, fork, and spoon specially fashioned for Lizzy.

"Mr. Tanner made the fork. He showed me how to make the spoon and knife."

The gift touched Abby's heart. Every time she ran an errand with Lizzy in tow, Mr. Tanner would stop and speak to the little girl. Sometimes, he'd whip out a small, wrapped peppermint, like a magic trick, from his pocket. He'd make her guess which hand, then give it to her even if she guessed wrong. Lizzy giggled, and clapped, making him grin.

Touched by his kindness and generosity, Abigail looked forward to bumping into him in the small village. She welcomed a friendly face amid so many strangers, some cold and hostile, looking down their noses at her in her threadbare dress.

"Never you mind what other folks say. You go about your business and make your own friends. Caleb has been loyal to me from the moment he arrived. Don't let the gossips make you shun him," Martha had said over an evening cup of tea.

Perhaps having only two friends, Caleb Tanner and Virginia Rhodes in a town the size of Fitch's Eddy wasn't so bad.

One hot afternoon, Sarah and Lizzy came home with a note from the teacher, Mr. Edmond Hammond.

"I have to go to the school, Martha. Seems the school master, a Mr. Hammond, needs to speak to me."

"Sarah will help with supper today. Go on. We'll be fine."

Abby crossed over to the other side of the street to reach the schoolhouse. Too bad she wouldn't be passing the blacksmith shop on her way. His friendly greeting always brightened her day. Ah, yes! She remembered Mrs. Fitch's yellow dress needed mending, which necessitated buying new thread. She guessed she'd be crossing over to the general store and passing the smithy shop on the way home after all.

When she arrived at the schoolhouse, she knocked. A man of medium height, with dull brown hair, wearing glasses, and sporting a beard opened the door.

"Mrs. Chesney?"

"Mr. Hammond?"

"Yes. Do come in." He eased out of the way to let her pass.

She sat in one of the classroom chairs and faced him. "Is there a problem?"

"Well, yes, and no. Sarah's a little old to be at school, you know." He paced slowly.

"She's here to accompany her little sister."

"Oh, Lizzy? Yes, yes. But she's proving a bit of a distraction."

"Really?" She raised her eyebrows.

"Yes. To some of the boys."

"Sarah can't be distracting ten-year-old boys, Mr. Hammond."

"No, no, of course not. But we have some boys who are thirteen and fourteen."

"What are they still doing in school?"

"They are not perhaps our fastest learners—if I may put it delicately."

"Sarah hasn't complained. What are they doing?"

"They are staring at your daughter when they are supposed to be doing silent reading." His face flushed and he stopped.

She hid a smirk behind her hand, then stood up. "I'm sorry, Mr. Hammond. Sarah is a lovely girl. Perhaps the people you need to speak with are the parents of the boys."

"I think you should take Sarah out of school."

"Really! I disagree. As long as I believe Lizzy needs her sister here with her, Sarah will remain." Her lips compressed into a frown.

Mr. Hammond sauntered closer and closer to her. "I see where she gets her good looks."

She backed up. "Mr. Hammond! Stop where you are."

"Oh, I beg pardon. Didn't mean to make you uncomfortable."

"You certainly did! You did it on purpose."

"I'm not a harsh man. I'm not hard-hearted. Quite the contrary. I can be easily persuaded to keep Sarah in school." He took her hand and kissed it.

She snatched it from his grasp and jumped away. "Mr. Hammond! How dare you!"

"Just being accommodating, Mrs. Chesney."

She stepped forward and slapped his face. He turned purple with rage.

"You'll regret this, Mrs. Chesney! And so will your daughters. I can make school mighty uncomfortable for troublemakers."

"Good. Then why don't you call those boys to task?"

His mouth fell open and he stared.

"Good day, Mr. Hammond."

She huffed out of the schoolhouse and high-tailed it across the street. Running to the general store left her breathless. She stopped, then regretted it.

"Someone chasing you, Mrs. Chesney?" Old Zeke asked with a licentious laugh.

She yanked open the door and collided with Caleb Tanner, who was on his way out.

"Pardon me, Mr. Tanner. Pardon me."

"Lucky for you, Caleb," Zeke said with a wink.

Chapter Eight

"Mrs. Chesney!" Caleb caught her elbow as she burst into the store. "Are you all right?"

Her face was flushed, and small wisps of hair had escaped her tight bun. Was she frightened or happy? Why she had come running? He stepped aside.

"Oh, that nasty Mr. Hammond!" She blew out a breath.

"Edmond? What has he done now?" Caleb stopped.

"He's hateful."

"What's he done?"

"So rude!" She leaned against the wall and slowed her breathing. Her color returned to normal.

"Rude? Do I need to teach him a lesson?" Caleb's right hand fisted at his side.

She made eye contact with him. "I don't think so. I slapped him pretty hard."

Caleb raised his eyebrows. "You what?"

"I slapped him." She broke into a smile and giggled.

"What did he do?" Caleb opened his eyes wide.

"I really couldn't say. It's not proper. But he was out of line."

"I'll take care of him." Caleb frowned.

"I think I did. For now, at least."

"Stay away from him." Caleb inched closer and softened his voice. "He has a reputation."

"Oh? What for?"

"I couldn't recount in front of a lady. But trust me, it's well deserved."

"Maybe I shouldn't send my girls to his school." She bit her lip.

"It's the only school for miles. Oh, he's safe during the school day. When there are children in the schoolhouse. But tell your girls to clear out as soon as class is over."

"Oh? So, he misbehaves after class?"

Caleb nodded.

"Have you witnessed this?"

"I have. Once I gave him a sound beating, too. He's afraid of me. If he bothers you again, mention you're going to tell me."

She laughed. "Thank you so much, Mr. Tanner. I will. And I'll make sure my girls come straight home from school the second they are dismissed."

"Good."

"Thank you."

"Happy to oblige, Mrs. Chesney. Fine day, isn't it?" Caleb glanced out the door, then returned his gaze to the handsome woman standing before him.

"That it is, Mr. Tanner. Good day."

He tipped his hat. "Good day."

Grinning, he returned to his shop.

Sam waited in the doorway. "Were you talking to my mother?"

"In fact, I was."

"What about?" Sam donned his apron.

"Mr. Hammond. The schoolmaster." Caleb checked on his utensils in the quenching bucket.

"What about him? Sarah doesn't like him."

"Nobody likes him. Seems he was rude to your mother."

"Don't you mind. I'll take care of her. Ain't none of your business." Two angry red circles appeared on Sam's cheeks as he faced Caleb,

"I ran into her in Rhodes'. Why do you care if I talk to your mother?"

"'Cause you're up to no good. I see your eyes. I see the way you look at her."

Caleb sensed heat creeping up his neck. "What way is that?" As soon as the question was out of his mouth, he regretted it.

"The way a fox looks at chickens."

Caleb burst out laughing. "Your mother is a beautiful woman. Any man with eyes can see it." He picked up the tools from the bucket and dried them off.

"You'll take my father's place over my dead body. Stay away from her."

"Don't be messing where you shouldn't be. There's nothing going on between your mother and me. We're simply friends."

"I got eyes. All I'm sayin' is I got eyes."

"Let's finish your project. Get the hammer." Caleb stoked the fire.

Silently, Sam did as he was told, but Caleb sensed a wall between them. As soon as he thought he was making progress with Sam, boom! Something happened to shatter his confidence and make the boy wary and suspicious. He certainly was an observant lad. He had Caleb pegged correctly.

Ashamed his admiration of Mrs. Chesney was so obvious, Caleb turned away from Sam and focused on his work. What could he do? If Sam could see it, soon everyone in town would. Zeke had already been teasing him before Caleb even met Mrs. Chesney. Sure, no one listens to the old man, crazy as a loon, but soon they might be getting those notions on their own.

He'd try to avoid her. Make sure not to be where she was. In such a small town, how could he manage it? He had to go to the general store for supplies, and groceries. It seemed Abby was there every other day.

Soon his secret would be out. She'd be horrified, and he'd lose her friendship. Or any chance he had of getting her friendship. He sighed. How long could a man hide what was in his heart?

AUGUST

It was rare for Caleb to close his shop early in August because of heat. The scorching sun added to the burning of his fire had wrung every extra drop of water from him. He returned home and sought relief at the water pump. He stuck his head under the faucet and pumped until his hair was soaked. Then he drank until his belly was full enough to float.

He shook the water off and brushed his hair back from his forehead with his fingers. But the unrelenting sun dried it quickly, leaving him as hot and uncomfortable as before. There was only one answer, Willow lake.

He tramped through the tall grass and weeds until he came upon the secret path he'd cut through the underbrush leading straight to the lake. It was the perfect place to wash and cool off. He kept his path to himself so he could bathe privately in a secluded cove.

The heat was unbearable. Hiking up the hill, he'd worked up a sweat. Wiping his face on his sleeve, he ignored his discomfort and hurried along, driven by the knowledge that relief was only a few feet away. When he spied the lake, he broke into a run.

Once on the shore, Caleb looked around to be certain he was alone. He didn't need some faint-hearted maiden to stumble upon him and run screaming into town about the naked man at the lake. Chuckling to himself, he pictured a couple of the stuffier, more proper women in Fitch's Eddy discovering him. An incident like that would seal his fate. He'd probably be run out of town.

Convinced no one could see him, he stripped off his clothes so fast anyone would have thought they were on fire. Naked, he waded into the water to his waist, then plunged in all the way. When he surfaced, he swam across, then turned around. Lying on his back, he floated, eyes closed, feeling his body temperature cool down.

Oh, the blessed relief! After paddling around for twenty minutes, he swam toward shore. Bare, he waded through the shallow water and up onto the little embankment. After pulling on his pants, he searched for his shirt, but couldn't find it. The rustling of a bush and a little giggle caught his attention. Shock washed over him as a familiar figure rose up amid the brush.

"Mrs. Chesney!"

THE SUN DIDN'T USUALLY get so hot in early August. At least not in Danbury. July was the most brutal month there, when working in the field did a body in. But today, resembled the middle of July. Abby wiped her forehead with the hem of her apron.

"Too hot to work today. Dinner's done. Supper will be cold food. We need to stop or the heat'll kill us," Martha said, mopping her face with a hand towel.

Abby remembered seeing a lake in the distance. Might be worth the walk in the hot sun to take a quiet dip alone. Best way to cool off.

"I'm going to walk to the lake."

"Take this with you. There're wild raspberries up there. They ought to be ripe about now. We can have 'em with milk tonight." Martha handed her a basket then plopped down in a chair.

As she wandered, she recalled the hot July nights when she and George were first married, before the children came. After dark, they'd sneak off to the pond nearby, rip off their clothes and jump in. She closed her eyes, remembering how cool and wonderful the water felt against her hot flesh. He would swim up underneath and scare her. They'd laugh and splash, chilling their bodies down to a comfortable temperature.

Usually the water play sparked mutual desire. When they returned to the cabin, they'd make love. Sometimes, he couldn't wait, and he'd take her in the shallow end, her body sliding up and down, against his. He was strong and held her up as if she were a ragdoll. Abby smiled at the sweet memory of her beloved husband and the fun they'd had.

Opening her eyes, she returned to present day and her lonely existence. Were days of naughty fun gone forever? Some nights, as darkness blanketed the sky, she fell straight into bed, as exhausted as an old woman. But she wasn't an old woman. She worked too hard and had little leisure time—and no fun, no laughter, no love.

Her mouth remembered the sweet taste of wild raspberries. As she pushed her way through thickets and tall grass, to the lake, she hummed a tune. The sight of bright red dots, clusters of berries peeking out from the greenery, caught her eye. She increased her pace. First, she'd pick the berries, then she'd wade into the lake to cool off.

The branches of the first bush were laden with ripe, juicy fruit. She reached in carefully to avoid the thorns intent on keeping her away. Before she had half a basket, she'd pricked her fingers three times. Sucking on the wounds, she stopped gathering. Maybe now was a good time to get wet?

Although she wouldn't be shedding her clothes, she looked for a secluded area. Then maybe she could take off her skirt and wade in wearing only her stockings and petticoat. Picking up the basket, she moseyed along to the quiet cove, singing, "My Days Have Been So Wondrous Free" as she walked.

When she glanced at the lake, she saw a man's head and shoulders rise from the water. Ducking down, she crept closer, but didn't recognize him. She spied clothing she recognized as belonging to Caleb Tanner. An impish impulse grabbed her. She snatched his shirt and hunkered down in a nearby bush to watch.

She expected him to have on underwear, but as he reached the shallow end, she realized he was naked. There would be no retreat now, she was stuck. She held the shirt to her face and breathed in deeply of his scent. Masculine and uniquely Mr. Tanner's—it pleased her. Turning her eyes to the lake, she watched him wade to shore. She sucked in air to see such a handsome man as he was born into this world.

She studied every inch. He was as fine as her George had been. She'd never seen a naked man before, outside of her father and husband. After he pulled his pants on, he searched for his shirt. Attempting to suppress a laugh, she clung to the garment. There was no way to give it to him without revealing she'd been spying, watching him, enjoying her mischief. Her face heated. What would he think of her? Was she an improper woman?

She didn't care. The joke was too good to hide. She giggled, drawing his eye, then stood up. When he exclaimed, "Mrs. Chesney!" She burst out laughing.

"It is I who stole your shirt." She stared at his chest, perfectly formed and bared to her eyes.

"Were you there..." He coughed. "...the whole time?"

"Yes."

Part of his chest, shoulders, and neck reddened. She tossed him the garment. His gaze connected with hers. His eyes were curious, not angry.

The heat in her body rose to her cheeks. He fumbled with the garment.

"No sense trying to hide now." He laughed and took his time dressing.

"I'm so sorry." She covered her mouth with her hand.

"Are you?" He cocked an eyebrow at her and smiled.

"Not really," she confessed, picking at a stray thread on her blouse.

"I see. Well, now you know me much better. Much better than I know you." His stare spread over her from head to toe.

"Don't expect you'll ever catch me like, like that!" She shook her head.

"No? I'm disappointed you won't be returning the favor."

She laughed. "I bathe in a tub at the inn."

"You never come out for a swim on a hot afternoon?"

"Maybe. But then, I would only remove one or two things. Never everything."

"Such a shame." He chuckled, donned the rest of this clothing, and approached her. His blue eyes always so sympathetic and friendly, now held something else. She guessed there was more to Caleb Tanner than simply kindness.

Embarrassment at her boldness surged through her, accompanied by a feeling she hadn't felt since her husband's death. Attraction? No, it couldn't be, it couldn't. He was gone only two months. Still, her body tingled at the sight of Caleb.

He fastened the last button on his shirt. "I apologize. I should never have been...if I knew you'd be coming down the hill, I'd..."

"Don't apologize. I surprised you. It could happen to anyone."

"It's so hot today. I needed a swim. Did you come to cool off, too?"

"I came for raspberries. And yes, maybe to wade in a bit." Her gaze met his.

"Oh, my. I spoiled your chance for a private swim. I'm so very sorry."

"No, no. It's all right. I mean, I wouldn't have gone all the way in." The idea of her running around the lake in broad daylight without clothes deepened the heat in her cheeks.

"Come. Why don't you take off your shoes and put your feet in. I hear that's enough to cool you all the way to the top of your head."

"Really?" She stepped closer.

"It's what I heard." He offered his hand. "There's a rock in the shade over here. You can sit there and dangle your feet in the water. It's so wonderfully cool."

The temptation overwhelmed her sense of propriety. After all, who would know? She took his hand and picked her way through the tall grass. She placed the basket down, then eased onto the flat rock and took off her shoes. The stockings would have to remain. First one foot, then the other slipped under the water.

She closed her eyes and sighed as relief from the heat climbed up her body.

"It's wonderful, isn't it?" He sat next to her and slid his feet in the water, too.

"Oh, yes. It's so unbearably hot today."

Out of the sun, they sat quietly enjoying the moment.

She kicked her feet, splashing them. "Sorry. I couldn't resist. Have some berries?" She offered him the basket.

"How are you?" He took a few and popped them in his mouth.

"Fine."

"No, I mean inside. I know what grief feels like."

"You mentioned you lost your wife and child."

"Yes. Emily died in childbirth."

She reached over and squeezed his hand. "I'm so very sorry. It must have been horrible."

"It was. Loss is hard. People who haven't experienced it, don't understand."

"I know what you mean." She took three berries and ate them.

"If you ever want to talk about it, I'm a good listener."

"Thank you. There's really nothing to talk about. I simply have to get used to George not being here. Day by day. Seems there's no speeding it up."

"No. There isn't."

"Do you still miss your wife?" Her hand flew to her mouth. "Oh, my. Is that a terrible question?"

"I do miss her. Every day. I keep her picture next to my bed."

"A picture?"

"A drawing a friend did." Caleb picked up a small stone and threw it in the lake.

"Oh. I see. How nice."

"It's comforting. To remember. People think it's bad, but it isn't. It's comforting."

"Yes! I know! How strange for you to say so. I was thinking the very same thing as I walked up here. I like remembering George and the life we had together."

They munched on berries and kicked their feet gently up and down in the water. Her gaze met Caleb's. His light blue eyes were still warm and friendly, but there was a touch of something more. Seeing it embarrassed her. *No, no, this man is still grieving. I must be wrong.*

She pulled her feet out, fastened her shoes, and walked to shore.

"Cool now?" Caleb joined her.

"Oh, yes. Thank you. I need to finish picking berries."

"I'll help." He again offered her his hand. It was warm, dry, and strong, guiding her, holding her steady.

"Thank you." She led the way to the bushes.

Caleb picked several berries before getting stuck by a thorn.

Abby took his hand in both of hers and examined the wound. She plucked out the thorn, then rubbed her thumb over the wound.

"Thank you. Those bushes are treacherous!" Caleb wiped his hand on his pants.

"They are. Be careful."

"I will. You have such a nice family."

"Sam is so angry. I think he's mad at his father for dying. Lizzy doesn't really understand, and Sarah hasn't taken it in completely yet."

"I've always wanted a family. Emily and I wanted four children." He sighed. "But it wasn't meant to be."

She reached over to touch his hand. His eyes met hers sending a small jolt through her.

They harvested most of the berries.

"Let's stop at your house on the way, so you can take some of our bounty."

"Are you sure? If anyone sees you go into my house, there will be gossip."

"Well, then?" She pondered for a moment. "You can go inside and bring out a jar, and we'll fill it outside. Okay?"

He laughed. "You're an independent woman."

"I don't like to let others push me around. We have nothing to be ashamed about."

"No, we don't."

They walked on quietly. Caleb carried the basket, filled with ripe, juicy red berries. He whistled the same tune she had sung earlier, making her laugh, then join in, singing.

When she returned home, Martha gave her a strange look. "You all right?"

"I am, Martha. For the first time I think I'm going to like it here in Fitch's Eddy."

Martha smiled and took the basket. "Good job!"

"We picked the bushes dry."

Martha stopped short. "We?"

Abby stuttered. "Oh, I mean. I. Yes, I. I'm a fast picker."

Martha uttered a deep chuckle, shook her head, and carried the basket to the kitchen.

Chapter Nine

Caleb picked up a small container of fresh cream at the general store. At home he poured it over his share of the berries they'd picked. As he savored the fresh, sweet, and tart flavor of the fruit, he thought about his afternoon with Abby.

Something had happened, but he had no clue what. He saw something in her eyes he hadn't seen before. She'd seen him for the first time. Not the naked part, but the inner part. Thinking about being undressed when she arrived embarrassed him even though he was alone.

How could he let such a thing happen? He didn't know she was going to the lake. But the look on her face, well, it told him something he'd wished for—she wasn't repulsed; instead, she'd stared, almost fascinated. She'd been married for at least seventeen years, so the male body didn't shock her. Not like she was a silly little virgin or something.

Longing! Yes, that's what it was. Obviously, she missed her husband in the same way he missed his wife. He wished he could have stayed at the lake for the rest of the day, and all night, talking to her, simply to be near her. As she spoke, he sensed her grief had burrowed into her bones, and yet she carried on, not letting sadness defeat her.

Was he ready to move on? Taste life again...with Abigail Chesney? If she could carry on, so could he. And the time had arrived. A small smile tugged at his lips. His heart lurched. He couldn't deny it—he was falling in love.

But what woman in Fitch's Eddy would welcome into her family a man the town didn't trust? He dreaded the heartbreak lying ahead. Maybe she was different.

He finished eating. There were some berries left over. He picked up the jar and returned to his shop. Sam stood outside, waiting.

"I closed down. The heat was too much." Caleb glanced at the sky. The sun had shifted, heading west toward sundown. The heat had lifted enough for him to resume work.

Caleb led the boy inside, then remembered what he held in his hand.

"I have some fresh berries. More than I could eat. Would you like these?"

Sam stared at the jar. His face became red as his brow furrowed. "Where'd you get those?"

Caleb realized his error too late. The last person he wanted to know about his time with Abby was Sam.

"Picked 'em." He poked around at the quenching bucket, facing away from the boy.

Sam grabbed Caleb's sleeve. "Where? Where'd you pick 'em?"

"Oh, I don't know. Wherever the bushes grow. Went for a walk. Found 'em." Caleb had always been a bad liar.

"You were out with my mother, weren't you?" The anger in the boy's eyes stopped the blacksmith cold. "Admit it. You been keepin' company with her? You got no right. No right at all."

"We bumped into each other by the lake."

"You what?" Sam's voice rose.

"You heard me." Caleb's dander kicked up. He'd be damned if he'd explain his actions to this mere boy. They had done nothing wrong.

"Stay away from my mother."

"Watch your step. What I do is none of your business! If I want to spend an hour or two with Mrs. Chesney, I will. She didn't object."

Sam took a swing at Caleb's jaw. He dodged, but Sam kept coming. Ducking and weaving worked for a while. Then Sam took a new tack and aimed at the stomach. He landed one, knocking Caleb back. He bent over, grabbing his middle, giving Sam an open invitation to connect with his nose.

The blow sent Caleb into the wall, knocking down a dozen tools. The clang of metal on metal reverberated, traveling to the street.

"Owww!" Sam shook his hand. The knuckles he'd scraped against Caleb's scruff appeared raw.

Caleb saw red. After wiping blood from his face with his sleeve, he grabbed the boy, fisting the neck of his shirt in his hand. Though Sam had some meat on his bones, he was no match for the blacksmith.

Nose to nose, Caleb hollered, "Don't ever do that again!" Desire to pummel the boy rose in Caleb's chest.

Fear lit in Sam's eyes, and he cowered. Caleb regained control and unhanded him. "Go home. Go home and let your mother look at your hand."

Sam burst into tears and took off, running. Caleb sank down on a stool. Shaking his head, he looked up when a feminine voice spoke.

"I declare. The Chesneys are wild, simply wild. Oh my! Look at what her boy did to you!" It was Charity Bloodgoode.

"I'm fine, Miss Bloodgoode. I'm fine. No need to fuss."

"You need a doctor!" Flustered, she flapped her way out of his shop.

When he looked up, Sam and his mother stood in the doorway. Caleb cringed.

"Sam has something to say to you, don't you, Sam?" Abby gave her son's arm a shake.

Sam rubbed his hand and stared at his shoes.

"Sam!" His mother barked.

"I'm sorry. Sorry I hit you. It was wrong."

Caleb managed a smile. "Apology accepted."

Sam faced the blacksmith, defiance in his eyes. "But I'm not sorry about what I said. You keep away." With those final words, Sam turned and fled.

Abigail got closer. "Oh, my. You're bleeding! I guess Sam's stronger than I realized. Let me help you."

Who was Caleb to argue with such a generous offer? He sat while she opened her bag, took out a clean cloth, wet it, then dabbed at his face. With her so close he could kiss her, his heart pounded. The more she touched him, the more he liked it. Perhaps a bloody nose had its advantages. When his gaze met hers, she smiled.

"Well, well! Isn't this cozy? I leave you alone for a minute and Mrs. Chesney takes over! I say, Mrs. Chesney, your husband isn't in the grave even three months yet and you have notions about the blacksmith? Scandalous!"

Charity Bloodgoode stood for a moment, then turned and flounced out of the shop.

Caleb shook his head.

"Don't worry. I don't care what she thinks."

"Soon it will be all over town," he said, and winced when she touched his split skin.

"I don't care. Do you?"

"No, I don't. Except people suspect me of all kinds of bad things."

"Are you guilty?" She dabbed the cloth gently, applying a salve.

"No."

"Then I don't care."

"Neither do I. Maybe it's about time the truth came out." He took a breath.

"The truth?"

Eye to eye, it was time. "You're the finest woman in this town. And I don't care who knows I think so." He eased her closer and brushed his bruised lips against hers.

AT THE WARM PRESS OF his lips, Abby closed her eyes. To steady herself, she gripped his shoulder. Well aware by not pulling away and slapping his face, she permitted this liberty. She didn't care. She trusted Caleb Tanner because he'd shown kindness to her and her family from the moment they'd arrived.

After their flirtation at the lake, she'd seen him as more than a friend—as a man. Perhaps her life, as a woman, wasn't over yet? Without her husband, she'd been a drudge, a drone—working until exhaustion made her quit. Falling into dreamless sleep every night—alone.

Martha told her "You haven't died with George, Abby. You can have a life again."

She hadn't believed it. Some of the unattached men in town, like Edmond Hammond, had shown aggression toward her, not kindness, not understanding—except Caleb. Sharing her grief drew her to him, like a moth to a flame. He understood and didn't make salacious comments or make unwelcomed advances. Except now. But this kiss was not unwanted.

She stood up.

"I'm sorry. I shouldn't have taken such a liberty." He met her eyes.

She cocked an eyebrow at him. "Sorry? Really?"

His face flushed. "Well, no. To be quite honest. Not one bit sorry. But I have taken a liberty."

"I could have stopped you."

"And yet you didn't. Why?" He shot her a curious look.

"You're not like the rest. I like you."

He chuckled. "I figured."

She finished ministering to his wounds, then packed up her belongings.

Caleb put his hand on her forearm. "I hope I haven't offended you."

"You haven't." She folded the leftover cloth

"But now?" He raised his eyebrows.

"I'm still a new widow, Mr. Tanner. Please don't expect much from me." She tucked it into her bag.

"Of course. You're right. But it would please me if you'd call me Caleb. At least in private."

She smiled. "All right—Caleb."

"May I call you Abigail?" He pushed to his feet.

After a brisk nod, she answered, "But don't tell Sam. He's still hurting."

"I understand."

"I appreciate you not giving him what he deserved." She ladled some water over her hands, then dried them.

"He's only a boy." Caleb touched the dressing she had applied.

"Yes, he is. He'll be all right. He needs time."

"He does. Thank you so much for this." He gestured to his face.

"It's the least I could do."

"He's got a powerful punch." Caleb wiggled his jaw from left to right.

"He's almost a man." She sighed.

"I'll be all right. Please tell Sam he can continue his apprentice work."

"Really? I know he feels bad. He talks about what you're teaching him."

"He does? I didn't think he much liked blacksmithing."

"I think he does. But nothing beats being out in the woods with Lucky. I'll send him along tomorrow. And he'll bring you a fine dinner as his apology."

"Not necessary."

"Yes, it is. I have to go."

"Thank you, again—Abigail."

"You're welcome—Caleb."

Caleb squeezed her hand before she left the shop.

On her way home, her emotions bounced from happy to scared. Confused, she didn't know her own mind. What should she do? What should she not do? Life had been so easy to figure out before, but now, the rules had changed. She was a grown woman alone.

Maybe Martha would share her wisdom. Abby picked up her pace. Chores awaited, and she had a growing pile of sewing to do. A smile tugged at her lips. Right or wrong, it felt good to be wanted again.

When she arrived at the inn, Sarah was setting the tables.

"What's to be done for supper?"

"Nothing. You fixed up Caleb?" Martha stood in the kitchen doorway.

"Yes."

"He's a good man. Didn't deserve a beating."

"Where's Sam?"

"I sent him to his room. He can't go beatin' up people."

"No, he can't. I need to talk to him." She made her way to her son's room, knocked on the door, then opened it.

"I know what you're gonna say before you say it." A sullen expression on her son's face put her off.

"Don't be mouthing off to me. I'm still your mother."

"I'm sorry." Sam sat up on his bed.

"You should be. You hurt Caleb. I fixed him up, but he's in pain."

"Caleb? You call him Caleb now? Pickin' berries together and now you calling him Caleb? What would Daddy say?" Anger shot from Sam's eyes. He pushed to his feet.

"Daddy isn't here. Daddy's gone. Forever. Never coming back. Sam, you have to accept it."

"No, I don't! And Caleb Tanner's not going to replace him."

"I never said he would. No one could replace your father. He was a special man."

"Darn right!"

"But Caleb is a good man, too. He's been very kind, and generous with you."

"So?"

"No more hitting. No more rude behavior. You must respect him, or you'll have to stop being his apprentice."

"Did he say so?"

"No. I'm saying it."

"Do you love him?"

"We're friends." She prayed silently for forgiveness for such a bold lie. "You go back tomorrow. And bring a good dinner with you. As an apology."

"Do I have to?"

"Yes. And we'll move on."

"All right. But he's up to something."

"He likes me. First person to be nice to us, except Martha, since we got here. You should be grateful. I am."

"You're grateful enough for both of us." Sam slid down on his bed.

"Sam!"

"Sorry. Sorry, Mama. Sorry."

She perched on the corner of her son's bed. "You're grown now, so I'm going to tell you the real reason I'm sending you to apprentice with Mr. Tanner."

Sam sat up.

"What happened to us, to your father, happened because we were tenant farmers."

"Dad loved to farm."

"Don't interrupt!" She shot a stern look at her son.

He kept his gaze riveted to his mother.

"I don't want you to go through what we did. When you're a tenant farmer, you can be put out at any time, like we were." Remembering, the pain of their move filled her again. Her eyes watered, but she blinked the tears back. Sam took his mother's hand.

"It's all right, Mama."

She took a deep breath and swallowed. "I want you to have a trade. To be good enough at something so no one can ever take your living away. If you become a good blacksmith, you'll be able to work anywhere. You can live where you want and will always be able to find work and support your family."

"That's why you took Mr. Tanner up on his offer?"

"Yes."

"Guess I was wrong. I thought you were sweet on him."

She bit back the words on her tongue. Sam didn't need to know how she felt about Caleb Tanner. Not yet anyway.

"I did it for your own good. To make you safe. You'll never have to lose everything, like we did."

"I understand. I'll do it."

"Thank you. You bring relief to your mother's heart." She hugged her son and returned to the parlor, where she'd set up her needlework. Focusing on the mending would take her mind off Caleb's kiss. She licked her lower lip before picking up a torn shirt.

She'd found out a little more about Caleb Tanner today. Besides what he looked like, she learned he knew how to kiss.

END OF AUGUST

At dinner, with the Chesneys gathered at one table, Martha spoke up. "Harvest festival is coming."

"What's a harvest festival?" Sarah stabbed a piece of meat with her fork.

"After the crops are harvested, animals slaughtered, folks celebrate. Right after is Thanksgiving. We put on a nice dinner here for folks with no family."

"What kind of celebration, Martha?" She trained her gaze on her mother-in-law.

"Singing, a bit of dancing. The wagon pull. Pie baking contest. Biggest squash contest. Candy-making, candles for sale. And the women dress up."

"Dress up?" Sarah turned a questioning glance at Martha.

"Yep. Of course, Ann Fitch outdoes everyone. She parades around in finery like you've never seen. You'd think her husband was a governor, or even president!"

Abigail's heart sank. She and Sarah had nothing but worn skirts and dresses. They would be the shabbiest ones in town. Her one decent dress had been left in Danbury because the wagon was too full. She sighed.

Martha patted her hand.

"Don't you worry. We'll have you and Sarah outfitted like the finest. I figure you and Sarah need some new things. Dresses."

"Fabric is expensive." She speared a piece of squash.

"Before John and I got married, I was quite the belle in Coventry. I had some nice things I didn't need here. They've been packed away in a chest in the attic. None of those will fit me now, but they might be perfect for you."

Sarah glanced at her mother. "Can we?"

"Of course." She smiled.

"I figure you can make whatever changes necessary to make them fit. Right?"

"I can."

"After dinner, let's go upstairs and see what's there."

Gratified to see a smile on Martha's face, her heart warmed at her mother-in-law's generosity. Excitement stirred in her, and she couldn't wait to see the treasure trove of elegant gowns her mother-in-law had squirreled away.

Martha rose from her seat, toddled off to the kitchen and returned, holding a small jar.

"This is for you, Sam. Put your earnings from the blacksmith shop in here."

"Don't we need the money?"

"No, son. I want you to keep it. Save it. Someday you'll need it. We can get along on earnings from the inn, the dining room, and your mother's sewing."

"Thanks, Grandma. Is this okay, Mama?"

"Yes, dear." Happiness spread through Abby. Sam was so much like his father, strong, proud, and independent.

Martha welcomed the help Sarah, Sam, and Abby provided. Sometimes, she'd stare out the window, almost as if she expected to see George marching down the street to the inn. Martha would put an arm around her and speak softly. She could only imagine the grief Martha bore, having lost both her husband and her son.

When they finished and cleared away the dishes, Martha spoke.

"Let's dig into the chest and see what we can find."

"I ain't goin' up there. It's women things." Sam shook his head and pretended to shudder. Sarah gave him a playful slap on the shoulder.

"It's all right, Sam. You can sit at the front desk, in case we have new arrivals," Martha said.

The womenfolk climbed the three stories to the attic. Each held a candlestick which cast shadows around the old wooden walls, making it hard to find the trunk.

"There! There it is," Martha pointed.

Abby handed her candle to Sarah and yanked the heavy piece from the eaves. With her hand, she swept the dust off the top, coughing in the process.

"Is it locked?"

"I don't think so. Try it." Martha took a candlestick and stood back.

Abby tugged hard on the latch once, twice, and the third time it gave way. She pulled up the lid. Brightly colored fabric, folded neatly, and piled to the top greeted her.

"Oh, Grandma!" Sarah squealed.

Martha beamed.

Shiny fabrics in greens, blues, golds, and pinks peeked out from the deep chest. One by one they took out the garments. Woolens, linens, cottons, silks, and, finally, Martha's white silk wedding dress.

"These are beautiful." Abigail fingered the fine fabrics gently as she lifted each from its resting place.

"They've kept pretty well. Try them on." Martha put her candlestick down and dragged an old bench over.

Abby examined each one. "Try this one, Sarah." She handed a ruffled pink silk dress to her daughter. Sarah shed her clothing and pulled it on. Her mother laced up the fastenings in the back.

"I can take in some of these bodices and shorten the skirts, if need be."

Martha blew off the dust on old mirror standing forlornly in a corner of the attic. Sarah skipped over to admire her image. There were three layers of lace at the bodice and ruffles at the wrists and the hem. A layer of lace covered the bodice to the waist.

"It's beautiful on you, dear." Martha beamed.

"Now you, Mama." Twirling, Sarah swished her skirt and gazed at her mother.

"Try the green one," Martha urged.

Abby took off her old dress and slipped the new one over her head. Martha laced it up. The forest green velvet skirt and vest complimented her eyes. The white silk bodice shimmered in the candlelight.

"It's a perfect fit." She fingered the soft, plush fabric and sauntered to the mirror. The low-cut bodice revealed more cleavage than Abigail was accustomed to, even with a modesty ruffle along the edge. She tugged at it, but it wouldn't rise. The full skirt fell softly around her body. Double white silk ruffles at the hem gave the dress a bouncy quality. The long sleeves, gathered at the shoulder, ended in lace at the wrist.

"Don't be so modest, my dear," Martha grinned. "You're a beautiful woman, show it off."

"But George..." she put her hand over her mouth.

"He would be proud. He wrote me what a beauty he'd married. And he was right."

Emotion choked her for a moment as she stared in the mirror. For a split second she saw his image standing next to her, his face smiling approval. As quickly as it came, his image in the mirror vanished into dust.

"Of course, they'll need pressing. I wouldn't trust those Whiting twins to take a hot iron to either of these."

"I'll do it, Mama!"

Abby grinned. "Okay, Sarah. If you think you can do it."

"I can. I can. You'll see."

The women took out other garments, many made of fine wool and some of cotton.

"They all need airing and pressing. The wool ones will be good for Thanksgiving and Christmas services." Martha handed a striped cotton dress to Sarah. "Can't have the Chesney women being made fun of because they don't have decent clothes. Let's refit these and when we get extra money, we'll buy some new fabric."

"Thank you, Grandma." Sarah hugged Martha.

"Wait 'til nasty ole Charity Bloodgoode sees you comin' to the Harvest Festival dressed in this. She'll drop her teeth." Martha laughed.

Abby pulled out each dress. She held them up to see who they would fit better, Sarah or herself. They spent an hour sorting and planning. They each took two dresses and descended the stairs.

"John and George would be proud to see their women taking their rightful place in Fitch's Eddy. There'll be no more whispering in church or anywhere else about my gals."

She didn't say a word about the gossip likely all over town about Charity discovering her at Caleb's house. Most likely it will lead to plenty of whispering about her among the church folks.

Thunder rumbled through the attic.

"Best we get downstairs. Get our chores done before the rain, if it's not already too late." Martha led the way.

"Sarah, let's take the dresses to our room."

They folded them neatly and laid them on the beds.

"I'm going to need more thread."

"I can get it, Mama." Sarah piped up.

She stroked her daughter's hair. "I'll need to match the colors, dear."

"Will you teach me how?"

"Of course." She hugged her daughter.

ON HER WAY TO THE KITCHEN, Abby remembered the white silk George had bought her. Wrapped up and tucked away in the attic, the fabric would be perfect for a new dress. There wouldn't be time to remake Martha's dresses and sew a new one before the Harvest Festival. But maybe for Christmas?

A new dress for the Harvest Festival didn't mean she'd stopped mourning her husband. It was simply about looking her best and being proud to be a Chesney.

As she passed by Sam's room, she peeked in. The jar Martha had given him sat on the small dresser. Already it held half a dozen coins.

Her mind turned to Caleb Tanner. She was surprised he'd agreed to continue working with Sam. She figured it wasn't because Caleb liked her son as much as it was that he fancied her. Sam would benefit, so she kept quiet. Having a trade would be a good thing for him. Look at all the coins he'd collected already.

Caleb crept into her thoughts often. She laughed to herself at the transparent flirtation Charity Bloodgoode heaped on the blacksmith.

Caleb fended the girl off politely. Now he'd revealed how he felt about her, poor Charity would have to find another target.

As she waited for the bread dough to rise, her mind traveled to days past, before she had married. The way George had flirted with her whenever they were together. They'd had a mutual attraction right away. Even when her mother tried to talk her out of marrying, him, she hadn't listened. He had owned her heart.

But what about now? She was still young. Would working at the inn and raising her children be enough? She missed George's wisdom, his humor. At night, the small bed was cold and lonely. She'd never dreaded cold winter nights when she slept with him. He had produced enough heat to keep her comfortable all night.

But now? Was it fair she'd have to pile on more blankets this winter? How could life be so cruel to take him away when she needed him? He'd been a hero, sacrificing his own life to save his children by keeping the wagon from going over the cliff. She'd relived the day over and over in her mind. There was nothing they could have done to save both George and the children. She sighed.

Being alone didn't suit her. A month ago, she didn't think there could be anyone in Fitch's Eddy for her. The Reverend Bloodgoode? She laughed out loud. Obnoxious and taking liberties, as he tended to do, she'd never be interested in him. And schoolmaster Edmund Hammond? She'd had to slap him for his aggressive and rude manner.

A small smile captured her lips as she remembered a pair of sympathetic blue eyes and a soft, coaxing kiss. Caleb had been empathetic in a way no other could. She wondered how he handled his grief. How long ago had he lost his family? Tears stung her eyes to think of the tragedy in his life. At least she had her children. He had no one except maybe her.

She'd heard the gossip. Old Zeke parked outside the general store in a chair tried to get her to listen to his nonsense. He rambled on and on about Caleb Tanner. He hinted the blacksmith was an evil man who had done in his own family.

She refused to believe it. He'd only shown kindness and understanding to her. Some people spread nasty rumors about him. What did she care? She knew the truth. Perhaps he needed a friend as much as she did?

"I think the bread's risen," Martha said, poking into Abby's thoughts.

"Oh, yes. Sorry." She stretched her arms out before standing up. She prepared the dough for the oven.

The clip-clop of horses' hooves and the bump of wagon wheels drew her attention.

"Looks like we got visitors. Best make another loaf, dear. Might be more people for supper tonight."

Abby opened the flour cannister.

Chapter Ten

E*arly September*
Before the afternoon sun faded to darkness, Caleb dismissed Sam and closed up shop. Since their fight, the two men worked side-by-side with no discussion outside of Caleb's teaching. Sam had proved to be a quick learner. Surprised the young lad could provide any significant help, Caleb had been impressed with Sam's growing skills, enabling the blacksmith to take on more business than usual.

September had not yet brought cooler days. He'd taken to regular jaunts to the lake after a hot afternoon in the shop. He told himself he didn't expect to find Abby there, but it was a lie. He cooled off there almost every day in hopes she'd join him.

Remembering the first time, he no longer stripped down completely, but waded in the with his drawers on instead. After he cooled off, he'd lie against the tree and close his eyes, remembering the day she'd tricked him and then her soft touch doctoring him.

She was a remarkable woman. Strong, a good listener, and a flirt! She haunted his dreams. Amazed to think he could have a life again, he knew if he could win her, he'd be the happiest man in town, maybe even in the whole state. But he was far from reaching his goal. And then there was Sam, who hated his guts.

The Harvest Festival was only three weeks away. Caleb had volunteered for the wagon pull. Knowing he was the strongest man in town, he figured to win handily over weaklings like Edmond Hammond and the reverend. If winning meant getting another kiss from her, he'd put his full force behind it.

The festival started on a Monday. Every day there was a new event. Friday was the dance. Saturday ended the festivities with a church supper. He'd make sure his clothes were clean. He'd take a bath, too. And not let those vipers near his Abigail. His Abigail. Did he have the right to call her his own? Not yet, but maybe someday.

After his swim, his gaze searched the horizon, but saw no signs of her marching over the hill. He sighed, finished dressing, and set out for home. While he walked, he pondered different gifts he might craft for her and her family for the coming holiday.

He whistled as he tramped through the high grass. Soon the snow and cold winds would be upon them. Would he see her then? Maybe only in the general store and during Sunday dinners at the inn. The chances of being alone with her grew slim.

Lost in thought, not looking where he was going, he barreled right into her. She had bent over to pick flowers and he knocked her to the ground.

"Oh my gosh! I'm so sorry. Pardon me." He helped her up, grabbing her elbow with one hand and her upper arm with the other. She lost her balance, falling against his chest, flattening her palms on his shirt to steady herself. Her touch started a fire in him.

"It's all right." She pushed off, stepping away. Her hand fussed with her hair. She stuffed stray strands into her bun. "I'm fine."

His fingers twitched. He wanted to pull the pins out of her bun and watch her golden locks cascade to her shoulders. He directed his gaze to her face.

"You're picking flowers?"

"I love the wild ones. My mother used to scoff, saying they were weeds. But those weeds have brightened many a table of mine."

"They are lovely, though not as perfect as garden flowers."

"It's what I like about them. They're imperfect. Like me."

"There's nothing imperfect about you." He took her hand.

She blushed a becoming shade of pink and cast her gaze to the ground. "You are too kind, Caleb."

"I speak the truth." He raised her hand to his lips.

"Sam told me you are going to do the wagon pull at the festival." She closed her fingers around his thumb.

"I am."

"We're entering an apple pie in the pie contest and my mother-in-law's famous raisin bread in the bread baking one."

"I've had her raisin bread. It's sure to win as will your pie."

"I don't know. Gossip has it Mrs. Fitch wins every year."

"Yes, and they say it's because her cook makes the pie!" He laughed.

"Really? That's cheating."

"Rules don't apply to Ann Fitch."

"We'll try our best."

"Anything you bake will be sweeter by far than any other." He kissed her palm.

"You flatter me." She removed her hand.

Stupid! I went too far. "I'm sorry."

"I just, it's...I don't..." she stammered, looking away.

Caleb stepped closer and took her in his arms. When she raised her gaze to his, he kissed her slowly, sensuously, and she melted against him. When they broke, he was breathing heavy.

She touched her lower lip. "I've got to go. It's supper time. I'll be missed."

"Of course. Until we meet again." His gaze connected with hers. The rosiness in her cheeks added to her beauty. He sensed there was fire buried deep within her. What a lucky man her husband had been to find such a woman.

He watched her hurry away and took his time returning home. After dinner, he stripped down and got into bed. Oh, yes, someday she would be his. Even if she didn't know it yet, he did.

ABBY OPENED THE DOOR to Rhodes' General Store. She needed thread and supplies for the inn.

Virginia Rhodes greeted her.

"Morning, Mrs. Chesney. What can I do for you today?"

"I need thread, and some other things."

"I hear you're fixing up a dress for Ann Fitch?"

"Yes. And getting one ready for Sarah and myself."

Virginia patted Abby's hand. "Glad to hear it. I'm sure you and your daughter will outshine everyone in our little village."

"You're too kind."

"What else do you need?"

She recited the list.

"I'll be right back. You know where the thread is. Please help yourself."

"Thank you."

The tinkle of the bell over the door drew her attention. Caleb Tanner entered. His gaze connected with hers. He tipped his hat. "Mrs. Chesney. How nice to see you."

She gave a small curtsy. "Likewise, Mr. Tanner."

Another tinkle and the door opened again. It was the Reverend Bloodgoode.

"Ah, Mrs. Chesney. What a pleasure." He took off his hat and stared.

"Reverend." She did another curtsy, then turned her attention to the boxes of thread.

"Getting ready for the Harvest Festival?" The reverend sidled up to her.

She took a step away. "I am."

Out of the corner of her eye, she could see Caleb easing closer as he examined a box of matches.

"Are you entering any of the contests?" The reverend approached her.

"My daughter swore me to secrecy." She didn't mind the lie if it got the man to move away.

"Ah, I see. Well, I'm proud to say, my daughter, Charity, is entering both the pie and the bread baking contests."

She should be entering the biggest gossip contest.

She gave him a small smile and returned to her task.

"Tanner." The reverend turned to Caleb. "I understand you've been luring Mrs. Chesney to your abode. Undoubtedly under nefarious pretenses." The clergyman huffed and puffed.

"I have no idea what you're talking about. Please don't slander Mrs. Chesney with your accusations."

"I'm directing my words to you, not to her. Obviously, she's an innocent."

"Obviously, you're putting your nose where it doesn't belong." Caleb's hand fisted at his side.

"We'll see about that." The reverend picked up a box of salt.

"I have your items, Mrs. Chesney." Virginia held a sack in her hand.

She picked two spools of thread and brought them to the counter. Glancing up, her eyes met Caleb's. He joined her and the reverend.

"Gentlemen, we're looking for some strong men to help set up the archery contest and the tables for the church supper. Would either of you care to volunteer?"

"I will, Mrs. Rhodes." Caleb spoke up.

Virginia smiled.

"We don't need the likes of you in our church, Tanner. We don't need your help with anything. You're dangerous. And stay away from Mrs. Chesney!" The reverend slammed his box of seasoning on the counter.

"Now, now, Reverend. I'm in charge of volunteers this year. And I think it's mighty neighborly of Mr. Tanner to volunteer. Thank you, Mr. Tanner. I'll put your name down and let you know where and when we'll need you."

"Thank you, Mrs. Rhodes."

"I don't think I need you to defend me, Mr. Bloodgoode. I can take care of myself. And I certainly don't need anyone to tell Mr. Tanner to stay away from me. If I don't want to be his friend, I'll speak up on my own."

The Reverend slapped a coin on the counter and strode to the door. With a snort and mumbling under his breath, he left, slamming the door.

The sound startled her.

Virginia laughed. She patted Abby's hand. "Don't let his gruff manner scare you. He's really a coward, you know." Then she added up the cost of Abby's purchases.

"Don't worry, Mrs. Rhodes, if anyone bothers Mrs. Chesney, they'll answer to me." Caleb raised a fist.

Virginia shot a knowing look, first at Abigail then at Caleb.

Heat rose in Abby's cheeks.

"Well, well. New friendship blossoms in Fitch's Eddy. How nice. Eight shillings, please, Mrs. Chesney."

She fished the coins out of her pocket and opened the leather bag she toted. Virginia loaded the dry goods and thread in and took the money.

Caleb placed a box of matches on the counter.

"Good day, Mr. Tanner," she said.

"Good day, Mrs. Chesney." Caleb tipped his hat.

WHEN CALEB RETURNED, Sam stood outside the shop. Caleb left his matches on a small table. Silently, the boy followed the blacksmith in and picked up the work he'd started the day before.

"There'll be a shooting contest at the Harvest Festival." Caleb threw more coal in the fire.

Sam looked up.

"You good with a musket?" Caleb asked.

"Yep. I'm the best shot in the family." Sam put a tool in the forge.

"You should enter."

"What do I have to do?"

"Mrs. Rhodes at the general store is keeping a list of men doing the events. You can put your name in with her."

"Is there a prize?"

"Yes." Caleb picked up a hammer.

"What is it?"

"A silver dollar. Put the piece over there in next, will you?"

Sam's eyes widened. He picked up the piece of metal with the big tongs and put it in the fire. A silver dollar was a lot of money.

Caleb took out a piece and set it on the forge. He hammered. Wiping the sweat from his brow on his sleeve, he faced Sam again. "Why don't you go there now and get your name listed."

"I will." Sam lit out like a flash. He'd never been to the general store before. His mother had always done whatever purchasing was necessary. The tinkling of the bell when he opened the door startled him. A sweet, soft voice drew his attention.

"Can I help you?"

A pretty red-headed girl stood behind the counter. His mouth went dry as he noticed her rosy cheeks, freckles, and curls. He couldn't stop staring at her hair.

"Can I touch it?" His fingers itched.

"Touch what?" she replied.

"Your hair."

Before the girl could answer, a deeper female voice broke into Sam's reverie.

"What do you want, young man?" Mrs. Rhodes stood staunchly by the young woman's side.

"The shooting contest?" Sam managed to utter, still staring at the girl.

Tapping her pencil on the counter, Virginia cocked an eyebrow and stared. "You are?"

"Sam Chesney."

"Son of Abigail Chesney?" She narrowed her eyes.

The boy nodded.

Mrs. Rhodes frowned. "Becky, please get the logbook."

The girl disappeared in the back.

"Becky," Sam murmured to himself.

The older woman drew herself up. "Her name is Rebecca Rhodes. She's my daughter. And you will address her as Miss Rhodes, if you address her at all."

"Yes, ma'am."

"Don't get any ideas. We keep a close eye on Becky and don't want any young men sweet talking her."

He reassured Mrs. Rhodes, even though he didn't know exactly what "sweet talking" meant. "No, ma'am. I'd never do that." Sam wiped his damp hands on his pants.

The girl returned with a long ledger. She laid it down on the table, raised pretty green eyes, and smiled at Sam.

"Pleased to meet you, Miss Rhodes." Sam gave a short bow.

Virginia Rhodes opened the book and thumbed through several pages. She dipped a quill pen in a small bottle of ink and wrote Sam's name down. Sam watched for a moment, then turned his gaze to Becky. She wore a dark green dress matching her eyes. He'd never seen a girl as pretty as her before.

"I see here Benjamin Fitch is signed up, too. He'll be sharp competition. I hope you're practicing, Sam."

"I practice every day when I go hunting. I hit more than I miss."

Virginia smiled. "You're confident. Good. I wish you good luck."

"Me, too," Becky piped up.

"Thank you kindly."

"Was there anything else?" Virginia closed the book and handed it to her daughter.

"No, ma'am. No."

"Best you get to work. Mr. Tanner teaching you?"

"Yes, ma'am."

"Good. Run along. He'll be wondering where you are."

"I will. Thank you for putting my name down. Pleased to meet you, ladies." Sam tipped his hat.

Becky blushed. Sam turned and hurried out the door, afraid he'd say the wrong thing. From the moment he'd arrived, he'd hated Fitch's Eddy. He'd kept telling his mother all the things he liked about Danbury and the ones he didn't about this small town. But today, he changed his mind. He'd never seen a pretty girl with hair the color of fire in Danbury before. Maybe Fitch's Eddy had its good points after all?

He stumbled his way to the blacksmith shop. His mind whirled with images of Miss Rebecca Rhodes, prettiest girl in Fitch's Eddy, and maybe in the whole state, even the country!

When he stepped inside the shop, Caleb spoke.

"Okay?"

"Yep. I'm signed up. Mrs. Rhodes said I should practice. But I get all the practice I need when I'm out hunting. She said Benjamin Fitch is signed up, too. Who's he?"

Caleb put down his hammer. "He's the son of the man who runs Fitch's Eddy, Elijah Fitch. The richest people in town."

"Money don't make you a good shot. We'll see who's better." Sam looked in the quenching bucket.

"Confident?" Caleb asked.

"Yep. Gotta show Miss Rhodes I'm the best."

Caleb laughed. "Miss Rebecca Rhodes?"

"Yep." Sam took a piece of iron out of the fire and picked up a hammer. "How come Fitch is so rich?"

"You know about logging?" Caleb put his tools down and sat on a bench.

"Not much." Sam shrugged.

"Fitch owns thousands of acres. He harvests trees every spring. Floats 'em down the river to Philadelphia, where he sells them to sawmills." He wiped his face with a rag.

"Trees?" Sam put the nail he'd finished in the quenching bucket.

"Huge trees. They cut 'em down and sell them for lumber to build houses, or make masts for ships. He makes a fortune"

"Huh, and I thought trees were only good for shade, firewood, and fruit."

"You'll see come March, when the river's high, and logging begins."

Caleb pushed to his feet and checked a piece of iron he had in the fire.

"Money don't mean he can shoot good."

"Nope. It don't."

Chapter Eleven

The murmur of voices drew Caleb's attention from his work. He moseyed over to the door and spied a crowd gathering in front of the general store. One head, a bit taller than the rest and crowned with bright red hair caught his eye. Sam came up behind him.

"What's going on?"

"I'm guessing Daniel Rhodes is posting the schedule of events for the Harvest Festival."

"What's a schedule?"

"When things are happening. On what day. Let's go." Caleb motioned to Sam.

"Pie contest is Saturday afternoon," Mrs. Rhodes said. She turned to Sam. "So we can eat the pies at the church supper."

The boy's gaze ran down the list until he spotted the shooting contest.

"Friday. Two o'clock." Sam read from the list.

"Who are you?" The voice came from another young man.

"Sam Chesney. You?"

"Benjamin Fitch. So, you're my competition?" Ben looked Sam up and down.

"I am." Sam pulled himself up to his full height, but Ben was still a few inches taller.

"Good luck. Or you could drop out now. I'm the best shot in town." Ben crowed.

"We'll see who's the best shot. You may be taller. And you may be richer, but I'm a crack shot."

"Not Friday. My father owns this town, and I own the shooting contest." Benjamin hitched up his pants.

"Money don't mean nothing when you're shooting," Sam replied.

"We'll see."

"I hit more than I miss."

"I don't miss at all." Benjamin shot a nasty glance at Sam and turned to walk away.

Sam's face reddened.

"Don't let him rattle you, Sam. You'll do fine." Caleb clapped the boy on the back.

Sam shook off Caleb's hand. "I don't need you to tell me I'm the best shot in Fitch's Eddy. I'll show him, and the whole town who's the best."

Ben Fitch stopped at the door to the general store. Becky Rhodes leaned against the doorframe. Caleb and Sam watched Ben speak to her. Sam's face grew dark.

The boy's got it bad for Becky.

Ben kept talking, but Becky turned her head. She stared directly at Sam and smiled. The anger drained from his face. Caleb chuckled behind his hand, his eyes darting from the girl to Sam and back again. Looked like there were two lovesick men working at the blacksmith shop.

"She'll be there at the shooting match." Caleb glanced at Sam.

"Then she'll know who the best is in Fitch's Eddy." Sam returned to the shop. Caleb studied the schedule then joined Sam.

"The wagon pull's on Friday morning, right before the shoot." Caleb took a new piece of iron. "Your mother's entering an apple pie? My favorite" He smacked his lips.

"Yep. And Sarah's helping my grandma bake raisin bread for the bread contest."

Caleb's mouth watered. "Martha's raisin bread will win."

"She's made it for us twice. I'd never eaten raisin bread before."

Caleb shut his eyes and let his mind remember. "Oh, and the cinnamon! The sugar!"

"You've tasted it?" Sam's eyebrows shot up.

"Oh, yes. Every time she bakes it, I can smell it. Once she brought me a whole loaf for fixing a loose step."

"She's nice to folks. Wish I had some now." Sam licked his lips.

"Me, too. How many loaves is she making?"

"I don't know."

"Mrs. Rhodes said the winner has to bring some to the church supper." Caleb put the iron in the fire.

"And the pies, too. Right?" Sam took the tools from the quenching bucket.

"So I hear."

"You ain't done this before?"

"This is my first time. I'm kinda new here myself."

"Explains why you don't have any friends."

Caleb sensed heat in his cheeks. "Folks here think things about me that aren't true."

"Same about us. Especially my mother."

"Your mother is a fine woman."

"Don't you go talking about my mother." Sam's hand fisted at his side.

Caleb held up his hands. "I mean it only in the most respectful way." He hoped Sam would believe his lie. "How about we make some new bullets for your gun?"

"Really?"

"Sort of like good luck for the contest."

"Thanks. Yeah. I guess I'm gonna need all the luck I can get."

"I don't know. Looks like Miss Becky Rhodes is rooting for you to win."

"Think so?"

"I do. Get the mold ready, this iron is almost hot enough."

"Yes, sir."

STARTING MONDAY, ABIGAIL, Sarah, and Sam set out to visit the wagons and carts set up in the street. One woman sold candles, a dozen for a shilling. Sam dug a shilling from his pocket.

"Here, Mama. For you."

She accepted the tapers and lightly touched her son's cheek.

One tall farmer stood behind a small table loaded with ripe squash, potatoes, and fresh carrots. They stopped to buy. Sam munched on a carrot while they strolled from farmer to farmer.

At the end of the street were the farm displays for the contests. One woman had entered a ten- pound zucchini. Next to it was the biggest peach the Chesneys had ever seen. A young woman displayed a huge chicken in a cage. The Chesney family marveled at the giant vegetables, fruit, and farm animals all vying for top prize in their category. They placed guesses with each other who would win in each category.

Every day, they rushed through morning chores and hurried to Main Street to see new exhibits. One woman sold hand-knitted baby clothes in pinks and blues. Abby fingered the fine wool, remembering when her children were babes, and the outfit her sister had given her when Sam was born.

Their favorite, by far, was the booth selling flavored candy sticks. She bought one for each of her children, cinnamon for Sam, licorice for Sara, and peppermint to bring home to Martha and Lizzy.

Early Friday morning, Abby and Sarah sat examining apples at the long table in the kitchen. They slowly emptied two small bushel baskets. The smell of baking bread surrounded them like a heavenly cloud, making their mouths water. Soon the scent of cooking apples and cinnamon would fill the air.

"We need perfect ones for the pies." She picked up a rosy red piece of fruit.

Sarah put one in the basket.

"No, dear. Put that one in this bowl. We'll make applesauce or an apple dumpling from it instead of pie."

"Sam's shooting contest is today, Mama. What if he doesn't win?"

"He'll win." She turned an apple around. "Hand me the peeler, Sarah."

"Mr. Benjamin Fitch told me he's going to win," Sarah said.

"When did you meet him?"

"At the general store when I got the cinnamon. He kept staring at me. Mrs. Rhodes introduced him."

"Was he polite?"

"He's handsome, Mama."

"And rich. You stay away from him. The likes of Benjamin Fitch don't marry poor girls like you, Sarah."

"He seemed kinda stuck up. Not like Mr. Josiah Quint."

"Now there's a good young man." She smiled.

A knock interrupted them. Abby opened the door.

"The twenty-five-pound sack of flour Martha ordered." Caleb stepped inside and slung the bag over his shoulder to the floor.

"Thank you. Can we offer you a cup of tea?"

"I'd be grateful. Where do you want this?"

"Right in here, Martha appeared in the doorway. She hurried over to the pantry. "Thank you kindly, Caleb. Saved me a trip."

"Happy to oblige."

"Sit. Sarah, fetch a cup for Mr. Tanner, dear." Martha joined him at the table.

Sarah put down a cup in front of Caleb and one in front of her grandmother.

"Getting ready for the pie contest?" he asked.

"She picks only the ripest, most juicy ones for the pie. She's gonna show me how she slices 'em up fancy." Martha sipped her tea.

Caleb caught Abby's eye and shot her a shy smile.

"I'm sure you ladies will win. Is Sam ready? I brought the bullets we made."

"You made bullets for Sam?" She looked up.

Caleb shrugged. "He seemed worried. I thought if he had the best bullets, he'd feel better."

"Very kind of you," Martha said. "He's out in the woods with Lucky."

He took a leather pouch from his pocket and placed it in Abby's palm. "Here, give these to Sam. I've got to get ready for the wagon pull." He pushed to his feet and was gone before she could utter another word. She bounced the pouch of bullets in her hand.

"He's a dear friend," Martha said, eyeing her daughter-in-law and cocking an eyebrow.

Abby sensed heat in her face. "What?"

Martha turned her attention to the cooling loaves. "Nothing my dear. Nothing. Caleb...nothing."

"Mama, are we going to watch the wagon pull?" Sarah put down an apple.

Silence blanketed the room. Sam entered.

"Bread ready?" He grabbed a knife and sat down.

"Are we?" Sarah insisted.

"Are we what?" Sam interrupted.

"Going to watch the wagon pull?"

Both children and Martha cast their gazes at Abby.

She fussed with the butter, pulled out a knife and sliced bread.

"Of course, we are. Of course. Eat first. Then we'll go."

The Chesney children exchanged looks with their grandmother.

MAIN STREET BUSTLED with activity. Every farmer, cowhand, and logger from miles away crowded the streets of Fitch's Eddy. Two wagons stood ready at the center of Main Street.

Two bare-chested men lined up, waiting. Daniel Rhodes stood at the finish line, in front of the general store. Caleb held the rope tied to a large wagon loaded with four barrels. Next to him stood a man not nearly as brawny handling the rope for the other. They crouched down and wound the rope around their hands.

Benjamin Fitch raised the starting gun in the air and fired. Caleb and his opponent pulled the ropes taut as they inched forward, dragging the wagons through the muddy street. Abby watched Caleb's muscles tighten as he strained to move the heavy load.

They pulled and pulled. Caleb lost his footing. He slipped in the mud and went down, face first. He rose, spitting dirt and words under his breath. He wiped his face with his hands, grabbed the rope and secured his footing before trudging forward. His opponent had gained ground. Caleb had to catch up.

"Come on Mr. Tanner! You can do it!" Sam's voice rang out among the cheers of the spectators. The two men grunted as they kept going. Sinews stretched as the men struggled under the weight of the wagons. Caleb grimaced, his jaw set, his lips pulled back, revealing his teeth. She sensed the strain on his body as he forged ahead, sheer will forcing him forward. As the men approached the finish line, with Caleb inching closer, his opponent fell. He lay in the mud, crying and rubbing his upper arms.

"Go, Mr. Tanner! Go!"

Again, Sam hollered words of encouragement. She stared at her son.

"He's a friend, right?"

"Right, Sam."

With a short burst of speed, Caleb gained ground, passing his opponent. The wagon bumped along faster, with more ease than before as it rolled toward the finish line. Abby's pulse kicked up.

"Go, Mr. Tanner!" she yelled.

Chants from the spectators to the man in the mud spurred him to try again, but he could barely stand. Caleb grunted louder as the wagon bumped its way across the finish line.

Abby, Sam, and Sarah jumped up, clapping and cheering. Martha grinned.

After he made it over, Caleb collapsed. Mrs. Rhodes handed him a towel. He wiped his face and chest, then faced the crowd, raising his fist in victory. Daniel Rhodes approached Caleb. He handed him a ribbon with a medal attached.

"Award for the winner of the wagon pull goes to Mr. Caleb Tanner!"

The crowd cheered. Caleb bowed once, then glanced over at Abby and her family. He slipped the ribbon over his head and ran home.

Shaking her head, Martha spoke, "He's gotta clean up for the dance tonight." Abby glanced at her. Martha continued, "Don't worry, he'll be a little sore, but he'll be okay." A suggestive grin tugged at Martha's lips.

"Amazing," Sam said, shaking his head.

"Come. We must serve dinner before the shooting contest. We don't have much time." Martha hustled her family to the inn. The helpers had set up the dining room. With so many people in town, they expected it would be packed.

At the front desk, Sam collected money from the hungry diners.

"This is one of our biggest days of the year, Sam. Please write down how many people come in for dinner, would you? I like to keep a record."

"Yes, ma'am."

She patted his arm. "Don't worry. It'll be over in plenty of time for the shooting contest."

Abigail, Sarah, and the helpers scurried about, delivering plates loaded with mashed potatoes, freshly harvested and roasted vegetables, roast beef, and bread baked in the wee hours of the morning. As people finished, the women wasted no time clearing plates, and setting new places. People lined up outside, waiting for their turn to sample the fare of the famous Martha Chesney.

When Caleb arrived, Martha escorted him to a small table she'd set aside. The diners stood and gave him a round of applause. His shining face, devoid of mud, beamed as he nodded to the crowd before he sat down.

"Bring him a double helping of everything," Martha instructed.

Abby filled a plate to overflowing and set it on his table.

"You've scraped all the mud off." She grinned.

"Can't eat at Mrs. Chesney's inn covered in dirt, can I? Besides, after the shooting contest is the cookie competition and the dance."

"The dance?" She feigned ignorance.

"Surely you've heard about it?" He raised his eyebrows.

"I may have overheard a word or two."

"May I claim the first and last dances with you?" Caleb picked up his fork.

Embarrassed, she cast her gaze to the table. "I guess."

"And maybe all the rest in between," he whispered.

She met his gaze and laughed. "Yes. I've got to go." She wiped her hands on her apron.

His gaze took in the room. "Many people are waiting to eat."

"It's wonderful."

"I'm so hungry, I could eat a whole deer," he said. His gaze lingered on her for a moment before he attacked the food on his plate.

She watched him dig in, then she returned to the kitchen. Abby didn't have long to ponder his suggestive glance as there were hungry people waiting.

As she rushed from tables to the kitchen and back again, she smiled to herself. George would want her to be proud of their son and to go on living. Yes, she would go to the dance. Yes, she would dance with Caleb, and maybe only him. And if it was scandalous, so be it. She didn't care.

SAM FINGERED THE POUCH of bullets before he shoved it into his pocket and shouldered his musket.

"Ready?" His mother called from the front hall.

"Yep."

The helpers were cleaning up the dinner dishes and putting away leftovers. According to Martha, in three sittings, they had served thirty-five people—a record!

"I couldn't have done it without you, and the children. This money will help us through the winter dry spell." Martha beamed as she transferred money to a small chest. Sam's counting skills were put to the test at the front desk as people poured through the doors, eager to taste Martha Chesney's cooking.

He'd never seen so many people on the streets of Fitch's Eddy, and at the inn. They filled the dining room and waited in the hall. All the bread was gone—mashed potatoes, too. There was a little meat left and some carrots and zucchini. Sam had eaten his fill from a special plate Martha had put aside before the customers came.

"You can't go hungry and win the shooting contest," she'd said as she placed the food before him.

A bark reminded Sam Lucky wanted to tag along.

"Let's go." He pushed through the door and the women followed. They marched down past the town square to the edge of town. Benjamin Fitch had already arrived. Sam shook hands with Mr. Rhodes.

Daniel Rhodes had set up apples as targets for the shooting contest on a fence railing. He drew a line in the dirt with a stick.

"This is where you boys stand. Don't step over the line or you're disqualified. Understood?"

The young men nodded.

"Draw straws to see who goes first." Daniel held three pieces in his hand. Ben picked first. His was long. Sam's was shorter.

"Benjamin Fitch will shoot first."

Ben stepped up to the line. His musket was shiny and new. Sam glanced at his old beat-up gun and his spirits fell.

"Seven apples. You shoot until you miss. Man who hits the most apples wins this bright, shiny silver dollar." Daniel held up the prize. The crowd applauded. Murmurs circulated as more and more people came to watch.

"Benjamin, step up. And may the best man win."

Ben sneered at Sam. "Me, of course." He spoke low so only Sam could hear him.

Sam stepped back, closer to the crowd, giving Ben room. Sam's nerves ratcheted up. His palms sweated. He wiped them on his pants. Lucky sat at his feet.

Ben took aim and fired. One shot, one apple down. He fired again—another one down. He hit three in a row. Then four, then five. Then he missed! The crowd groaned.

"Sam Chesney, your turn." Daniel set up the apples.

Sam fingered the special bullet before he loaded it in the gun. His gaze connected with Caleb's. A nod from the blacksmith boosted Sam's confidence.

You can do it. You can beat him. I know it.

Caleb's words ran through Sam's head. He patted his dog, straightened up, and raised his musket. "Lucky, I'm gonna pretend the apple is a bird. Then I won't miss."

He took a deep breath and closed one eye. The other peered through the sight and zeroed in on the piece of fruit. When he had it in the perfect place, he fired. Direct hit! Sam let out a breath. He raised it again, and again—hit after hit. He'd equaled Benjamin Fitch's five down and raised his musket for apple number six. Sweat ran down his forehead. He brushed it away quickly, then aimed carefully, and squeezed the trigger slowly. He missed! The crowd groaned.

"A tie! We have a tie! We need a tie breaker." Daniel announced. "Each man has a shot at three more apples. But first a break."

Both boys got a drink from a ladle in a bucket. When Sam looked up, he spied Becky Rhodes in the crowd. Who could miss her with her red hair shining like fire? She smiled at him. He returned it. His spirits rose. Becky wanted him to win? Well, then he'd have to do it, just for her.

He also locked gazes with his family. He'd never have believed he'd have the support of so many people. Benjamin Fitch, obviously rattled and no longer cocky, stepped up to the line.

His hands shook a bit as he raised his gun. He hit two of the three apples but fired wide of the third. Then it was Sam's turn. Ben's brows came together as he frowned. His teeth clenched, his hand fisted, and his face reddened. Even if he didn't win, Sam had given the overly confident Fitch boy a few moments of anger and agony.

With a pat to Lucky's head and the bullets from Caleb, Sam's confidence grew. All he had to do was hit all three and he'd win. He swallowed hard and stepped up to the line, careful not to go over.

Taking his time, he raised his gun, peered through the sight, and took aim. First shot hit the mark. Second shot blast the apple to bits. And here was the winning shot, number three. He put the gun down for a moment to take a deep breath, reload, and still the slight tremor in his hand.

He heard a familiar voice in his head. *You can do it, son. Try hard.* It was his father. Emotion squeezed Sam's heart. With his father alive inside him, Sam could do anything. After wiping his face with his shirt, he stepped up to the line, raised his musket, and mowed the third apple down.

He won! Sam had broken Fitch's winning streak. Benjamin shook Sam's hand, reluctantly.

"Congratulations, Chesney."

Sam grinned.

Daniel Rhodes presented the silver dollar to Sam, who held it up for the crowd to see. Then his family mobbed him with congratulations, ruffling his hair and hugging him. Caleb clapped him on the back.

"I knew you could beat him," came a sweet voice.

Sam looked up to see Becky Rhodes standing in front of him.

"Save a dance for me tonight, Miss Rhodes," Sam said.

"I surely will." She smiled before her mother dragged her away.

Chapter Twelve

Martha shepherded her brood to the inn. They had supper to serve before the dance. The meal consisted of corn chowder, salted pork, a slice of freshly baked bread, and apple dumplings, using apples rejected for pie.

When they returned to the inn, Martha's helpers were boiling up a mess of dumplings and heating up the corn chowder they'd made in the morning. Loaves of bread made hastily during the last meal were cooling on racks.

"I'll cut the pork." Martha selected her sharpest knife and set to the task. The women added small bowls of chowder to trays with apple dumplings and meat, then they carried them out to the hungry diners filling the seats. A half loaf of bread and butter were set in each table.

Most of the visitors ate their fill then set out on their journey home before dark. The dance was to be held in the large meeting house behind the general store. Only Fitch's Eddy folks would attend.

The Chesney women finished serving supper by six o'clock. Abby and Sarah hurried to their room to prepare for the dance.

Freshly altered gowns hung by the door. First, they washed in a basin of cold water. Then they dressed their hair. Abby braided Sarah's blonde hair, plaiting pink and white ribbons in the long single braid. Sarah pulled Abigail's hair up on the sides to meet at the top of her head. A green ribbon fastened the hair in place and ran down the back. Her hair hung in loose curls.

"Mama, you never wear your hair down."

Abby turned her head left to right and back again. "I need to keep it out of my way most days. Don't want to get it in food or stitched into someone's dress." She laughed.

Sarah brushed it again and again. "It's so pretty."

She cupped Sarah's cheek. "Thank you, sweetheart."

Martha poked her head in. "Piety has agreed to stay with Lizzy tonight while we're at the dance."

"Thank you, Martha." She took down the dress. Sarah shed her workday clothes. She held the bodice for her daughter.

Martha sat on a bed. "I have to see this. Hope you don't mind."

"It's fine," she said, lacing up the front. The fabric was a smooth pink linen, the neckline dipped, but a layer of silk organza trim kept it modest. The sleeves were fitted with a flounce at the shoulder and a ruffle at the wrist. Next came the petticoats. Layered over them was the skirt, a silk taffeta in pink a shade darker than the bodice with narrow white vertical stripes. There was a matching ruffle at the bottom.

Sarah beamed. She picked up the sides of the full skirt and twirled around.

As Abby watched, tears clouded her eyes. Thoughts of George squeezed her heart. "How I wish your father could be here to see you. You're such a grown up young lady."

"Well, I am fifteen." Sarah raised her chin.

"She's the spitting image of George." Martha wiped her eyes with a handkerchief.

"Now you, Mama."

Martha stood to help Abigail dress. She slipped on the dark green velvet bodice, and waited for her mother-in-law to lace it up. White lace trimmed the scooped neckline and the wrists of the fitted white organza sleeves. She tugged a little at the neck, but it didn't budge.

Abby bit her lip and knitted her brows. "This is too revealing."

"It's a dance. All the women will be dressed like that," Martha said.

"Mama, you look beautiful."

She slid the petticoat up and fastened the waist. Next came the white silk taffeta skirt. The fabric shimmered in the candlelight. Dark green velvet trim about six inches from the bottom of the skirt matched the bodice. The rich green caught the touch of green in her hazel eyes. Her hair, streaked naturally by the sunlight, glowed against the dark velvet.

"Oh, my! The Chesney women will be the handsomest at the dance." Martha clasped her hands together in front of her chest.

"What about you, Grandma?" Sarah reached out to the older woman.

"Nothing fancy like you ladies. My old blue linen. I'm an old woman, no one will want to dance with me. But you two! You won't be able to sit out one single Virginia Reel!"

Hand knit white wool shawls were passed to Abigail and Sarah.

"I'll get dressed now." Martha stopped in the doorway.

"We'll wait for you."

"Nonsense, dear. Go now, while the night is still young. I'll be along."

In the lobby of the inn, they met up with Sam. He wore his father's finery, tailored in by his mother. Clad in a waistcoat, coat, and breeches all in a dark brown linen, his shirt was white, with a single frill down the front. He reminded her of her husband.

Her hand flew to her mouth. "You look like your father!"

Sam grinned. "You look beautiful, Mama. And Sarah? I'll have to watch you all night. Don't you dare dance with Mr. Benjamin Fitch." Sam's brows knitted.

"This is a dance. And I'll dance with whomever I please," Sarah sniffed, raising her chin slightly.

"Let's go. I'll keep my eye on both of you." She held her shawl close.

"I'll have to watch Mr. Tanner, too, I suppose," Sam grumbled under his breath as he held the door for his mother and sister.

CALEB YANKED UP BLACK breeches. He fastened his white shirt with a double ruffle down the front and tied the neck piece around twice before knotting it. A white silk brocade waistcoat was the next garment. Then he donned a gold coat, cutaway down to his knees in the back. His outfit had belonged to his grandfather, with whom he shared the same build.

He couldn't remember the last time he'd had occasion to wear such fancy garments. But tonight would be special. He'd begin his courting of Abigail Chesney at the dance. He needed to look the part of a suitor and not a common man dressed in a blacksmith's filthy rags.

After brushing off his breeches with a clean rag, he left home for the meeting house. On the way, he wondered how she would look. He didn't care if she wore her usual poor clothing, because her beauty radiated like the sun. Nothing could dim her light for Caleb. His heart sped up as he increased his pace. Would she be there already, or would he have to wait for her to arrive? Anticipation made his hands sweat and his mouth go dry.

Fat candles burning in lanterns lit up the entrance. The night air had the slightly sweet fresh smell of harvest season. Caleb shook hands with Daniel Rhodes.

"Congratulations on winning the wagon pull, Mr. Tanner."

"Thank you. Do you know if the Chesneys have arrived yet?"

"I don't think so. Isn't that them, coming this way?" Daniel pointed.

Caleb turned and saw Abigail move out of the darkness and into the light. He caught his breath. Her hair was loose, with curls bouncing around her shoulders. The richness of the color of her dress contrasted with the delicate pink of her cheeks. Her eyes seemed to almost glow green, reflecting the deep hue of the bodice. The snowy white skirt rustled as she approached. He was speechless.

"Mr. Tanner, how nice to see you." She did a little curtsey.

He bowed, unable to speak for a few seconds. "Mrs. Chesney. You look beautiful." The words tumbled right out of his mouth. His heart pounded faster in his chest. His fingers itched to touch her luxurious hair. Going on impulse, he took her hand and kissed it. How could a hand always working as hard as hers feel as soft as a calfskin glove?

He stepped away, allowing her to enter first. "Allow me, Mrs. Chesney."

"Thank you." She stepped across the threshold.

He stayed to the side so Sarah Chesney could enter. Sam drew up beside him.

"Well, well. Look at you, all dressed up." Caleb grinned.

"I could say the same. Those are mighty fancy clothes. Where'd you get 'em?" Sam blurted out.

"My grandfather. Though it's none of your concern."

"Sorry. Don't mean to be disrespectful. But it sure is a change from the smithy shop."

"And the same for you."

Sam laughed. "Blacksmiths can look like gentlemen, too, I reckon."

Caleb gestured to the door. "Let's go in. I believe Becky Rhodes is already inside."

"Why didn't you say so?" Sam pushed ahead.

Caleb laughed as he followed his apprentice.

The place must have had a hundred candles burning. The sound of three fiddles and a banjo met his ears. People were already lined up and dancing. On the left was a long table covered in two crocheted lace cloths. A large bowl holding iced tea was flanked by cups. Three platters were piled high with cookies. Molasses, chocolate, and sugar cookies all drew his eye. Two more platters held stacks and stacks of shortbread squares.

While the music played, Caleb and Sam stopped for refreshments. Caleb only had eyes for Abigail. He did notice a few women staring at Abby and whispering behind fans. He frowned. Jealous women made him sick. She deserved better. She never bothered anyone or gossiped. Why couldn't they leave her alone?

She was the most beautiful woman in the room. And even though Ann Fitch was dressed in the finest, and, probably the most expensive dress, Abby outshined her easily. Caleb spied Reverend Bloodgoode and his daughters at the door. The reverend had better steer clear of Abigail or Caleb would step in.

Charity Bloodgoode shot him a nasty look, raised her nose in the air, and flounced into the room accompanied by her sister. They gave him a wide berth. Relief flooded him. The last thing he needed was more of Charity's flirtations.

When he finished his shortbread, he faced Sam.

"Good luck with Becky."

Sam grabbed his arm. "One dance with my mother. No more."

Caleb shrugged the boy's hand off. "Watch it, Sam. Remember who you're talking to. Your mother is perfectly capable of refusing to dance with me if she wants to. Don't interfere." And with those words, he made a beeline for her, arriving seconds before the reverend showed up.

ABIGAIL HADN'T BEEN to a dance since she'd been sixteen. After being formally introduced, she'd bumped into George at a dance in Danbury. When her mother left, she spent the evening dancing with him. It wasn't long afterward they started keeping company, then he proposed.

The lights, the music, the smell of the baked goods made her giddy. The curious looks aimed her way, and the outright rude stares made her uncomfortable at first. Then Virginia Rhodes sidled up to her.

"Lord, Mrs. Chesney. You are the prettiest woman in the room. Where did you get this dress?"

"Thank you, Mrs. Rhodes. From a friend."

"Have you tried the cookies yet? The winners from this afternoon are over there." She pointed.

"Thank you." She wandered over to the table and picked up a molasses cookie. Caleb was by her side in a heartbeat.

"Mrs. Chesney, how nice to see you."

"Same, Mr. Tanner."

She sensed his gaze roll over her like a warm hand, making her tingle. The music stopped. When it started up again, the Reverend Bloodgoode appeared behind her.

"Mrs. Chesney may I have this dance?"

She glanced at Caleb, whose face colored. She cleared her throat.

"I'm so sorry, Reverend. But I've promised this dance to Mr. Tanner." She held out her hand and Caleb grabbed it quickly. Shooting a bright smile to the reverend, she followed Caleb to the dance floor.

"You read my mind, Mrs. Chesney. I will be forever grateful." He bowed before taking his place.

"It's the first time I ever asked a man to dance, Mr. Tanner." She lowered her lashes, struggling to keep a grin from her lips.

As they glided across the floor, sometimes taking hands, sometimes not, she couldn't break her gaze from his. He drew her in. She saw passion, warmth, and desire flickering in his eyes. Her body responded. As if his wants had bypassed her brain and gone right inside her heart and soul.

He held her steady when they slid past the two lines of dancers. She couldn't stop grinning. She had forgotten how much she liked to dance. Her hair bounced around her shoulders as they skipped to and fro to the music. Light on his feet, Caleb knew the steps and guided her when she needed it.

They danced and danced. And when the reverend tried to cut in, she politely told him she'd already promised the dance to "Mr. Tanner." She moved gracefully, quickly, and easily. She danced and laughed with

Caleb as if he were the only man there, and she didn't care if anyone noticed or commented.

Life was for the living. She had come back to life, resurrected herself. Her feet skipped along, sometimes barely touching the floor, yet she didn't tire. She wished the evening would never end.

SARAH STOOD BY THE table nervously munching on a cookie and watching the dancers.

"You look very nice this evening, Miss Chesney."

She whipped around to see Benjamin Fitch's smiling face. She curtsied.

"Mr. Fitch."

"May I have the next dance?"

"Dance?" Sarah swallowed; her hands grew damp.

"Would you care to be my partner?"

"I— I— I've never danced." She wrung her hands and pulled at a lacy handkerchief.

"It's easy. I'll show you." He held out his hand.

Before she could speak, the musicians struck up another song. She put her hand in his, flinching at his strong grip.

"Sorry. Sometimes I don't know my own strength."

He guided her to the dance floor.

"Do everything I do." He took both her hands.

Sarah had dreamed of going to dances and having young men courting her, but she never thought it would happen. And now the richest boy in town wanted to dance with her. *It must be grandma's beautiful dress.* She didn't think it could be her. What was she but an awkward girl of fifteen who worked hard to help her family? Sarah Chesney was no princess. But maybe, only for tonight, dressed in her grandmother's elegant gown, she could be?

She watched his feet and followed along. The steps repeated. The lively music and his warm hands got her heart pumping. She grinned at him, and he returned it. When they had to step close, then back again, she sensed something, but didn't know what it was. How confusing life had become since she'd arrived at Fitch's Eddy.

When the music ended, he kept hold of her hand.

"Tea? Cookies?"

"Yes, please."

"Stay right here." He rushed over to the refreshment table. While he was gone, the schoolmaster, Mr. Hammond sidled up.

"Enjoying yourself, Miss Chesney?" He leered.

Something in the way he stared made her recoil. "Oh, Mr. Hammond. What are you doing here?"

"Having a good time. I know you're young, but you dance well. I was wondering..."

But Benjamin Fitch broke in.

"Ah, ah, old man. Miss Chesney is dancing the next one with me. Right?" He looked at her and winked.

"Oh, yes. Yes. I am." Relief flooded through her.

"Well, the next one then?"

"I don't think so. In fact, she's promised to me for the entire evening." Ben tried to look regretful but didn't succeed.

Sarah drew close until their arms touched. In the safety of Ben's presence, she relaxed. Edmond Hammond scowled and snorted.

"You Fitches think you own everything and everyone." With his chin in the air, he stalked away.

Sarah let out a breath.

"You don't really have to dance every dance with me." He gazed at his hands.

"Oh, I don't mind." Her cheeks heated. "I mean, I know you don't want to. You were being nice. Polite."

"I sure foiled old man Hammond, didn't I?" He chuckled. "I was serious about every dance. You don't have to, but I'd be honored."

"Me?"

"Miss Chesney..." Benjamin lowered his voice. "...you are the most beautiful girl in the room."

Embarrassment heated her face, neck, and chest. There was no place to escape. She raised her gaze to him, and saw he meant what he said.

"Oh."

"Sorry if I embarrassed you."

"I didn't expect you to say something so, so — nice." She fanned her face with her hand.

"I'm not the stuck-up ogre some people think I am. If you'd rather get a new partner, I understand."

With the boldest move of her young life, Sarah took his hand. "No, no. I'd be happy to dance every dance with you."

"Here. Eat first." He handed her a cookie and a cup of iced tea.

"Thank you." Sarah took a bite of the sugar cookie but kept her eyes on his.

Oh, what would her father have thought? He probably would have punched Benjamin Fitch for his statement. But she didn't mind at all. When she finished the drink, Ben extended his hand again.

"Can't make a liar out of me. And old man Hammond is lurking in the corner."

Sarah placed her hand in his and let the magic of the night sweep her away.

SAM STOOD, FROZEN, at the refreshment table.

"Faint heart never won fair maiden, or something like that." Martha Chesney's voice startled him.

"Grandma! What?"

"Go on. If you don't ask Becky to dance, someone else will."

Sam sensed color flooding his cheeks. "I don't know what you mean."

"Go on. Stop standing here mooning over the girl."

Sam stood silently, staring at his hands. He glanced up, spying Becky across the floor. She wore a pretty green and gold plaid dress. He recognized the garment as one his mother had spent days sewing, often working late into the evening.

"I know you want to, Sam."

"How do you know?"

"I'm a wise old lady. Go on. She's over there, talking to her mother. Looks like music's going to start up again. Don't be dilly-dallying. Someone else will swoop down and you'll be out of luck."

Sam's gaze connected with Martha's. He knew she was right. When he looked around, he saw a young man about his age or older heading in Becky's direction.

"Thanks, Grandma," Sam muttered as he hurried across the floor.

Sliding a bit across the wood floor, he came to a stop right in front of Becky. A frown from Mrs. Rhodes didn't deter him. As soon as the sound of the fiddle reached his ears, he spoke up.

"Miss Rhodes. Would you like to dance with me?" Sam wiped his sweaty hand on his pants and then extended it.

Before her mother could speak, Becky put her hand in his. "I believe I would, Mr. Chesney."

Sam bowed and eased her out onto the dance floor. Although he'd never been to a dance, he'd watched Caleb and his mother. The steps didn't look difficult and if he tripped a couple of times, so what? He'd still be holding hands with Becky Rhodes.

Guiding him through the Virginia Reel, she smiled warmly as they skipped and bowed their way to the music. The melodies inspired his agile form, urging it to move fast and to the rhythm. Her tiny hand felt warm and soft in his.

He prayed the music wouldn't stop. When it did, they were a bit winded. As holding hands with Becky had made his hands damp and his mouth dry, he needed to wet his whistle.

"Tea?" he asked.

"Yes."

Sam kept hold of her hand and led her to the refreshment table. He filled a cup with tea and handed it to her. As he poured one for himself, he heard a squeaky, male voice.

"Miss Rhodes, can I have the next dance?"

Sam whipped around to face a tall, skinny boy, obviously younger than he.

"Miss Rhodes has promised the next dance to me. The next several, in fact. Why don't you come back when you grow up?" He sipped the cold drink.

The boy's face flushed. He bowed slightly to Becky and ran off.

Becky's gaze met Sam's. She giggled, covering her mouth with her hand.

"I hope you don't mind, Miss Rhodes, but I figured you didn't want to dance with someone who wasn't out of knee pants yet."

"Now I'm going to hold you to that, Mr. Chesney."

"What?"

"You promised to dance every dance with me."

Sam beamed. "My pleasure, Miss Rhodes, my pleasure. Shortbread?"

"I'd be delighted."

They wandered over to the cookies, standing close, whispering, and laughing. Sam caught his grandmother's eye. The older woman gave one nod. Sam returned his gaze to Becky's. Darn if she didn't have the prettiest eyes this side of Danbury.

For a boy whose world had crashed, who'd had nothing mere months ago, he'd bounced back and risen to the top in Fitch's Eddy.

As he moved toward the dance floor with Becky in tow, he spotted his sister dancing with the braggart, Benjamin Fitch.

Anger seethed in his chest. What was he doing with Sarah, anyway? Everybody knew rich folk didn't mingle with poor ones. There was only one conclusion left. Fitch had bad intentions regarding Sarah. Sam sidled up to Ben, who gave him a brief, unsmiling nod. Sam barely contained his anger.

"Lay one finger on my sister and you're a dead man," Sam hissed. Becky gave Sam's hand a tug, and he turned his attention to his partner. Now the warning had been made, he relaxed a little. Fitch knew where Sam stood, and Sarah should be safe—at least for now.

What a job being man of the family was. Was Sam up to the challenge? He didn't rightly know, but figured he'd be finding out sooner rather than later.

Chapter Thirteen

*E**arly Saturday morning***
Though Sarah lay fast asleep, Abby awoke at sunrise. Against the early morning autumn chill, she pulled the blanket up to cover her shoulders, and revisited last night. Closing her eyes, she recalled how she had returned home with her family but had promised Caleb she'd sneak out for a private goodnight.

She smiled at the memory of Sarah wanting to sit up and talk all night about the sterling qualities of Mr. Benjamin Fitch. Fortunately, she fell asleep after extolling only two, and Abigail had tucked her daughter into bed. Sam had disappeared into his room, and Martha had left the dance early and was snoring soundly in her room.

Still wearing her elegant attire, Abigail had wrapped her knitted shawl around her shoulders and stolen soundlessly down the steps. Even the creak of the kitchen door didn't wake the household.

The moon had shone gold in the black night, barely lighting her way down the path to the garden. Caleb had perched on the wooden bench and waited. She stopped for a moment to make out his handsome profile in the moonlight.

She and her husband had had many illicit meetings before marriage without chaperones or parents even knowing. She chuckled, remembering how dense her mother had been when Abby declared a new passion for taking a walk after dark. Of course, George was there to meet her and keep her safe from harm.

This seemed similar, yet now she was much older, more experienced. In the early days of their courtship, she and George had skirted the edges of decorum, always careful not to go too far. Now, the same excitement, the same thrill pulsed through her veins as it had at sixteen. Then, her ignorance of intimacy and youthful fear of it had kept her safe. But now? Well, she knew the delights of the marriage bed and had been deprived. Would she be able to resist?

When she entered the garden, Caleb rose.

"You look even more beautiful in the moonlight." He reached for her, slipping his hands around her waist.

Their bodies touched, igniting a fire within her. He had wasted no time and kissed her quickly. When she wound her arms around his neck, he kissed her again, more slowly, sensuously. It was dark. The world was asleep. There was no reason to hurry. She relaxed in his embrace, softening against his hard chest as his tongue explored her mouth.

Desire filled her. After marriage, when her feelings were aroused, she'd simply follow through with George. But Caleb wasn't her husband. They weren't married— she needed to show restraint. While her mind warred with her passion, she enjoyed the headiness of his body pressed against hers, his male scent, mixed with a little sweat teasing her nose, and the slight rub of the scruff on his face.

Warmth spread through her as she lay in bed, remembering his embrace. Eyes still closed, she recalled the frustration of shutting down their little lovemaking session. Attempting to calm her breathing, she had stepped away, out of his arms.

"Is something wrong?" Caleb had looked perplexed.

She shook her head. "It's best to stop now. Before we can't."

"Do you mean it?"

She met his gaze.

"I mean, do you mean you don't want to stop?"

Grateful for the darkness to hide her blush, she chuckled.

"Oh, you've given me the best news." He hugged her tightly then released her. "I'm so glad you're not repulsed by me."

"Repulsed?" she laughed. "Quite the contrary."

"Some women are."

"Not me."

He took her hand and fell to one knee. "Marry me, Abby. Marry me and we won't have to stop."

Shocked at his proposal, she covered her mouth with her hand. "Marry you? Oh, no. It's too soon. Too soon to marry again."

"Will you think about it?" Caleb rose, but kept hold of her hand.

"I will. But in the light of day, you might feel differently."

"I won't. I love you. And I'll never stop."

She took a deep breath. Confusion filled her head. "I've got to go."

"Why?"

"I don't trust myself."

"You can trust me," he said, raising her hand to his lips.

She laughed. "You're a man. You may think you have control, but after a certain point, no man has control."

His sheepish expression confirmed her words. "I suppose you're right. But I'd never do anything to hurt you."

She cupped his cheek and ran her thumb along his skin. "I know. But nature is strong in us."

"Then marry me."

She shook her head slowly.

"But you have agreed to think about it?"

"I have. I will."

"Good. I'll take you home." Caleb took her hand and led them out of the garden. At the kitchen door, they shared a passionate kiss, and then Caleb departed.

She stole upstairs as silent as a ghost and slid into bed. But she couldn't fall asleep for some time. Thoughts flooded her mind, keeping her awake. Did she love Caleb Tanner? How could she know? Did he truly love her or did he simply want someone to do wifely duties? Before she'd made up her mind, she'd fallen asleep.

In the light of day, she decided not to make a decision, but to take each day as it came. Eventually, the right thing to do would come to her. That was what her husband had always said. And he'd been right. She told no one of Caleb's intentions.

DURING HARVEST FESTIVAL, the inn served breakfast only to those who were boarding there. Hot oatmeal, bread, apple butter, and tea were set out on a sideboard. Abigail turned her energies away from thoughts about the seductive Mr. Caleb Tanner and on to making winning apple pies.

Women entering had to bake four pies, then pick one for the judges. The pies would be served at the church supper, commencing at four in the afternoon, right before sundown. While she worked in the kitchen, Sarah and Martha pressed more dresses handed down and refitted for the event.

She rolled out pie dough and sliced apples. After coating them with cinnamon and sugar, she laid them out perfectly in each pie plate. She baked them, one at a time. By the time she finished, breakfast was cleared away, the dishes done, and it was one o'clock. They barely had time to dress and get to the church for the judging.

Both Sarah and Abigail wore white muslin dresses. Sarah's had a dark pink sash and pink ribbons woven down the long sleeves with a muslin ruffle at the wrist. Abby's dress, slightly lower cut than Sarah's had a large turquoise blue sash with a big bow in the back. A turquoise ribbon was laced along the neckline.

She wrapped her dark blue knitted shawl tighter against the brisk October air. Pies for judging were laid out on a long table in the church foyer, With the Chesney pie, there were six—Abby's apple pie, one custard, one gooseberry, one pumpkin, one sweet potato, and another apple—from Ann Fitch.

Wearing a navy blue, silk taffeta dress, Ann Fitch stood proudly by her pie. Each baker lined up. The judges, the Reverend Bloodgoode, Daniel Rhodes, and a visiting circuit magistrate each took a plate with a piece of pie. They tasted it and then placed a number next to the confection. The winning pie would be the one accumulating the highest total.

People crowded into the church, hovering around the judges, and eyeing each pie. Abigail was proud of hers, but she had to admit Ann Fitch's pie looked a bit nicer. She caught Caleb's eye as he stood by the door. He nodded.

A murmur rippled through the crowd, growing louder as the judges placed their numbers by each pie. Tension, almost palpable, filled the air. Winning the contest was an honor a woman carried for an entire year. Martha claimed a winning pie would bring diners to the inn.

Finally, the votes were cast. Daniel Rhodes tallied each score.

"And the winner is...Ann Fitch!"

A roar arose from a handful of spectators. But one voice screamed louder than the rest.

"Not fair! Ann Fitch should be disqualified! She didn't bake the pie! Her cook did!" The screamer was Charity Bloodgoode.

A gasp hissed through the audience. Then silence. Daniel Rhodes cleared his throat. He spoke quietly.

"Mrs. Fitch, is it true?"

Ann Fitch covered her mouth with her hand and ran out of the church. The crowd murmured. Angry voices rose. Abigail hurried out after Mrs. Fitch.

She caught up with her at the town square. Grabbing her upper arm, she stopped her. Ann was crying, hiding her eyes with her hand.

"Is it true?" Abigail asked softly.

Ann spoke. "It is. I can't lie anymore."

"Why?"

"Giselle is from France. She's a better cook, a better baker than I am. I can't bake a decent pie to save my life. But Elijah insists I enter the contest and I must win. Every year. She can cook and bake better than anyone in the world. And I'm useless. Just useless. I can't let Elijah down. Now, he'll know the truth. I'll be humiliated."

She hugged Ann. "Wait, wait. Let's go back. I have an idea."

"You? Why would you help me? I've never been nice to you."

"You give me sewing to do and pay me for it. You deserve a chance to explain."

"Oh, I can't. I can't." Ann stiffened. "I can't."

"Wait outside. Come in when you feel ready." She stepped across the threshold of the church. The dissenting voices fell to a low murmur but didn't let up. She clapped her hands. When the spectators didn't quiet down, Caleb put two fingers in his mouth and whistled.

"Please, everyone! Listen!"

They turned their attention to Abby.

"I've talked to Mrs. Fitch. Here's the story." She said a silent prayer to excuse her lie yet to come. "Mrs. Fitch's cook is too shy to enter. She's from France. Doesn't speak English well. She's afraid to enter her pie. She begged Mrs. Fitch to enter it for her as Mrs. Fitch's pie. Ann Fitch did her cook a favor. If you think it's the best pie, then you must give the medal to Mrs. Fitch."

Unnoticed by the crowd, Ann Fitch stepped quietly into the church.

"Well, it got the highest scores from all three judges," Daniel Rhodes said.

"Give the medal to the best pie," a man called out.

"Who cares who made it?" another one said.

"The medal goes to Mrs. Fitch!" a woman cried.

Daniel spoke. "Quiet, quiet! We'll take a vote. All in favor of giving the medal to the pie with the highest score— no matter who baked it— raise your hands." Daniel counted. "Those opposed?" He counted again.

"Medal goes to best pie. Mrs. Fitch— you win!"

Daniel looked around. Ann Fitch, beaming, stepped forward. "Here I am."

She held the medal as if it were life itself.

"Now, it's time to eat the pies and decide which one is best yourself!" Daniel Rhodes announced.

People filed out to the meeting hall behind the general store.

Ann Fitch drew Abby aside.

"Thank you. From the bottom of my heart. I owe you. How can I ever repay you?"

"Don't worry."

"And your pie came in second."

"I guess I need to talk to Giselle and find out what her secret is."

"I think you might have to learn French first," Ann replied.

Abigail laughed.

TABLES WERE STILL SET up from the dance the night before. The Reverend Bloodgoode commandeered his flock. He ordered the men to haul out the benches and the women to lay out supper with pie for dessert.

Elijah Fitch had donated a roast pig and a turkey. Each family brought a dish. Martha brought raisin bread. Bowls of mashed potatoes, sweetened with cream, were set to one side of the meat with a platter of roasted potatoes on the other.

Vegetables, fresh from farms graced the table. Boiled turnips, Creamed celery, and creamed asparagus were favorites. A pot of mashed winter squash swimming in butter and Mrs. Rhodes' carrot and apple casserole was gobbled up quickly. Boiled peas with salt pork added a bit of saltiness to the meal. Martha placed three of her fat raisin bread loaves next to half a dozen loaves of white bread and a slab of soft butter.

A dozen pans of cornbread, Fitch's Eddy's traditional dish to honor the end of the harvest, crowned the table near the pies. Due to abundant rainfall, the corn had grown taller than ever. Kernels bursting with natural sweetness were plentiful in the moist bread.

The Chesney family sat together. But Sam searched the crowd for a glimpse of Becky Rhodes.

"May I join you?" Caleb asked Martha.

"Yes. Of course." She slid down to make room. He sat between Martha and Abby. Once seated, he pressed her hand under the table for a moment before turning his attention to the reverend for the blessing.

Reverend Bloodgoode, never at a loss for words, stood up and droned on for twenty minutes. Caleb noted the restless shifting of people in their seats didn't encourage old Ebenezer to shorten his message.

Caleb could hardly focus. Almost embarrassed he'd proposed late the night before, he frowned, wondering if he had rushed her. She had not been a widow long, and he should have shown more restraint. By comparison, he'd been widowed for a long time. He knew what he wanted; he wanted Abigail Chesney as his wife. Would she turn away from him due to his eager pursuit?

Suddenly, a small, soft hand curled around his fingers. Surprised, he stole a glance at her and raised his eyebrows, then regained his composure. As quickly as the hand warmed his, it retreated. Perhaps his words were not in vain and she might return his affection and agree to marry. Of course, it wouldn't happen right away, but he was a patient man. He'd waited this long to find another woman equal to his Emily, he could wait for however long it took for her to agree.

Finally, the Reverend wound it up.

"And we bless this bounty, Our Lord. Amen."

Somber faces broke into smiles. Rumbling stomachs would receive their due. People rose and formed a line at the food table. Charity Bloodgoode supervised the women serving.

"Not too much. There are many more waiting to be served."

Caleb wasn't surprised to hear her demand the servers reduce portion sizes. Chuckling to himself, he wondered when he reached the table if she'd serve him more than a teaspoon of anything. He let the Chesney family go before him. Sam stood between him and Abigail.

"You danced more than one dance with my mother."

"Yep."

"But I said—"

"It was her choice. And none of your business."

Sam moseyed forward with the line. "You'd better not be disrespectful of her."

"Never. I would never be disrespectful."

If they'd been on better terms, he would have ruffled Sam's hair or at least had a handshake with the lad.

"You spent all evening dancing with Becky Rhodes."

"Yeah. And it's none of your business." Sam gave as good as he got.

Caleb roared with laughter as he made his way to the front of the line. Virginia Rhodes placed a large portion of turkey and pork on his plate. She winked. Lord, one would think she knew about his secret meeting with Abigail! Although he figured most folks would have been asleep by midnight, maybe someone had been awake and seen them. The idea made him weak. He'd rather die than ruin her reputation.

"Man who can pull a wagon like you did needs a bit of extra meat, wouldn't you say, Mr. Tanner?" Virginia asked.

Caleb blew out a breath and sighed in relief. "Wouldn't want more than my fair share."

"We can spare a bit extra for the strongest man in town."

"Thank you."

With his plate loaded, he took the seat next to Sam Chesney. The men ate quietly. Caleb listened to the chatter from other tables. He got bits and pieces of conversations.

"The redheaded girl with the Chesney boy."

"Danced every dance with her. I counted."

"Mr. Fitch ain't gonna like his son courting Miss Chesney."

"I tell you he danced every dance with that Mrs. Chesney!"

There it was. Someone had noticed. He swallowed.

"Silence!" The Reverend hollered. "I believe we need a special blessing for these beautiful pies, created for our enjoyment." Wearing a salacious grin, he turned to face Abby. "And apple is my favorite."

Anger grew in Caleb's chest. While words of prayer were uttered by Ebenezer, Caleb watched him carefully. *The old windbag isn't going to give up.* She turned away from the reverend's leer. Caleb laughed. Perhaps he didn't need to defend her from Ebenezer after all.

WHEN THE CHURCH SUPPER was over, there wasn't a smidgeon of pie left. Martha pushed to her feet, full up from eating food, thankfully, she had not cooked. She had closed the dining room of the inn during the event. Darkness settled around Fitch's Eddy like a cloak. The slight chill in the air hinted at cooler days to come.

Martha drew her wrap tighter around her waist. Sarah held Lizzy's hand. Sam stepped back a few paces to talk to Becky Rhodes. Caleb and Abigail lagged behind. When Martha reached the inn, she put out bread, butter, cheese and tea for her boarders who had not attended the church supper.

As she walked home from the town square, the smell of burning wood from the church fire blended with the smoke of the inn, created a pleasant scent. Martha had enjoyed the warm spring and summer days, but winter ones by the fire with hot apple cider and pumpkin muffins had their appeal.

After the holidays, the loggers would return. She looked forward to their arrival. Not only would she have a full house during the season, but she'd also enjoy the companionship of the men, some old friends by now, who came to find work in the spring. After supper, around a crackling fire, she'd hear many a story of their adventures.

The short walk refreshed her spirit. It wouldn't be long before she, Abby, and Sarah would be working on a Thanksgiving feast for travelers, and townsfolk. The crisp air cooled her as she hustled Sarah and Lizzy along. Martha put a good distance between herself and her daughter-in-law. The older woman had made up her mind to leave her Abigail and Caleb alone. It would be mighty hard to get to know each other with children about, asking questions and interrupting. Besides, endearments couldn't be shared with young ears eagerly listening in, could they?

Martha understood how hard it was to be a widow. After her husband, John, had died, how many nights had she cried herself to sleep? She'd lost track. With one foolish attempt to keep up with the younger loggers, John had lost his life, and had taken her dreams with him. As she grew older, Martha's goals had shifted, but she still had plans, until John died.

When she got word from her son, that he'd bring his family to Fitch's Eddy, Martha's hopes of a new life grew. The inn, Abby, and the children filled her days, but her nights were still cold and empty. She missed John's affection, his warmth and closeness at night. His presence made her feel safe. And since he'd been gone, she found herself fearful for the first time in her life.

While she mourned the passing of the son she hadn't known in his adult life, her heart broke for his wife. Martha had had many happy years with John. But Abby's happiness had been cut short. Weighed down with the burden of raising her children alone, her daughter-in-law had trudged on ahead with few complaints.

The way Abby hid her pain, accepted loneliness, and attended to her children spoke well of her. Martha admired her and determined to help her any way she could.

She was still young and beautiful. She could get another husband, a man to take care of her, Sarah, and Lizzy. Sam was practically a man already. Not long after she learned of her son's death did Martha size-up Caleb for her daughter-in-law.

Once the notion of Caleb as a possible husband for Abby entered her head, Martha encouraged a union. Why should she waste away alone when Caleb, a strapping, handsome man with a thriving trade, was mired in loneliness himself? No reason, Martha decided.

From her observations, it appeared he'd gotten the idea all on his own. It warmed her heart to think of her daughter-in-law safely joined with another good man. Lord knew Martha wouldn't be around forever.

She lit the lantern by the rocking chairs on the front porch, then opened the door for her granddaughters.

"Sarah, stoke the fire. Lizzy, come upstairs. Grandma will tell you a story." Martha took the child's hand. Maybe Caleb and Abby would linger, snuggled close against the chill of the night air. Maybe love would ignite and light the darkness in two hearts?

Chapter Fourteen

N *ovember*
Days were short. Early sunsets and cold winds swirled around the inn as the Chesneys prepared for the coming holiday. Reduced time for hunting due to darkness prompted Caleb to increase Sam's apprentice days to four each week.

Abby brought a simple meal to her son at the blacksmith shop at noon every day—a good excuse to see Caleb. When she entered the shop, his face lit up. While warming herself by the fire, she exchanged pleasantries with the blacksmith. She'd drop hints of impending trips to the general store hoping he could make an excuse and meet her there.

Noting Sam's expression sour when Caleb stood too close to her or laughed too loudly, she'd made up her mind her son would simply have to get over his aversion to the man. Sam had ceased dropping disparaging comments about Caleb in front of his mother. Was it a sign he'd accepted him? Though undecided about his proposal, she hoped Sam wouldn't make her decision any harder.

At dusk, she hurried to the woodpile in the inn's backyard to fetch a log or two to keep their fires hot throughout the evening—or it was her excuse. No one knew she met Caleb at the wood pile. When she arrived, he'd snake one arm around her waist. Then he'd draw her close and kiss her passionately.

He raised his head. "When can we stop hiding and let people know I'm courting you?"

"Soon."

"Right after Thanksgiving. I'm not one for sneaking around. We're not doing anything wrong. Let's clear the air and stop the gossip."

She fidgeted with the ties on her coat. "You're right. After Thanksgiving."

"I don't know if I can wait." He stepped closer.

She raised her arms. Linking them behind his neck, she eased into his embrace. Closing her eyes, she breathed in his unique smoky scent mixed with a bit of sweat. She liked the way he smelled. He tightened his arms around her. She sighed.

"I love you." His soft whisper warmed her ear.

"I love you, too." She'd not said it aloud before. But she'd known for some time. Relief at admitting the truth washed over her.

With her words, his grip tightened.

"I think Martha knows," she said.

"I'm not surprised. She's no fool." He released her, sliding his hands down her arms to connect with her hands. "Did she say anything?"

She shook her head. "I think she approves. I'd better get back."

"Soon, we'll have regular time to be together."

"I know. I hate sneaking around," she said.

He leaned in for one last kiss, then took her hand. Together they walked to the kitchen door of the inn. Caleb turned toward his house.

As she faced an overload of work during the holidays as well as dealing with the bitter cold, Caleb's love warmed her heart and eased her burden.

Of course, she wasn't alone—she had Martha's loving support. But if Martha should suddenly pass away, how would she cope? She pushed the terrifying thought out of her mind as she hurried to get out of the cold and warm up by the fire.

"VIRGINIA RHODES SAID she'd sell our jars of pickles. The extra money could buy some gifts for the children," Martha said.

"She said she'd take some of my needlework, too. She said handkerchiefs sell well at the holidays." Abby chimed in.

Oranges, peppermint, licorice sticks, and chocolates from the general store topped the list of goodies to fill the children's stockings. Although Abigail and George gave more homemade items to their children at the holiday, this year, the young'uns had suffered the greatest loss of their lives. Though gifts wouldn't bring their father back, the sweets would put smiles on their faces, even if only for a little while.

At dinner, Martha spoke. "We need to be getting ready for the holiday. Broken chairs need fixin'. Any curtains or bed linens need mending? Tomorrow we'll get started. We'll have a full house from Thanksgiving right through Christmas. Oh, Sam, please get a twenty-five-pound sack of flour at the general store tomorrow."

Grateful to be busy, Abigail had less time to focus on celebrating her first holiday without her husband. The holidays had been her favorite time of the year. George, always a hard worker, had never failed to take time off to play games and read stories with his family. Together, he and Sam had hunted for their Thanksgiving turkey.

"Christmas," she murmured to herself, anxiety making her head pound.

In the evenings, George would whittle small toys. Sam still had the whistle his father had fashioned. And the girls each had a small doll made by him. The cold winter nights had made cuddling up with her husband even more enjoyable. She'd miss his kisses and hugs, his laughter ringing out when the children beat him at a game.

The memories brought tears to her eyes. Sam took his mother's hand.

"I know, Mama. I miss him, too."

She hugged him hard, spilling her tears on his shirt.

SAM DAWDLED HIS WAY through the street to the town square and Rhodes' General Store. He hated carrying the heavy bag of flour, but he was the only one in the family strong enough to do it. The minute he stepped into the store, his gaze settled on the shiny, new hunting knife on display. Next to it lay a new musket, its barrel gleaming in the light. Although he was saving his wages from the blacksmith, he had a long way to go before he could buy either of those.

"Sam Chesney?" It was Virginia Rhodes.

"Yes, ma'am."

"Come to see Becky? She's busy in the kitchen, baking brownies."

"No, ma'am. Not that I wouldn't like to see her. But I've come for a sack of flour for the inn."

"I'll be right back."

The tinkle of the bell drew Sam's attention. Benjamin Fitch, dressed in clean clothes, looking like the son of wealth, strode in. He motioned to Sam, who returned the greeting.

"Hunting for your Thanksgiving turkey, Chesney?"

"In a bit."

"It'll take you ten years to find the best place to hunt turkeys," Benjamin Fitch said.

"Yeah? I don't think so. And stay away from my sister."

"Good luck. I hope you enjoy your Thanksgiving chicken." Benjamin snickered.

Sam confronted him, grabbing his shirt. "So where are the best places to hunt turkeys?"

"What'll you give me in return?"

"Nothing."

"How about you lay off me about your sister?" Benjamin pushed his advantage.

"No way!"

"Okay then. Tough luck, Chesney."

Sam weighed the pros and cons. "Okay. I'll lay off until after Thanksgiving."

"Deal."

"So, where's the best place?"

"Old Zachariah Lee's place. Come on. I'll show you."

The boys returned to the inn. Sam entered quietly, grabbed his musket, and joined Ben. They tromped through tall grass and woods to the Lee place.

"Gotta be careful. Stay away from the big pasture. Old man Lee's got a nasty bull in there. He's mean as the day is long."

"Probably no turkeys in there anyway."

"Sometimes they go where Lee keeps his chickens. Turkeys eat some of the feed. Come on. I'll show you."

Sam followed.

AN HOUR LATER, ABIGAIL washed her hands and pulled out her bread board. She looked around, her lips compressing in a frown.

"Where's the flour?"

"I sent Sam to the general store a while ago." Martha rested her hands on her hips.

"I'll find him. Probably stopped to play with Lucky." She set out for the store. When she entered, Daniel Rhodes was opening up a barrel of crackers.

"Mr. Rhodes, have you seen my son?"

"He was here not too long ago. He and Ben Fitch set out to hunt turkeys."

"Oh?"

"Didn't he tell you? They went up to Zachariah Lee's place."

"Can you show me?"

"Of course." Daniel stood by the window and pointed as he spoke.

"Thank you." She pushed through the door.

Daniel returned to his task, but a moment later spoke up. "Oh, don't go in the pasture. There's a mighty mean bull in there. Mrs. Chesney. Mrs. Chesney?" He looked around, but she was gone. He shrugged.

She drew her brows together. As she trudged through the dense weeds, she spoke to herself.

"When I find the boy, he's gonna get a talking to."

When she reached the split rail fence, she slipped right through. In the distance, cows lay on the grass or stood. Huddled together, sharing their warmth, they switched their tails. Feeling a chill, she pulled the belt on her coat tighter.

In the distance she saw something large and black. It ambled slowly toward her. Squinting, she made out large horns and long legs. The creature's walk became a trot. It must have been at least two hundred yards away. As a ray of sun broke through the clouds and cast bright light on the creature, she saw it was a bull—a very large bull. Abby swallowed hard and made tracks to the fence.

Afraid to break into a run, because the bull might charge, she backpedaled as fast as she could. But the bull gained ground. Unable to contain her fear, she turned, gripped her skirt, raised it, and ran full out.

As soon as she took off, the bull put his head down, snorted, and chased after her.

One glance over her shoulder and she screamed. She ran full out toward the fence. But the bull cut her off. Turning, she searched desperately for a way out. When she spied a gate, she sped straight for it. The bull followed. She screamed again, though she was uncertain anyone could hear.

"Mama!" A familiar voice came from the woods. She saw her son running. Benjamin Fitch beat Sam to the pasture.

"Stay away!" She hollered, still moving, attempting to get out of the path of the bull.

He pawed the ground twice. Almost out of breath, Abby pushed herself to keep going. A sound from her left caught her attention.

"Here! Here! Here!" Then a loud whistle which drew the animal's attention.

She stopped. Ben Fitch had hopped the fence. He lobbed rocks at the bull. One came down straight between the large animal's shoulders. The bull snorted. The lad threw another rock, and the bull charged. Ben placed his hands on the top fence rail, and vaulted over, landing on the other side. The bull stopped short of crashing into the wood.

Now free to flee, Abby dashed to the fence and climbed through.

"Mama, what are you doing here?"

"Looking for you! You didn't come back from the store. Daniel Rhodes told me you were up here, hunting turkeys!"

Benjamin Fitch, red-faced, stood beside Sam.

"Thank you for saving me."

"You're welcome, Mrs. Chesney." Ben smiled.

"Sam, we need flour." She pointed. "To the store!"

The bull made one more charge at the fence, startling her.

"I thought everyone knew about old Zachariah's bull." Ben brushed himself off.

"I know now. Find any turkeys?"

The boys shook their heads.

"Sam, you can come join Benjamin after you get the flour."

"I'll wait here," Ben said.

Sam walked side by side with his mother. "What were you doing hunting with Benjamin Fitch?"

"Aw, he's not so bad." Sam's long legs kept an easy pace with his mother.

She cocked an eyebrow at her son. "Really? I thought he was a dirty dog?"

"Naw. He's okay. He knows where the turkeys are."

"Good. Get a big, plump, juicy one for us."

They arrived at Main Street. Sam hurried to the store, and Abby returned home. Benjamin Fitch had risked his neck to save her. She shook her head. *What a surprise—who would have thought he could be bothered with someone like me? Maybe he's all right for Sarah?*

Sam arrived home with the flour and lit out again. *Always good to make a friend from an enemy, George said.* She watched her son run off with his musket on his shoulder. She grinned as she ripped open the sack and shoved the measuring cup in the silky flour.

THANKSGIVING DAY

Abby watched as the chairs filled with folks celebrating Thanksgiving at the inn. She blew some strands of hair from her face and leaned against the door frame. It was noon and she'd been cooking for hours. The Chesneys had been working since dawn preparing the feast. The Reverend Bloodgoode insisted on giving a prayer of thanks before the meal each year. Martha bristled at the idea but decided not to interfere. Best to stay on his good side.

Martha had used the last of the corn to fashion a thick corn chowder to start the meal.

"Fill 'em up with a bit of soup, then they won't eat as much." Her philosophy was not based on a miserly attitude, but on a realistic assessment of the amount of food they had and how many they had to feed. Sarah had made corn bread and helped with sweet smelling loaves of Martha's raisin bread.

"What a mighty fine turkey you got, Sam. He'll do nicely." Martha looked over the bird. Early in the morning, they had prepared it and put it in to roast.

The pungent smell of cabbage boiling mixed with the aroma of the roasting bird made her stomach rumble. She loved cabbage. A large cast iron pan held turnips, parsnips, and carrots. Fat yams sat on a rack high over the fire to cook slowly. White potatoes were in a pot of water, waiting their turn at the fire.

Abigail and Sarah had made the desserts the day before. Taking leftover bread she'd stored in the pantry all week, they made bread pudding along with apple pie and pumpkin pie.

Martha strolled out of the kitchen and stood next to her daughter-in-law.

"Biggest crowd we've had yet," she said. "Looks like we'll have enough money left over to buy sweets for the children for Christmas."

Abby hugged her mother-in-law. She had given up hope of any kind of happiness during her first Christmas without George. Leave it to Martha to inject something to smile about.

Sam showed the last of the diners to their tables. Caleb entered and approached Abby.

"Today's the day."

"But we said after Thanksgiving?"

"I can't wait." Caleb took her hand in his before taking the place next to her at the Chesney table.

Ebenezer Bloodgoode burst through the door.

"Heathens and believers come together to give thanks!"

Martha raised her eyebrows, and shot a glance at Abby, who hid a chuckle behind her hand. The women returned to the kitchen. While the reverend blathered on, they set out the dishes on the groaning board. Next to the turkey were mashed potatoes and a plate of roasted yams. There were three bowls of vegetables. Along with all that, six loaves of white bread and three of raisin bread graced the table.

"That's everything, Grandma." Sarah wiped sweat from her forehead with the hem of her apron.

Martha reached over and cupped her granddaughter's cheek. "Great job, sweetheart."

The family sat down at their own table in the back. Caleb occupied the extra chair. Abby stood. Sam put his hand on her arm.

"What are you doing, Mama?"

"Mr. Tanner, Caleb, is eating with us."

"He's not a member of this family."

She stared straight into her son's eyes. "Not yet."

Sam swallowed and let go of his mother's arm.

"Thank you kindly for offering me a seat at your table."

Little Lizzy patted Caleb's hand and grinned. He stroked her hair. "Thank you, Lizzy."

"You're family to me, already, Caleb Tanner." Martha speared a piece of turkey with her fork.

When the meal was over, Sam, Sarah, and Martha's helpers cleared the table. The weather outside had turned nasty, with hard rain and chilling temperatures, so people stayed to visit with their neighbors. Sam put more logs on the fire.

Caleb joined Abby in the kitchen where she put on two kettles for tea. As she stood next to him, the reverend entered.

"No folks in the kitchen, Reverend." Martha attempted to shoo him out.

"Tanner is here. And I see he's taking up Mrs. Chesney's time." Ebenezer cast a jaundiced eye in their direction.

"It's none of your concern, Reverend. Thank you for doing the blessing. Don't you have to make preparations for Christmas?" Martha asked.

"Tanner, are you courting Mrs. Chesney?"

"If it's any of your business, Reverend, yes, I am. Run along."

"You've sullied her reputation by being seen alone with her on many occasions. People are talking." The reverend faced her. "Are you aware this man may be a murderer?"

"What are you talking about?"

"People are saying he killed his wife."

"Let 'em." Caleb turned away from Ebenezer.

She bristled. "Ridiculous! Mr. Tanner's business is his own. Town people ought to keep their noses in their own back yards."

Ignoring her, Bloodgoode raised his voice. "Not very chivalrous, Tanner, letting your presence ruin Mrs. Chesney's reputation."

"Mr. Tanner understands neither he nor I can control what other people talk about or think. Frankly, I don't care." she straightened up.

"Really, Mrs. Chesney! You shock me!"

"Please don't spoil this special day. Go back to your church and the jealous gossips who want to ruin the happiness of others." She turned away.

He huffed out of the kitchen and slammed out of the inn.

"See, Mama?" Sam raised his eyebrows.

"Your mother's right. Can't control the minds of others. So don't bother," Martha said.

As Sam left the kitchen, Caleb grabbed his upper arm. "I'd never do anything to harm your mother."

"What about her reputation?" Sam asked.

"There is no way to protect against jealous people who make up stories. We're courting now. It's official. Settle yourself to this, Sam. Accept it."

"Never!" Sam pulled away from Caleb and returned to the dining room.

After Caleb left for his home. Abigail stood at the door and gazed at the mountains. Martha joined her. The leaves had turned, splashing brilliant gold, bright red, and orange across the foothills.

"Such a shame George never got to see the Catskills." She sighed. "They are so beautiful."

"He would have appreciated their beauty. Whenever I feel bad about losing John and George, I look at the mountains and know how blessed we are to live here. Their bounty sustains us."

"You're right, Martha."

"And this Thanksgiving, though I've lost so much, I have gained family." She patted Abby. "I'm mighty grateful for you and yours, my dear. Mighty grateful."

CHRISTMAS EVE

Soft, fat snowflakes fell, blanketing Fitch's Eddy in a clean, white coat. Abigail stood at the front window of the inn. Memories of her husband flooded her mind. Each year for Christmas, he had cut down low-hanging boughs from a pine tree and brought them inside. She loved the fresh sharp scent. Short winter days were spent preparing food to last for the winter. He had built a small shed where they kept potatoes, apples, and meat.

She'd stewed vegetables and fruit. They pressed apples to wring out every tangy drop for cider, which they drank warmed in front of the fire. They'd eat their supper of fluffy slices of warm bread covered in sweet butter, apples, and salted pork by the light of a mighty blaze. He would spin tales of his boyhood in Danbury. Although he said he wasn't a storyteller and all his were true, Abigail knew the adventures were fictitious, but never let on.

After the children were snuggled into their beds and the logs burned down some, he would retrieve a small bottle of brandy he'd kept under the bed. They would take a nip to ward off the chill of the winter's night.

Then they'd crawl into bed and douse the candles. Off in their room with the door closed and the children asleep in the front of the tidy cabin, they had privacy and time for intimacy. He would make love to her. Afterward, she'd cuddle up to him and they'd share their dreams.

"Ten years they said before the farm is ours. We only have four more left. Can you stand it?"

"As long as I'm with you, George, I can stand anything."

What had once been sweet memories were now bittersweet. Those words haunted her. She had always known that as long as she was with him, she could walk through fire. But now she was alone, and at this special time of year, pain seared through her heart. She watched the heavy snow fall and sighed.

"I know where your mind is." Martha's voice startled her. "Yes, I think about John on nights like this, too."

"Do you miss him much?" She faced her mother-in-law.

Tears dampened Martha's eyes. "Every day. I miss him every day."

"Does it get easier?"

"Yes, my dear, it does." Martha patted her on the shoulder. "Someday soon you will have someone else. And it will be good and right."

She smiled. "Thank you."

"You're a fine woman. Caleb Tanner is a fine man. The match would be most suitable."

"But Sam?"

"He'll get over himself. He's already doing better with Caleb. He's confused, is all. Doesn't know quite how much he's supposed to guide his family. He's smart. He'll figure out he doesn't need to tell his mother what to do. Or his sister, either."

She laughed. "You've got him figured out."

"I raised his father, didn't I?"

"And you did a good job." She hugged Martha.

"Come, let's get the stockings filled. I've got the goodies hidden under my bed."

The women crept quietly to the dining room to fill each stocking, then hang them by the fireplace. They whispered and laughed as they divided up the sweets, sharing the joy of giving.

"No licorice for Sam. Give his to Sarah. Give him an extra cinnamon stick." She sorted through the treats, doling them out evenly. "Oh, Lizzy is partial to peppermint."

"Me, too. Settles my stomach," Martha added.

When they were done, they buttered bread, made tea, and nibbled their snack by the fire.

"This will be my best Christmas in years, having you all beside me."

How could she grouse when her mother-in-law was so independent and brave? This was the first Christmas of her new life. She raised her teacup.

"To you, Martha. Brave and wise. Thank you for taking us in."

Martha smiled and clinked her cup with Abby's.

"'Tis you and the children who have saved me."

Chapter Fifteen

A bby couldn't sleep on the eve of her first Christmas without George. Always such a special day in their house, now, they'd have to create new traditions. Life at the inn meant fewer outdoor chores. Of course, they'd be cooking from the early morning hours throughout the day.

At least they'd still salivate over the wonderful smells of a goose or turkey roasting. And turnips and carrots, maybe with a dash of precious cinnamon to turn the carrots as sweet as yams.

This year there would be only apple pie as an early frost had killed the last of the berries. Without George to fill the children's stockings the night before and stash them under the bed, Abby had taken over the task, and placed them on the mantle.

She sighed. When he died, her dreams had died with him. She no longer yearned for a grand home and acres and acres of farmland to call her own. She spent each day scrubbing, cooking, and sewing until her fingers grew numb. There was no time for dreams beyond the thought of simply making it through the day.

But it was Christmas and she made up her mind it had to continue to be a happy time, of relaxation, laughter, storytelling, and dining better than any other night of the year— except maybe Thanksgiving.

Now Caleb had come into her life. Could he provide a strong and constant love, like George? Did she dare to dream again? She trusted him because Martha did and didn't understand why the town gossips vilified him. He refused to bare his soul to strangers and steadfastly kept his secret sadness to himself, rather than open himself up to pity. If people thought him sinister with no facts or proof, then let them, he'd said to her more than once.

While she admired his pride and refusal to give in to pressure, she wondered how hard must it be to be an outcast in such a small town? Besides Martha, Caleb was the only person who understood her without explanation. She saw acceptance in his eyes.

If a journey like hers could go so wrong as to take her husband, would she ever be safe again? Was she safe with Caleb? She sensed him watching over her from time to time. Then there was Sam. She shook her head and frowned. *Will my boy ever learn to back off and let me live? He's not my keeper, though he'd disagree.*

She wanted to dream again, to anticipate happier times, to smile more than she frowned. Caleb was so handsome and sweet, so strong and willing to help at every turn. His shy passion made her feel like a girl again, being courted by the best man in town.

"George would say not to borrow trouble because it will be knocking on your door soon enough." She climbed in bed and shut her eyes.

The sun was barely up when someone jostled her.

"Wake up, Mama. Wake up. It's Christmas!" Lizzy pulled and tugged on her mother.

She yawned and sat up. "All right, all right. I'm coming."

"Can we go downstairs and see our presents?" Sam poked his head in their room.

"The stockings are filled!" Sarah clapped her hands together.

"Did you go downstairs and peek?" Abby pretended to frown, but the cherubic face of her youngest child broke through her pretense. She grabbed Lizzy, pulling her onto the bed, hugging her.

"Yes, little one. The stockings are filled. Let's go downstairs and see what you got this year." She let the squealing, squirming, laughing child go. After combing her fingers through her hair, she reached for a wrapper. Bundling herself up in a woolen coat, she grabbed a pair of warm stockings and followed her children down the stairs.

The cavernous Inn dining room stood empty. But in the kitchen, on the fireplace mantle were three stockings. Already dressed, Martha added a spoonful of tea to a mug of hot water. Sam stoked the fire and added three new logs.

Abigail uncovered dough she'd made the day before. She cut it, rolled it out into ropes, added cinnamon and sugar and twirled it together to make cinnamon buns, their traditional Christmas breakfast. Martha made hot chocolate for the children and a cup of tea for Abby. She shoved the pan of buns into the oven. Sam poked the fire until it flamed.

"Can you make two batches, Mama?" He asked.

"While the buns are cooking and before you open your stockings, I have a special Christmas present for each of you. Sam, first." She opened the pantry door and slipped inside. She came out carrying a sheepskin coat.

"This belonged to your father. It's yours now. You'll need it for hunting and gathering wood in the winter." She handed Sam the garment. He fisted it and brought it up to his face. A slight shiver shook him. She snaked her arm around his middle and hugged him. Sam pushed his arms through the sleeves and fastened his new coat.

"And for Sarah, your father's Bible." She handed her daughter the book. Sarah ran her palm gently over the well-worn cover. "Thank you, Mama," she said, her voice low.

"And for Lizzy, something from grandma. She says this was your father's favorite book when he was a little boy."

"What's it say, Mama?"

"A Description of 300 Animals."

Lizzy smiled so broadly, she lit up the room.

"Now you may have your stockings," Martha said, handing one to each.

By the time the children took out their first candy stick, the cinnamon buns were done. She turned them out to cool. When they could be handled, she buttered each one and put them on a plate.

As they tore into the confections, there was a knock on the door. Martha peeked out.

"Who could be here so early?"

"Oh! It's Caleb! I invited him." Abby scurried up the stairs to dress.

CALEB WHISTLED AS HE strolled down the street. His breath puffed ahead in the frigid air like a fine mist. The sun had woken up, stretched, and cast her rays on him. On this perfect wintry day, he brimmed over with Christmas spirit. Today he would present the woman he loved with a fine gift he'd made. He'd kept it a secret even from Sam, which wasn't easy with the boy in the shop almost every day. He'd slung the heavy item over his shoulder, and he fairly bounced down the street to the inn. Still asleep, the town didn't utter a sound as he trod along the well-worn path.

His thoughts turned to Sam. Caleb had tried everything to win the boy over with no success. He had even crafted the perfect gift, but he doubted it would make a difference. He hoped to marry Abby right after the New Year. Would she agree, knowing Sam still opposed their union?

Caleb straightened his powerful shoulders and took a deep breath, trying to quell his nerves. His loud knock reverberated through the empty rooms of the inn. Maybe he should have tapped lightly in case the few boarders were still asleep? Martha didn't serve breakfast on Christmas until eight. Church service started at ten, so she had time to set up a small buffet. People needed to be a little hungry when they came to the inn for Christmas dinner, the biggest meal of the year, after Thanksgiving.

Caleb smacked his lips at the mental vision of roast duck or goose. Or maybe turkey and Martha's fine stuffing, potatoes, and vegetables. But the crowning glory would be Abby's pies. Hunger gnawed at his belly. Seductive aromas emanated from the inn. Closing his eyes, he pictured a table laden with the best food for a hundred miles. The scent of cinnamon teased his nose. Ah, yes, was it raisin bread he smelled?

Martha answered the door with a broad smile. "Come in, come in. You're in luck. The cinnamon buns are still warm." Martha pulled on his arm.

"Cinnamon buns?"

"Family tradition for Abby and the children. And now you, too."

He grinned. The sound of family traditions including him warmed his heart. Although being part of a family every day was good, it must be especially wonderful on Christmas, he mused.

"What have you got there?" Martha led him into the kitchen.

Abby hurried down the steps. He bowed to her, and she curtsied.

"This is for you. It's a bed warmer." He pulled the item out of the burlap sack and placed it on the floor. The finely polished brass gleamed in the candlelight. The wood handle was finished to a rich, smooth patina.

"Oh my goodness! Caleb! What a fine gift. Did you make it?" She clasped her hands in front of her heart.

"I did. Fill it with hot coals or wood and slip it under the mattress. The heat will travel through the brass, but not the wood, so the handle will never get hot."

"Wonderful. Thank you." She leaned over and kissed him—right in front of the children! Stunned silence fell.

"I have something for each of you." He pulled more gifts from his bag. "For Sarah, I have a copper necklace." He handed her a shiny copper circle with a hole and a thin strip of rawhide strung through it.

"Mama, tie it for me, will you?" Sarah held it up to her neck.

"For Sam, a new hunting knife. Be careful. It's sharp enough to carve a turkey." Caleb pulled an eight-inch knife sheathed in rawhide from the bag. "And for Lizzy? A new cup. Hammered copper."

She clapped her hands and spoke. "Thank you."

"And last of all, Martha. A small cast iron pot." Caleb handed her the pot, complete with a top perfectly fitted.

She nudged Sam. "Thank you, Mr. Tanner." The boy fingered the blade carefully. "This is pretty sharp."

"Thank you," Martha said to Caleb. "This is the perfect size for leftovers! Now we have some things for you. But first cinnamon buns." Martha handed him a plate with two big sweet-smelling buns on it. He took it.

"I finally finished this. It was supposed to be for you last year!" Martha laughed as she handed him a forest green hand-knitted sweater.

"And I made this for you." Abigail handed him a dark blue scarf made from the softest wool.

"Thank you, ladies. These are fine gifts. I'll be warm all winter long!"

Caleb relaxed in his seat as the Chesneys wolfed down more cinnamon buns, slices of white bread and raisin bread slathered with rich, creamy butter. The children drank hot chocolate, and the adults had tea.

When the church bell sounded nine times, Martha rose.

"Time to get breakfast on the table. Folks will be coming down soon."

The family got busy. They cleared away their dishes and arranged food on platters. Sam refilled the kettle and put it on the stove. Caleb drew Abby aside. Fingering the scarf, he spoke.

"Thank you for letting me be part of your family today."

"I feel you are already a part of my family. Christmas wouldn't be the same without you."

Caleb stared at the floor, blinking rapidly. He swallowed and took a deep breath. "This is the first Christmas I've celebrated since I lost Emily. You and your family are the best gift any man could receive."

They hugged. Caleb kissed her cheek before Sam nudged her.

"Yes, yes. We have work to do. I know." She cupped Caleb's cheek and smiled into his eyes. He had brought the spirit of the holiday to the Chesneys, even in their melancholy. Perhaps he was her best Christmas present, too.

Martha thrust a wad of cloth napkins into Caleb's hands. "Since you're now part of this family, you can put out the napkins and silverware."

Caleb laughed and followed instructions.

AFTER THE CHURCH SERVICE, the Chesneys bid quick farewells to their friends and hurried home to get Christmas dinner on the table. There were a few more dishes to make, like the squash and the mashed potatoes.

"Get some boughs in here, Caleb, would you? Cheer the place up a bit." Martha gave him a small hatchet.

Sam tackled the potatoes with the old masher while Sarah sliced bread. Martha cut up squash and put it in a pot with water. Abby arranged serving dishes on the sideboard. Even Lizzy helped by folding napkins and putting out silverware. People started lining up outside by one thirty, even though dinner wasn't going to be served until two.

Martha peeked out of the kitchen. "Open the doors. It's too cold for folks to be waiting outside."

She let in the half dozen diners. They bowed.

"Merry Christmas, Mrs. Chesney."

"Happy holiday."

Their customers greeted her warmly. Sam collected the money for the meal. When he returned to the kitchen, Martha put the shillings in her coin box.

"This is the most we'll take in until spring, when the loggers arrive." She squirreled away the money. "It's gotta last." She sighed and joined Caleb, placing festive boughs around the faded walls of the old Inn. She sighed.

"Most of the time, I'm okay. But come the holidays, I'm missing John something fierce."

She blinked rapidly to keep the tears at bay. Caleb gave her a gentle hug.

"I know what you mean."

Martha returned to the kitchen. "Caleb, give me a hand with this bird, will you?" She folded a kitchen cloth to protect her hands from the heat.

Sam pushed up next to her. "I can do it, Grandma."

Martha shrugged and shot Caleb a glance. "Okay, son."

By two, the long table, dressed in a white cloth, groaned under the weight of platters, bowls and baskets of delectable dishes. Martha counted. Every seat was filled except for the small table in the corner, reserved for family. The dining room could hold fifteen people. She smiled to see so many partaking of their Christmas dinner with the Chesneys. And the money didn't hurt one little bit.

"The Chesneys don't eat in the kitchen on Christmas." She set her lips together and motioned to the corner.

The bright sun shone off the snow, sending brilliant spikes of light into the room. The sounds of laughter mixed with the clink of utensils filled the air with festive spirit. Before she knew it, Martha was laughing at one of Caleb's stories, and downing her fourth cup of tea.

By four thirty, the last diner had left the inn. Stuffed with savory fare, Martha moaned.

"Sit still, Martha. We'll take care of everything." Caleb rose from his seat. Abby followed.

Before she could object, the family had jumped up and set to the task. Dishes and empty platters were whisked off tables and carried to the kitchen. The sound of dishes being dumped into water met her ears. She raised her gaze to the ceiling.

"They're a gift from God. Oh, John, how proud you would be."

When they were done, the tired children fell into their beds. Abby yawned as she walked Caleb to the door.

"What a wonderful day," he said. "Thank you. And Martha."

"Aw, Caleb. Thank you for the presents and for helping. You're a great addition to our family."

He wrapped his new scarf around his neck, bent his head in expectation of chilling wind, and forced himself out into the cold.

Martha pushed to her feet.

"And what now?" Abby asked.

"One more celebration. A small dinner for the New Year. Then the hard work of getting ready for logging season begins. We have mending to do, repairs to the inn, fruit and vegetables to put up to store for spring. You'll be surprised how busy we'll be.

"And boarders?"

"Not many in January and February. But we'll be full up from March through June."

"Tires me out just thinking about it." She yawned again.

"Up to bed, child. Dream sweet dreams of your wedding."

"Wedding?"

"When the wildflowers bloom, we'll have your wedding right here in the inn."

She kissed her mother-in-law on the cheek. "If the groom doesn't change his mind. The Chesneys are a handful."

Martha snorted.

THE SKY IN FITCH'S Eddy darkened. Angry clouds spit forth swirls of snow. Wind twirled the flakes up into miniature funnels, settling in deep drifts in the corners of buildings. With only three days left to prepare for the New Year's dinner, Abby had to brave the weather and trek to the general store for raisins and other foodstuffs.

Donning her coat, then draping a shawl over it, she pulled on her thickest shoes, and opened the front door. A biting wind pushed against her. Something brown and square fell in with the powdery snow and landed at her feet.

"What's this?" she said to herself. Picking up the smooth, cowskin bag, she saw a tag with Sarah's name on it. She closed the door, then squeezed the bag gently. Her fingers came up against something hard inside and something crinkly.

"Sarah?"

"Yes, Mama?" Her daughter appeared in the archway to the kitchen.

"Something here for you."

She handed the small package to her daughter. Sarah pulled at the knot keeping the drawstring closed tight. She worked it loose and opened the bag to find a small wooden box.

"Sam! Bring the chisel!" Abby was anxious to see what was inside.

Sarah unfolded the note accompanying the box. The lettering in black ink was precise. The note read.

A Christmas sweet for the prettiest girl in Fitch's Eddy.

With respect,

Benjamin Fitch

Sarah grinned. Sam joined his mother and sister. "What's wrong?"

"Can you open this?" Abby aarked.

"What is it?"

"A present for me." Sarah held the note to her chest so her family couldn't see.

"Who's it from?" Sam gripped the box and pried the top loose.

"None of your business." Stifling a smile, Sarah refolded the letter and stuffed it in her pocket.

"I bet I know." Sam used all his strength to pry up the nails.

Sarah raised her chin and put her nose in the air.

Finally, he got the top loose. He slid it aside, exposing an exquisite selection of nine chocolate candies.

"Oh!" Sarah's eyes grew and her face lit up.

"Candy? Someone sent you candy? Only a Fitch has money for something like this."

Sarah snatched the box from her brother's hand and ran up the stairs.

"I'll kill him." Sam muttered under his breath.

"Hmm. First you're going to kill Caleb and now you're going to kill Benjamin Fitch?"

"Yep."

She laughed. "You'll be putting your new knife to good use."

"Yes, I will!" Sam hollered. "What's the matter with the women in this family? Have they got no pride?"

"Pride? I don't think there's anything wrong with Mr. Benjamin Fitch's gift to your sister. He likes her. He's being nice. How can you object?"

"What would Papa say? He'd beat Mr. Tanner to death with his bare hands. And Fitch? I'll make fast work of him."

She frowned. "Your father would not hurt Caleb. He'd be grateful another man wanted to take us on. Who can a widow with three children hope to find to support her and her brood? Most men would run for the hills. But not Caleb."

"He has bad thoughts about you, Mama. He's not interested in the rest of us."

"Yes, he is."

"Why, because he made us things? He's buying us with gifts, so we won't object to him marrying you."

"Why should you object? He's a good man."

"I don't think so. He's trying to replace Papa. Not even cold in his grave, and Mr. Tanner has bad ideas about Papa's wife. Shame on him. And on you, Mama, for encouraging him."

She grabbed Sam's upper arm hard. "Look here, my self-righteous child. You have no call to judge me. I'm entitled to some happiness. I'm not dead yet. And finding a man willing to support my family is a gift from God. Your father wouldn't object. He'd be glad I won't be alone forever. Shame on you for judging me, Caleb, and for thinking you know everything about your father. Well, you don't."

"My father was a God-fearing, righteous man!"

"But not a hard one. He loved me. Loved us all. And he'd want what's best for us. And I'm to decide what that is, not you!"

Sam's lower lip trembled. "You'll forget him. You'll marry Caleb Tanner, and it'll be like Papa never existed."

She pulled Sam into a hug. "I'll never forget your father. He was my first love. He lives inside me every day. And I see him in you, Sarah, and Lizzy all the time. I feel he's here with me, in my heart, and so much in you, Sam. You are much like him, but you need to temper your feelings with wisdom. Calm down. Things will work out."

Sam gripped Abigail.

She felt telltale wetness on her shoulder and softened her tone. "You're going to be a great man, Sam. Learn to trust those who love you."

Sam sniffled and stepped back. "I'm sorry, Mama. I'm trying to do what I think Papa would."

"Be yourself, Sam. You don't have to be him. You couldn't. It'll be enough, you being Sam."

After Sam put the chisel in his pocket and headed for the kitchen, she opened the door. Blustery wind stung her face. Putting her head down, she pushed forward, into the blast. Snow swirled around her as she trudged along to the general store.

What if I'm wrong? What if Sam is right? Does he know something, feel something about Caleb? Or is he simply headstrong and wrong on all counts? She believed in her instincts. Still a shred of doubt crept in. Was Caleb the right man for her family? She shoved her misgivings aside and scooted inside the store, ready to warm her hands and face by the wood-burning stove.

AFTER THE NEW YEAR'S dinner, cold, snowy, dark days stretched ahead endlessly. Folks stayed inside, hovering around fireplaces and wood-burning stoves. The inn had only an occasional boarder. Their footsteps echoed in the empty dining room.

By the second week in January, Chesney family spirits were low. Over a dinner of soup and bread, they bemoaned their fate.

"Seems like we'll never see summer again," Sarah moaned.

"How much snow is gonna fall? I keep shoveling, but it's no use. Next day, more covers the path." Sam shook his head.

"These are hard days. But they'll pass. Three chairs need fixing." Martha buttered a piece of white bread.

"The mending filled two baskets. I'll get to it when I come back."

"Check on the pickle sales, dear."

When they finished their meal, the Chesneys got to work. Sam tackled the three chairs. Sarah threaded a needle and started sewing. And Lizzy tagged along after Martha, fetching things and helping out where she could. The inn needed sprucing up before logging season. Abby donned her coat. She spread a shawl over her shoulders, too, for added warmth. As she approached the door, there was a knock.

When she opened it, her eyes widened, and her mouth flew open.

"Howdy, Mrs. Chesney. You got a room to let?"

"Oh my God! Josiah Quint!"

"Yes, ma'am. I'm here to stay a while." She stepped aside to let him in.

Chapter Sixteen

"Sam! Sarah! Martha! Look who's come to Fitch's Eddy!"
Wearing no gloves and a coat too thin for the wind, Josiah shivered. Snowflakes lodged in his eyebrows and on his shoulders.

Abby threw the door open wide. "Come in, come in, Josiah. What brings you here?" The young man appeared exhausted. He staggered into the inn. She pulled up a chair.

"I've been traveling all the way from Sawyer's Bend in Pennsylvania. About fifty miles. Snow made the trip hard."

"I thought you were going to Ohio with your brother?"

"I found a job on a farm in Sawyer's Bend. Thought I'd stay a spell."

"What happened?"

"I got tired of working for someone else. I want a place of my own. Get a job and save up to buy my own land."

Sam ran across the room. He embraced his friend. "Josiah!"

Sarah hesitated in the archway. As Josiah faced her his smile grew. She curtsied

He stepped closer. "How nice to see you again, Miss Chesney."

"Same, Mr. Quint." Sarah licked a smidge of chocolate off her lip. Abby watched her daughter's face color.

"Well, shear my sheep! It's young Mr. Quint. You staying with us for a bit?" Martha asked, wiping her hand on her apron.

"Yes, ma'am. I plan to. I'm looking to settle down and Fitch's Eddy might be the place." He turned his gaze on Sarah, who's face flushed a deeper red.

"Well, well. Have something to warm your bones." Martha tugged on his sleeve.

"Sounds mighty good." He followed her.

"I'll be getting along to the store. Sam, you going to the smith's today?"

"But Josiah's just arrived."

"Don't you have work? Doesn't Caleb need you?"

"You're blacksmithing now?" Josiah lifted his eyebrows.

"I'm apprenticing. Mr. Tanner's teaching me."

"Like it?"

"Doesn't beat hunting, but yeah. It's all right."

"I need to get me a profession or a piece of land. Or a job. I'd appreciate any help you folks can give."

"Logging season's starting in a couple of months, Mr. Quint. I'm sure Elijah Fitch can find work for you." Martha addressed the young man. "Smart to come here, Mr. Quint. Fitch's Eddy is growing. Seems like new families move in every week."

"That's what I heard, Mrs. Chesney."

Sarah's mouth fell open, she covered it with her hand.

While she straightened her shawl, Abigail chuckled to herself. Goodness, could her young daughter have two men courting her? Josiah hadn't stopped staring at her for a second. What will Sam say when he figures out Josiah is here for Sarah? Is Josiah going to want to work for Fitch when he finds out about Benjamin?

She was still smiling when she stopped at the blacksmith shop.

"My dear Mrs. Chesney, what a pleasure to see you today. Come, warm yourself by the fire. Where's your rascally son?"

"An old friend arrived on our doorstep this morning. You remember Josiah Quint, don't you?" She shed her shawl and coat, then cozied up to the heat.

"Yes. A fine young man."

"He turned up on our doorstep. Claims he wants to settle in Fitch's Eddy."

"I see. We can always use another young man to start a family here."

"He kept staring at Sarah." She raised her palms to the fire.

"You think he's interested in her?" Caleb put a knife in the quenching bucket.

"I do." She rubbed her hands together.

He chuckled. "There will be quite a battle between Mr. Quint and Benjamin Fitch. The Fitches don't like to lose."

"I doubt Josiah does, either. Sarah will have her hands full."

Caleb pulled hot iron from the fire. "Mind she doesn't spend time alone with your friend."

"Time alone?"

"People talk. And things happen." Caleb picked up his hammer.

"What do you mean? Sarah's a good girl. And Josiah is our friend."

"He's also a man. Can't be too careful with your daughter's virtue." Caleb took a swing at the iron.

"You've got a lot to say about it." She stiffened.

"I'm only trying to look out for the girl who I hope to make my daughter soon."

"Well, she's *my* daughter. So, you can keep your opinion to yourself."

Caleb looked up. "I didn't mean to overstep."

She wrapped her shawl tighter around her shoulders. "You don't need to be giving advice. You don't have children. You don't know what you're talking about."

Caleb's face froze. "Correct. I don't. God didn't see fit to give my daughter life. Thank you for reminding me."

She reached for his forearm, but he yanked it away. "Oh, Caleb. I'm so sorry. I didn't mean it."

His eyes grew cold.

Her heart squeezed. "I apologize. I hope you'll forgive me."

"Don't you have somewhere to be?" He moved to the forge.

She hesitated but only for a moment. "Yes, the general store. Good day to you, sir." She bowed her head and pushed out against the wind.

Caleb followed. "Abby, I..." but the door closed before she could hear the rest.

The cold penetrated her clothing, chilling her to the bone. Or was it Caleb's words? He had been so sweet and supportive, but she hadn't considered he'd take the place of a father to her children. She knew he'd support them, but have a say in what they did or who they spent time with? She hadn't considered it at all.

What would George have said? Of course, he knew Josiah Quint better than Caleb did. Her husband was protective, but he wasn't blind. Their daughter was beautiful. He would have wanted her to make the best match she could— for love, not money.

Was Caleb right not to trust Josiah? Did it mean Caleb couldn't be trusted with Abby? Did he mean all men were base and would take any advantage they could? She shivered. Perhaps she had to rethink marrying again. If she married Caleb, he'd have more rights over her children than she would.

Preoccupied, she bent her head against the wind and trudged through the ever-deepening snow. She noticed Old Zeke on a chair by the woodstove in the store. He shot her a toothless grin.

"Morning, Mrs. Chesney. How are the little ones?"

"Fine, Mr. Zeke." She tried to hurry past the old gossip before he could trap her into a conversation, but he put out his leg and stopped her.

"I hear you're expecting a new arrival?"

"What?" She faced him.

"Looks like Caleb Tanner might get the babe he says he's always wanted."

"I don't know what you're talking about. Mind now, move away and let me pass."

"Don't play coy with me, Mrs. Chesney. Charity Bloodgood's been hinting you've taken up residence in Mr. Tanner's place."

"Nonsense! Move away, let me pass." She pushed by. Her lips compressed and her brow drew into a stern frown, which she shot at Old Zeke. "Don't be spreading gossip about me. Or about Mr. Tanner either. He's a decent man. Don't go telling tales that aren't true!"

"Just passing on the news."

"Keep your wicked ideas to yourself!" She turned her back to the old man, who cackled as she strode to the counter.

"You should chase away that nasty old man," she said to Virginia Rhodes.

"He's something, isn't he?" She shook her head.

"He spreads lies."

"I don't think anyone believes him. Now what can I get for you today, Mrs. Chesney?"

ABIGAIL SLUNG THE FULL-to-bursting bag over her shoulder. She pushed past Old Zeke and stepped out on freshly fallen snow. With the wind at her back, she hiked faster than she'd intended. The strong force behind pushed her. In front of the blacksmith shop, she slid and fell on her rump in the snow. Tears formed, but she blinked them away. The hard dirt under the snow would leave a bruise, but it wasn't pain making her cry.

"Abby! Abby! Are you hurt?" Caleb rushed out of the shop. He lifted her to her feet, then picked up the spilled sack of brown sugar, candles, and meat and packed them back in the bag. "Are you all right?"

She struggled to control her emotions. After taking a deep breath, she spoke.

"I'm fine, thank you." She grabbed Caleb's arm. "Caleb, I'm so sorry. So very sorry."

He brushed her words aside. "It's forgotten."

She brushed the snow off her skirt and picked up the sack.

"Let me carry it to the inn for you."

"I can manage."

"I know." He shouldered the bag with ease and took her elbow. Although she wouldn't admit it, she was happy to have him close on this blustery day. She tucked her hand into the crook of his arm as they made their way down the street.

When they reached the inn, he cupped her cheek and drew her gloved hand to his lips.

"Take care. Rest."

She shook her head. "No time to rest. Thank you." She took the bag from him and opened the door. "You're a good man, Caleb Tanner."

He bowed, then turned.

"Wait! I'm here, Mr. Tanner." Sam scooted out the door and joined Caleb.

"Come on, Sam. We have a big order from Elijah Fitch for axes and hatchets to fill."

"Bye, Mama."

She smiled at her son, then closed the door against the frigid air.

"Come by the fire, dear. You must be frozen solid," Martha said.

She watched Caleb and Sam falling in together as they hurried along to the blacksmith shop. Was Sam right? Was it too soon? Was Caleb the right man? She chewed a fingernail. George always said the heart should come before the head. Was he right this time, too?

"Did Mrs. Rhodes sell all our raisin loaves? Does she want more? And the pickles?" Martha chattered away as Abby made her way to the kitchen. She shed her gloves and opened her hands to the fire. Steam from the kettle moistened the air.

"Tea?" Sarah stood by the stove. Josiah sat on a stool by the door.

"Yes."

"Warm your bones, Mama," Sarah said, as she filled the teapot.

Abby trained questioning eyes on Josiah Quint. Could he be trusted. His smile, his face—so open— she wanted to believe. Without her husband, she would have to become protective, like a father would be. Could Caleb step into the role? Would the children listen to him?

"Mrs. Rhodes sold all the raisin loaves and requested six more. Half the pickles sold and she's putting the other jars on the counter to encourage sales." She fished shillings out of her pocket. "Here's the money for the loaves. She gave me meat for the pickles."

"Oh, good. Good. Yes. We need meat. Now we'll have enough stew to feed Josiah tonight, too. Sarah, start the stew, dear. I'll get the potatoes." Martha took her hand. "You look pale, dear."

"I fell on the way home." She rubbed her sore rump.

"Oh, my! Are you all right? Anything broken?"

"Just my pride." Abby managed a small smile. "I'm going upstairs."

"Rest. Sarah will bring your tea. You need to get better." Martha knitted her brows. Her dark eyes perused Abigail with concern.

"I'll be fine. Need some rest." She trudged up the stairs slowly. Exhaustion from her conversation with Caleb, Ole Zeke, and the fall overwhelmed her. Feeling weak she crawled into bed. Her mind whirled with thoughts of what marrying Caleb might mean to her children.

Have I been selfish? Thinking only of what the marriage would mean for me? What about Sarah and Sam? And Lizzy? He would be the only father she'd remember. Could he be a good father so quickly?

She made up her mind there would be no wedding until she was completely sure he was the right man. Her decision eased her mind enough to fall asleep.

SINCE MOST OF THE ROOMS at the inn were empty, Martha made a deal with Josiah. If he agreed to make his own bed, fill his own bowl with water in the morning, and tend to his own fire, she'd let him have the room for free until she had a boarder who needed it.

Josiah shoveled snow, chopped wood, and hunted for game to pay for his meals. Pleased with the deal and Josiah's hunting skills, the Chesneys frequently added duck or turkey to their table. Josiah's stories of settling in Pennsylvania brightened cold, dark winter evenings by the fire. Abby and Sarah knitted while Josiah wove his tales. Sam took up whittling, under instructions from Caleb, who gave him a special knife.

Martha took Josiah to the general store. He'd agreed to haul flour sacks for her on the days Sam worked.

"Morning, Mrs. Chesney. Who's this young man?" Virginia Rhodes looked Josiah up and down.

"This is Mr. Josiah Quint. He's an old friend. Came across from Danbury with my boy, Abby, and the children."

"Pleasure to meet you. Welcome to Fitch's Eddy."

"Pleasure's all mine, ma'am," Josiah replied, tipping his hat.

"Martha, those raisin loaves are selling faster than you can make 'em. I could use half a dozen every week."

"Wonderful! We'll deliver on Fridays."

"What do you need today?"

"Hmm, guess I have to add another sack of flour to my list!" Martha laughed.

"Becky, fetch Mrs. Chesney's goods."

Another man joined them at the counter.

"Mr. Fitch. What can I do for you today?" Virginia addressed Benjamin Fitch.

He shot a disdainful glance at Josiah. "My mother needs five yards of white lace and molasses, cinnamon, and brown sugar."

"Sounds like your cook is baking," Martha murmured.

"Indeed, Mrs. Chesney. Our French cook is the finest baker for many miles. Except for you and Mrs. Abigail Chesney, of course." Benjamin bowed.

Josiah nudged Martha.

"Oh, pardon me. Mr. Benjamin Fitch, this is our guest, Mr. Josiah Quint. He traveled from Danbury with my family."

Ben cast a sour eye on Josiah and gave a short bow.

"Pleased to meet you," Josiah said.

Virginia gathered Martha's purchases and put them in the leather bag. She handed the two flour sacks to Josiah.

As they headed for the door, Martha overhead Mrs. Rhodes speaking to Ben.

"Looks like you have competition, Mr. Fitch."

Martha closed the door quickly, hoping Josiah hadn't heard. He hoisted the two sacks over his shoulder and rested the leather bag on the other one.

"Why did you really come back, Josiah?" Martha never minced words.

"What do you mean?"

"Surely there was work you could do in Pennsylvania."

"Yes, there was."

"And?" Martha cocked an eyebrow at the boy.

"But no girl in all of Pennsylvania as pretty as Sarah Chesney." He laughed.

"Ain't it the truth!" Martha joined in. "But don't be getting any ideas. She's young yet—only fifteen. Too young to marry by at least a year."

"I got time, Mrs. Chesney. Nothing but time."

When they returned to the inn, Abby was pounding dough for bread. Josiah dropped the flour sacks, put down the leather bag, and grabbed his musket.

"Get us something juicy for dinner, Josiah," Martha called.

The young man waved as he strode toward the woods with Lucky following behind.

"You're right, dear."

Abigail put the kettle on the stove to heat.

"About what?"

"Josiah. He's got ideas about Sarah all right. It's why he came here." Martha eased down into a chair.

Abby kept pounding. "Caleb said I should keep an eye on them. Make sure he doesn't have time alone with her."

"Josiah?"

"Yes."

Martha laughed. "Leave it to a man to know a man better than a woman does."

"Then you agree?"

"I sure do. I married a man and I raised a man. I know all about the call of nature. Gotta keep an eye on Sarah. She's sweet and trusting."

"She's gotta learn how to handle herself. We can't be keeping an eye on her every minute of the day."

"True enough. Bet Sam could give her some advice. Caleb, too."

"Caleb's not her father. Let Sam speak to her."

Martha raised her eyebrows. What was she talking about? Caleb was almost Sarah's new father. And come spring— well, would there be a wedding come spring? Martha sighed. *Love never runs smooth. Always a bumpy road.*

THE NEXT DAY, AFTER breakfast, Abby spoke to Sarah.

"Come to the dining room. We'll sew."

"Me, too, Mama?" Lizzy chimed in.

"Not yet, sweetheart. When you get older. Stay in the kitchen with Grandma." She patted her youngest on the head and hugged her.

Mother and daughter settled by the fire in the dining room. Sarah picked up a sheet, and Abby a curtain. They threaded their needles.

"You seem happy to see Josiah," Abby began.

"I am. He's such a nice man."

"Yes, he is. And he seems happy to see you." She knotted the thread and picked up a curtain.

Sarah's face colored, but she said nothing.

"Has he said anything to you?" She shifted in her seat.

"He talks to me, like he does to everyone." Sarah focused on her work.

"I mean, does he flatter you?" She pretended to concentrate on her needlework.

"What do you mean, Mama?"

Frustrated, she took a deep breath. "Does he say how pretty you are? What a good wife you'd make?" She took in air.

Sarah looked up, her eyes wide as saucers, her face pink. "Oh no, Mama! He's never said anything like that to me."

"Good." She let out a breath.

"Is it bad for him to think I'm pretty? Benjamin Fitch said it at the Harvest Festival dance. Should I have slapped him or something?"

She laughed. "No, no. It's a compliment."

"Oh, good. Because I didn't."

"It's all right for a man to say you're pretty. But I think Josiah feels more."

"What does he feel, Mama?" Sarah kept her gaze on her work.

"You know. How a man feels for a woman? How a woman feels for a man?"

Sarah stuck herself. "Ouch!"

"Careful! Let me see." She examined the pinprick. She fetched a wet rag and wiped off Sarah's hand, then wrapped a clean cloth around it.

"I'm sorry. Well, when you said...I, I mean..."

"I know. You're young. But you enjoyed dancing with Mr. Fitch, didn't you? And I saw the way you smiled at Josiah. Kind of a flirt, aren't you?" She returned to repairing the hem on the curtain.

"I'm not a flirt!" Sarah threw down the sheet and glared at her mother.

She raised her palm. "No, no, of course not. But you're beginning to understand how things are—between a man and a woman." She swallowed.

"Maybe." Again, the young girl's face colored.

"You remember when I was expecting Lizzy? I told you where babies come from?" She prayed her daughter would remember so she wouldn't have to give the talk again.

"Yes, Mama."

"Well, you shouldn't be expecting a baby if you're not married." Relieved, Abby took a deep breath, sensing heat in her cheeks.

"I'd never do that, Mama." Sarah's face grew hot with indignation.

"I know you wouldn't, dear. But men, even young ones. Well, maybe especially young ones, don't always have good control over their desires. And they might pressure a girl into doing things she shouldn't." She let out a breath.

"Josiah and Benjamin would never do it, either."

"They might. Not because they don't like you, but maybe because they like you too much."

Again, Sarah shot a wide-eyed look at her mother. "You think so?"

"I do. Sometimes they don't think. Think about what might happen if they give in to their—uh, desires."

"Oh my!" Sarah covered her hand with her mouth.

"So it's up to you, sweetheart, to protect yourself. I don't want you to be alone much with either Josiah or Benjamin. Do you understand."

"You think they'd try to hurt me?"

She shook her head. "Not intentionally. Both seem to be sweet on you."

Sarah grinned. "I noticed."

"Mind my words. Be safe. Don't go anywhere with them alone. Or even spend much time in a room alone with either of them."

"I understand."

The howl of the wind drew their attention. Puffs of powdery snow blew up from the street, the bushes, and down from trees. The sun hid behind clouds making the day as gray as the one before. Abby inched closer to the fire.

I hope she does. The women worked on in silence for a while.

"Did grandma talk to you about Caleb?" Sarah asked.

She laughed out loud.

"How's the mending coming?" Martha poked her head into the dining room.

"Fine," Abby replied.

Martha gave her a knowing smile and retreated.

Chapter Seventeen

nd of January

E As if a gift from God, brilliant sun melted the dusting of snow from the day before. Caleb had stopped coming to the inn for every meal. Since his argument with Abby, a formality had sprung up between them. The cold prevented her from sneaking away to grab a log or two for the fire from the wood pile.

She didn't stop to visit in his shop on her way to the general store. Caleb blamed the cold and snow. But in his heart, he worried. Their meetings had become sporadic, accidental rather than regular or planned. Wishing he could take back his stupid remarks didn't make it so. He missed her but decided not to push. Frankly, he had no idea how to mend the tear in their relationship.

The sunshine gave him hope. As he hurried past the melting snow, he spied Abigail and her daughter setting the table for Saturday dinner for the family and their one boarder. He strode the wet, muddy street, wondering if he'd be welcome at the family table or if he should take his old spot at the table for two. Drawing closer, he saw her look up and smile. She stopped working and met him at the door.

"Mr. Tanner, how nice to see you."

He wiped his feet on the mat and stepped toward her.

His heart sank. "I hope we haven't gone back to formality?" he blurted out.

"No, no. Caleb. So happy you're joining us for dinner." She extended her hand.

Sarah scurried into the kitchen, leaving them alone.

Caleb drew her nearer. "Please, forgive my intrusion the other day. I should not have spoken out. Telling you what to do was a mistake. You know what you must do for your children. I'm sorry. I'm new at courting. It's been years."

She inched closer, resting her palm on his chest. "I'm so sorry for my harsh words."

"I love you. I deeply regret having upset you."

She looked up, and he seized the opportunity, lowering his mouth to hers. She softened against him. Her welcome of his kiss renewed hope.

"Now, now, save it for later." Martha bustled in from the kitchen, her arms laden with loaves of bread and a cutting board.

The couple broke apart abruptly. Martha laughed. "Don't be shy. Just teasing you is all."

Abby wiped her mouth. Her gaze eased over him from head to toe. Her eyes held the promise of fires within.

"Am I forgiven?" he whispered, his brows knitted.

The warmth of her grin sent relief coursing through him. "Yes. Of course."

His brow smoothed out. "Thank you."

She cupped his rough cheek.

"Come, dear, time to serve," Martha directed. "Caleb, sit here." She pointed to a seat at the family table. He knitted his brows and glanced at Abby.

He'd have to tamp down his eagerness for fatherhood. Perhaps stand back and take his lead from Abigail. Yes, men controlled the world, but she was a wise and sensitive woman. She could guide him into the role of father, smooth the way.

When the table was set and the food laid out, Caleb held a chair out for her. Sam, Sarah, Lizzy and Josiah raced in and grabbed their seats.

"Slow down, children. Elders first." Martha took a portion of meat, pickles, and bread, then passed the dishes to Caleb. He deferred to Abby before serving himself. If she consented to marry him, he would sit at the head of the table. He would be responsible for her welfare, Martha, and the children. He swallowed. Quite a load for a man used to living alone.

And what if he and Abby should have another child? And what if she should die in childbirth, like Emily? The idea made him weak, his stomach knotted. If anything happened to her, he'd be responsible for her children. Sam could take care of himself, but what about Sarah and little Lizzy? Abby was right—what did he know about being a father? He swallowed hard at the prospect.

"Are you all right?" Her gaze drew his.

"Fine." How could he tell her his fears for the future? He had to carry on, move forward, secure her heart, and take his place as the head of their family. A kernel of hope grew in his heart. Wasn't it time for him to have his dream? He squeezed her fingers for a moment, then bent his head for grace.

Martha said the short prayer before the family ate. Caleb prayed silently for a moment, for the welfare and happiness of his prospective family—and, thus, for himself.

A GUST OF COLD AIR drew Josiah and Martha's attention as they stood at the front desk. The Reverend Bloodgoode stood in the entryway.

"Yes, Reverend. What can I do for you?"

"I'm looking for an able-bodied young man with kindness in his heart."

Martha narrowed her eyes. "Oh?"

"Yes. With so much snow to shovel, I simply can't find the time to devote to my sermons. I was wondering if Sam Chesney would have some time to help us out."

"I can do it." Josiah piped up.

"Who's this young man?" The Reverend cocked an eyebrow.

"A friend. He's staying with us. Looking to work for Fitch logging, when the season starts. Josiah Quint, the Reverend Bloodgoode."

"I'd be glad to help." Josiah shook the reverend's hand.

"Thank you, young man. As soon as you can. Shovel is in the front. We need both the front and side walkways cleared."

"Consider it done."

Ebenezer Bloodgoode bowed slightly and exited the building.

"Very kind of you," Martha said.

"I got the time." He pushed to his feet and shrugged on his jacket.

"Wait a minute. You can't wear that thing. You'll freeze. I believe I have some of John's clothing in the attic. You're about his size."

While Martha climbed the stairs, Josiah stood at the window. The sky had cleared. The snow had let up, and the sun shone brightly, making the sparkling white powder glisten.

"Here you go." Martha handed a sheepskin jacket to Josiah. He fingered the heavy garment.

"Thank you. But with the sun out, I don't think I'll need it." He donned his own and opened the door.

As he drew closer to the town square, he spied someone shoveling snow off the front steps of the church.

"Benjamin Fitch, is it?" Josiah asked.

Ben looked up. "Yeah?"

"You can stop now. The reverend asked me to do this. Can I have the shovel, please?"

"You? You don't belong here. You're not from Fitch's Eddy. My father instructed me to do this, and I'm going to finish the job."

"Not necessary. I promised Reverend Bloodgoode I'd do it."

"Too bad. I've got it."

Josiah reached for the shovel, but Ben yanked it out of the way.

"You're living at the inn, aren't you?" Ben narrowed his eyes.

"What's it to you?" Again, Josiah reached for the tool, but Ben snatched it away.

"You stay away from Sarah Chesney."

Josiah raised his eyebrows. "Sarah Chesney? She your intended?"

"Not yet. But she's gonna be."

"Over my dead body."

Ben glared at Josiah. "I can arrange it."

Slightly taller and broader than Ben, Josiah stepped forward. "I dare you."

Ben pushed him, and he fell. Then Ben fell upon him. Josiah shoved Ben's shoulders, backing him off. The two men wrestled around, rolling in the snow, punching each other.

A woman's scream didn't deter them.

"Stay away from her!" Ben hollered through gritted teeth.

"Will not. You stay away." Josiah replied.

Another scream, and a crowd gathered. Josiah aimed for Ben's face but missed. Before they knew it, they were being torn apart. Caleb grabbed Josiah and Sam grabbed Ben, who landed one sucker punch on Josiah's face. Blood spurted from his nose.

"I'll kill you!" Josiah struggled against Caleb's tight grip.

"Stop! Stop it. Both of you!" Caleb raised his voice.

"I'm going to shovel this walk. Go back where you came from, Josiah Quint!"

"Never! I'm settling here."

"You'll never get a job from my father."

"We'll see about that."

The fighters struggled against the men holding them back.

"Josiah, we need to get the bleeding stopped. Come on. I'm taking you home." Caleb kept a grip on the young man and yanked him down the road.

Benjamin Fitch wiped his nose on his sleeve and busted out of Sam's hold. He picked up the shovel and finished removing the last bit of snow from the front walk.

"You shouldn't be fighting. Josiah is a good man," Sam said.

"Yeah? We'll see how good he is. He'd better stay away from Sarah."

"You'd both better stay away from Sarah," Sam muttered under his breath.

"I heard you!" Josiah yelled.

Caleb pushed open the door to the inn and shoved Josiah inside. "Martha!"

She hurried out from the kitchen, wiping her hands on her apron. "Good gracious! What happened?"

Caleb explained as he sat Josiah down.

"I'll get some clean cloths." She scurried away.

When she returned, she carried a small bottle of brandy, clean cloth, and a basin filled with water.

"Your jacket is ruined."

Josiah tried to smile. "Guess it's good I wasn't wearing John's, then."

Martha wiped his face, gently. "Here. Have a nip." She opened the brandy bottle and handed it to him. Then she put some on a cloth and wiped his nose with it.

Josiah jerked away. "Ow!"

"That's what you get for fighting. Who'd you fight with and why?"

"Benjamin Fitch," Josiah muttered.

"And it was about Sarah, I believe," Caleb put in.

"Oh, dear. Not good. She's just a young girl yet. You boys need to leave her be." Martha frowned.

"Tell it to Fitch." Josiah looked at his hands.

"I will. It won't do much good, though. Those Fitches own everything and think they can have whatever they want."

"Not Sarah Chesney, they can't," Josiah said.

"Right now, you need to go up to bed. Rest."

"I'm all right."

"Rest, I said! Now scoot!" Martha swatted his shoulder. Josiah obeyed.

As he climbed the stairs he wondered. Could a poor boy like him ever have a chance against a rich boy like Benjamin Fitch? Sarah would have to be crazy to choose him over Fitch. His spirits drooped, and his body ached. He'd have to do something spectacular to win Sarah. Gloom settled over him as he lay down and pulled the blanket up. But the Quint men never gave up.

What was it his brother always said? "Life ain't easy. Fight for what you want."

Josiah fell asleep dreaming of making Sarah his bride.

A WAGON PULLED UP TO the huge, white farmhouse on the hill where Elijah Fitch and his family lived. Thousands of acres of rich timberland, farmland, lakes, brooks, and streams belonged to Elijah Fitch, son of the late Elkanah Fitch, the man who'd accumulated the vast estate.

Elkanah had arranged for his son to marry the cream of Danbury society. He plucked Ann Hammond, the most beautiful young woman in the county with the biggest dowry, from her home. At the tender age of seventeen, she made the perilous journey to the raw countryside of Fitch's Eddy over twenty years ago. After two miscarriages, Ann carried the third pregnancy to term and gave birth to a healthy baby boy, Benjamin.

As he was their only surviving child, Ann doted on Ben, giving him everything his heart desired. His father turned a sterner eye to the boy, determined to make a strong man of the lad. Nevertheless, Elijah had a soft spot for his only progeny. After much bluster, he usually gave in to his wife's generosity regarding the boy.

A servant delivered mail to Elijah as he sat at the head of a vast oak table, crafted in Fitch's Eddy in the style of France. The table easily seated eighteen people. Elijah sat at the head, with his wife to his right and Benjamin to his left.

China imported from Limoges, France with a gold *fleur-de-lis* border graced each place. Sterling silver with an ornate rose pattern gleamed with light from the generous windows. The sideboard groaned with platters of roast pork, lamb with roasted potatoes, a pot of beef stew, and bowls of mashed potatoes, and creamed spinach. A six-layer chocolate cake stood proudly at the end.

Taking the letters, Elijah nodded to the messenger, then faced his wife.

"Where's Benjamin?"

"Washing up."

The young man scooted into the dining room and slid into his seat. He lowered his head, but his bruises were visible.

"Benjamin!" Ann exclaimed, raising her hand to her mouth.

"What happened?" his father asked.

"I was shoveling snow at the church, like you told me to, Father, when this new boy jumped me."

Ann narrowed her eyes. While she adored her son, she knew he had a temper and had been in fights before.

"As long as the other lad came out worse than you." Elijah buttered a piece of raisin bread. He took a bite. "This is delicious."

To deflect his attention from his son, Ann cooed. "Oh, yes. Martha Chesney makes it. She's the best baker, outside of our Giselle, of course."

"She John Chesney's wife, by chance?"

"Yes." Ann buttered a piece for herself.

"Sorry to lose him. He was one of my best."

"Father, if a Josiah Quint comes looking for a job, don't hire him." Ben took a piece of bread, too.

"I can't let your petty squabbles interfere with my business. If he's an able-bodied man, willing to work hard, I'll hire him."

Ben made a face but kept quiet.

"Not everyone is as lucky as you. Some young men have to work to earn their slice of bread."

"I know."

While a servant filled his plate, Elijah sorted through the mail quickly. He stopped at a small piece of folded paper addressed to his son. The woman put the plate filled with Elijah's favorite foods before him.

"Hm, here's one for you, Ben."

"For me?" Ben reached for the paper, but he was too late, his father held it out of reach.

Not bothering to hand it over to the boy, Elijah ripped it open and read the contents.

"What's this? A thank you for a Christmas present? From a Sarah Chesney? What the devil is this, Benjamin?" His father knitted his brows, his expression fierce.

Ann's mouth fell open, but she shut it before Elijah noticed.

"I sent her a small box of Giselle's Christmas chocolates."

"You what?" His father roared. "Who is this girl? John Chesney's daughter?"

"Granddaughter," Ben corrected.

"Granddaughter of an innkeeper?"

Ben cut a piece of meat.

"I married the best of Danbury society! Your mother was the most beautiful, most sought after belle in all of Danbury. And you've picked an innkeeper's granddaughter?"

"Don't judge, father. She's the most beautiful girl in Fitch's Eddy."

"Bosh! Nonsense! We'll pick your wife. Not you."

"No, you won't. I will pick my own wife."

"Now, Elijah. Remember what the doctor said. You must calm down. Ben's too young to get married."

"Yes, and when he's old enough he will marry a woman from a good family!"

"I'll marry whoever I want." Ben's chin jutted out.

"I haven't worked hard all these years to turn this over to some poor trash."

"She's not trash!" Ben rose from his seat.

"Sit, Ben. Elijah don't be hasty. It's much too soon for Ben to get married. The girl isn't even sixteen yet."

"Good. Then he's got plenty of time to forget her before she comes of age." Elijah tucked into his food.

"I'm not going to forget her." Ben raised his gaze to meet his father's.

"You'll do what I tell you to do. Your mother and I will decide who is right for you and when."

The meal continued in silence. Benjamin wolfed down his food.

"May I be excused?"

"For God's sake, yes! Get out of my sight. You've ruined this beautiful meal." Elijah waved his hand.

Ben gave a quick nod of his head to his mother, glared at his father, and pushed his chair back. When he'd left the room, Elijah turned to his wife.

"The boy is headstrong. This is your fault. You indulged him."

"Now, now, Elijah, no use getting all riled up. He's not even courting the girl—at least not formally yet."

"She's too young. And too poor."

"We don't know about her family."

"Find out. Find out everything you can about her. She's probably after his money. I bet every young woman in Fitch's Eddy would give their right arm to marry Benjamin!"

"Don't worry, dear. I'll stop by the general store first thing tomorrow. Virginia knows all there is to know. Or maybe I'll run into Mrs. Chesney there."

"Good. Save our boy from a disaster, Ann. I'm counting on you."

"Yes, dear. I know." She patted his arm. "Cora? Time for dessert."

Chapter Eighteen

F*ebruary 26*
First thing in the morning, Martha climbed down the back stairs, she put on her coat and popped outside to check the root cellar. Sam had loaded half the cellar with potatoes, turnips, and carrots in the fall. During the winter, Martha had acquired an ever-growing assembly of winter vegetables, like beets, onions, winter squash, and cabbage. He'd carved out a spot for salt meat, too.

She pondered as she examined her supplies. Potatoes were piled high all the way to the ceiling. Those would be a mainstay throughout the next two months. She'd have plenty of hungry mouths to feed. Once the men started working, each ate as if he were two men, not one.

"Looks good." Inside, she marched up to the top floor, then she opened the door to the attic. Inspecting the space, she spoke.

"Okay, Josiah. You and Sam can haul the apples up here. There's no room left in the root cellar. I've got a room for you on the third floor."

"Okay, Mrs. Chesney. Thank you."

Martha descended to each floor and inspected the rooms. They were clean, but spare, with only one or two beds and one dresser. Three had two narrow beds. Three had one larger bed each. All were made up, neat and tidy with clean sheets, pillows, and blankets. The loggers boarding with her didn't arrive with much. No one complained about the small space. Compared to the bunkhouse Elijah Fitch provided, the inn was paradise.

Martha's boarders ate breakfast and supper at the inn. Dinner was provided in the bunkhouse. Pinching pennies, Fitch put out meager fare for breakfast and supper. The dinner repast was hearty. He needed to keep the men fueled and working. The smartest loggers spent a few shillings and ate breakfast and supper at the inn. They had to stay at the site for dinner.

Some men spent their evenings, and their pay at The Black Dog saloon, eating, drinking, and hooking up with women in the private rooms upstairs.

No one provided as comfortable a bed or food as good food as Martha Chesney. At the end of the day. The handful of loggers lodging with the Chesneys warmed themselves by the fire, dug into good home cooking, and polished off loaf-after-loaf of freshly-baked, warm bread dripping with fresh, creamy butter.

After supper, a logger might play a tune on a guitar or banjo. The men would sit around the fire, maybe taking a nip from a hip flask.

"Sam? Did you pick up those extra sacks of flour I ordered from Virginia?"

"I'm getting those on the way home today."

"Good." Martha lit the fire under the kettle. Sarah pounded bread dough while Abby mended a shirt. Sarah put two loaves in the oven.

"These'll be baked by dinner today, Grandma."

"Good." Martha turned her gaze on Abigail. "I'm moving Josiah to the third-floor front room. We'll store the apples in the attic."

"I've put some in the larder."

"Perfect. Looks like we're ready."

A knock on the door drew her attention. She peeked around the corner and spied a scruffy-looking man waiting outside. She turned to her family. "Why it's old Lars Jorgensen! The season begins."

Icy rain fell, pelting him as he squeezed under the small overhang. She hurried to the door to let the man inside.

"Lars! You're a sight for sore eyes! Come on in."

Martha hustled the man into the dining room. "Sarah! Cup of tea for Mr. Jorgensen." She joined him at a table.

"Where's John?"

The smile fell off Martha's face as her heart almost stopped. "Oh, my God. You don't know. Of course, you don't know."

"What?" He put his leather bag on the chair next to him. "Know what?"

"John died last spring. End of the season. You'd already left."

"What happened?" Angus took off his hat.

As Martha retold the story, she wiped tears from her eyes. This would be her first logging season without him. Abby and her children were a godsend. Martha would have had to sell the inn if they hadn't shown up. No way could she run the place alone.

"What do I smell?"

"Bread baking. My granddaughter has become quite the baker." Martha boasted.

"I remember your bread. You makin' the one with the raisins in it?"

"Yep. In fact, I have a fresh loaf."

Sarah arrived with the tea. Martha introduced them. "Sarah, how about a couple of slices of our raisin bread and some butter for Mr. Jorgensen."

The girl hustled back to the kitchen.

"She's quite a looker," Lars said before taking a sip.

"Now don't you get any ideas. You're old enough to be her father. Besides, she's already got two young men interested."

"Too bad. Your kin would be something. I always told John luckiest thing he ever did was get you to marry him."

Martha laughed. "Flattery. Won't do you any good."

"You got my room ready?" He sat down.

"Sure do. How many you bringing with you this year?"

"Two so far. Maybe one more."

"We have someone already here who's fixing to work, too."

"Yeah? He any good?"

"He's young and strong."

"Guess we'll find out." Lars laughed.

Sarah carried a tray to the dining room and set it down on Mr. Jorgensen's table.

"Thank you kindly, Miss Chesney."

She made a small curtsey and left.

Martha narrowed her eyes. "Remember my words, Lars. Leave the girl be. My grandson is half your age and just as big. He'll beat the living hell out of you if you even go near his sister."

Lars' eyes widened. He held up his palm. "Don't worry about me, Martha. I won't be bothering her."

"Good. See you don't." Martha crossed her arms. "Now, what have you heard about the new sheriff?"

LARS AGREED TO INTRODUCE Josiah to Elijah Fitch and help him get hired. They trudged through snow to the outbuilding on the Fitch estate where Elijah made his office. The two men knocked.

"Come in." Elijah sat behind a vast wooden desk. He looked over wire-rimmed glasses at Lars and Josiah.

"Jorgensen, isn't it?" Elijah put down his pen.

"Yes, sir. And this is a friend of mine, Josiah Quint."

"I've heard of you. What are you doing here?"

"He's come for a job."

"Let the young man speak for himself, Jorgensen."

Lars nodded.

"I want to learn logging."

Fitch sat back and hooked his thumbs in his suspenders. "So you do, do you? Aren't you the young man who started a fight with my son?"

"He started it." Josiah shifted his weight.

"Doesn't matter who started it. Who finished it is what counts."

"Nobody. Caleb Tanner separated us."

"Too bad. I'd like to know who the winner was."

"I was ahead."

Elijah laughed. "I expected you to say so. You've got gumption, Quint. I'll give you a chance. Lars, take him down to the bunkhouse. Where's your gear?"

"I'm staying at the inn, sir." Josiah hated calling him "sir." He didn't even call his father "sir." Well, not anymore. Not since he turned twenty.

"Your choice. By the way, what was the fight about?"

"Shoveling snow for the church."

Fitch cocked an eyebrow. "I heard you were fighting over a young girl."

Anger filled Josiah's chest. His nostrils flared as he stared at Elijah.

"She's worth ten of any other girl in the county. In the state even. Don't say a word agin' her."

Elijah held up his hand. "Okay, okay. I get it. But a Chesney? Granddaughter of an innkeeper? You can have her. My son, Benjamin, is destined for more a more refined wife."

"Fine with me." Josiah turned on his heels and left before his temper got the best of him. *Imagine the rich windbag thinking he and his son are above everyone!* He kicked a clump of dirt out of his way. Lars grabbed his arm.

"Hey, boy. That's no way to talk to Mr. Fitch."

"I'm twenty-four. Ain't no boy."

"You are compared to him. And me. And when you act like you did? I think you're more like twelve."

Josiah kicked a small stone. "He makes me mad. He thinks he owns everyone. He doesn't own me and he doesn't own Sarah Chesney."

"Sarah Chesney? Oh, now I get it. You like her?"

"Who wouldn't?"

Lars laughed.

"She's the prettiest girl in town." Josiah shoved his hands in his pockets.

"I've no doubt. Guessing Fitch's son agrees with you." Lars matched Josiah stride-for-stride.

"He thinks because he's rich, he can have her. But she likes me better."

"Then why fight? Let the lady choose." Lars raised his hands. "Come on. We've got work to do."

"Thanks for helping me get this job."

"I hope you thank me later. This is hard work. Grueling. Dangerous."

"But it pays. And I'm saving up to get my own farm."

"Okay." Lars looked the young man over. "You look strong. You'll do fine."

They approached the bunkhouse. Johan Gustavson came out.

"Lars!" The two men embraced briefly. They launched into Swedish.

"Wait! Wait a minute. What are you speaking? Gibberish?"

"Our native language. Johan and I are from Sweden."

Josiah shook his head. "Talk English."

The men ignored him and continued speaking in their native tongue. Josiah turned away and stared at the thickly wooded forest in front of him. Trees with massive trunks stood proudly, their budding leaves a soft yellow green. Reaching to the sky, the oaks and elms defied Josiah to take them down and turn them into ships' masts or dining tables.

"I'll show you," he muttered at the trees, their leaves swaying defiantly in the brisk wind.

His resolve hardened. He'd show Elijah Fitch, Benjamin Fitch, Sam Chesney, and Sarah— anyone who questioned him, would be made to eat their words. He'd be successful, no matter what. He had to be. He was a Quint, and failure wasn't in his vocabulary.

ABBY STOPPED BY THE smithy shop on her way to the general store. She'd been so busy preparing for the new boarders, she hadn't seen Caleb in two days. She hankered for a glimpse of his handsome face and sunny smile.

"Hello, Abigail."

"So formal today, Caleb." She tossed him a coquettish grin.

"Can you come out for a walk with me tonight?"

"We're so busy. I doubt it. Martha has almost a full house. We'll be cooking and cleaning from dawn until dark."

"I gather Martha makes most of her money during the logging season."

"Yes," she said. He put down his hammer, wiped his hands and closed them around her fingers.

"Please try to get away. Even for only a short stroll?"

"I will." Although the kisses stolen in the shadows were wonderful, Caleb wanted more—her time and attention boosted his spirits. He truly enjoyed her company. She talked to him, honestly. Especially about her children. And he'd learned to listen without offering advice.

"With all the strange men in town, it doesn't feel safe for me or for Sarah. I'm not going to be sending her to the store at all."

"Maybe Sam or I should go with you?"

"Thank you. I'll go only in the early morning. They'll be in the woods, working."

"All right. But say the word if you want me along."

"You have work to do, too. Have you filled the order for axes from Elijah Fitch?"

"Almost. Sam and I only have a few more to make." He brought her hand to his lips. "Can we go for a walk right after supper?"

"Come early. When you've finished, the others will still be eating. I can't run out and leave Sarah and Martha with all the cleaning up to do. But I can go while they're still eating and return when they are done."

His face lit up with joy. "Excellent!"

"Be there about five thirty. I'll have your plate ready."

"I'll see you then, my love."

Impulse possessed her. She fisted his shirt and brought his lips to hers. He pulled her close, up against him. The feel of his hard body pressed to hers lit her fire. Her insides melted at the masterful way he held her, and the passion in his kiss. All doubts flew from her mind—her body ruled.

He bent down, his mouth to her ear. "Honey, I need you so much."

She gripped his middle tight, crushing her softness to him. She closed her eyes. Those were words she longed to hear. She'd missed being needed, being loved, not only by her children, but by a man. Her heart sang as he whispered how much he cared for her.

She breathed in his masculine scent mixed with the smell of the burning coal and hot metal. She wanted to drift away, in his arms, to leave the cares of her world behind. But unmarried people didn't do such a thing—not respectable ones.

Deep down in her heart, she didn't care about the opinions of others, but she had her children to consider. She'd not humiliate them by giving in to her feelings and desires. Calling on every ounce of strength to pull herself away from the man she wanted with every bone in her body, she slowly stepped back.

"I'm sorry. I didn't mean to get carried away."

She cupped his cheek. "I love when you get carried away."

He chuckled. "You're shameless."

"Yes, I am. When it comes to you."

He kissed her palm then helped her with her coat. She wrapped her shawl tight over the coat and hurried to the door.

"Until tonight."

"Tonight." His eyes filled with lust.

And then she was gone.

The bite of the late winter wind cooled her passions quickly. She bustled along to the general store, going over in her head what she needed to buy.

When she arrived, Ann Fitch stood at the counter.

"And I'll take five more yards of the pink lace. When is the silk I ordered coming in?"

"Let me check." Virginia Rhodes stepped into the back room.

"Mrs. Fitch, buying more fabric?"

"Yes. I'm hoping you'll have time to fashion a dress for me. I got a picture of what they're wearing in Paris, and I want one just like it."

"Let me see."

Ann handed Abby a well-worn newspaper clipping. She handled it gently.

"Recreating this dress will be a great deal of work. With the inn full to the brim with loggers, I barely have time to breathe."

Ann cocked an eyebrow. "I'm prepared to pay handsomely."

"I'm curious. Why would you want such a fancy dress? Where would you wear it out here?"

"I'm no fool. I know it will take months to sew this. I want it for the Harvest Festival next fall. I want to have the most dazzling dress anyone in Fitch's Eddy has ever seen..."

"This dress will certainly do the trick," Abigail said, handing the clipping to Mrs. Fitch.

"I've ordered the silk. I think I ordered enough. I want it in pink. The article said it was originally in pink."

"Pink would be beautiful." She fingered the lace on the counter.

"And with lots of lace."

"Of course, Mrs. Fitch." She stepped away.

"If you started when the season was over, could you finish it in time?"

"Probably."

"Good. Then I'd like to hire you." Ann gave a smile.

"I don't know how much to charge."

"I'll pay whatever you ask. Think it over." Ann tucked the clipping into her bag.

"Thank you. I will." With an order like this, they could put some money aside.

Virginia returned to the counter. "Becky is checking our records. I know we placed the order, but I'm not sure when they said it would arrive. Mrs. Chesney? Can I help you?"

She placed her order and put the items she took from the shelves on the counter.

"Credit? Or swap?"

"Cash." Feeling bolder than she had any right to, she pulled a few shillings from her pocket and placed them on the counter.

"Very good. Thank you. Always a pleasure to do business with you, Mrs. Chesney."

She thanked Virginia and wandered to the far corner of the store to look at thread.

Mrs. Fitch leaned over. Thinking Abby couldn't hear her, she spoke in a loud whisper.

"What do you know about Mrs. Chesney?" she asked Virginia.

"You mean Martha?" Virginia wound the lace around a piece of cardboard.

"No, the younger one."

"We've chatted. I know she comes from Danbury."

"I know. But I don't know her maiden name."

"Oh? She comes from a fine Danbury family. My cousin lives there. She told me." Virginia gathered fabric samples and placed them in a box.

"A fine family, you say?"

"Yes. Have you heard of the Wolcotts?" Virginia tucked the box under the counter.

"The Wolcotts of Danbury?"

"That's what I said. She's a Wolcott. On her father's side."

"Oh, my goodness. I had no idea. Yes, a fine family indeed. Wolcott—changes everything. Thank you, Virginia." Mrs. Fitch's brow furrowed and she chewed a nail.

"You're most welcome, Mrs. Fitch. I'll have Daniel deliver the silk to you as soon as it arrives." Virginia smiled as Ann Fitch hurried out of the store and into her carriage.

Abby had heard it all. What did it matter to Mrs. Fitch if she was a Wolcott? Her interest was piqued for a moment. But there were loaves of bread to be made and sewing to attend to, so she must be on her way. Tucking her bag firmly under her arm, she left the store, closing the door loudly behind her.

Yes, she was a Wolcott. Why did it matter?

CALEB SHOWED UP RIGHT on time. Abby brought his plate to the table.

"Is there some place where we can be alone?" The question burst forth, though he had decided not to ask. He no longer trusted himself to be alone with her. His heart wanted nothing more than stolen moments with her, but his desire flamed hot, threatening to consume him.

He wanted to put her above his own needs. But their wedding must be hastened, for his patience was wearing thin. He wanted to claim her as his own as soon as possible.

"Outside? By the root cellar?"

"Must we wait until the wildflowers bloom to marry?"

"Yes. There is no time for us to be together now. Martha needs me."

"And so do I."

"But you will still need me when logging season is over."

"True. I'm sorry. I don't mean to be selfish. But I've waited so long to find you."

She put her hand over his. "Only a little while longer. I promise."

"Then you do consent to marry me?"

"Yes, but privately, only between us. I have to talk to Sam first."

"I understand." He dug into his meal.

She buttered two slices of bread, handed one to her beloved and took a bite from the second one herself. When she finished, she returned to the kitchen.

Caleb ate quickly, passion driving him to be alone with Abby. She peeked out twice to see if he was finished yet. When he put down his fork for the final time, she glided across the floor and took his plate.

"Finished, Mr. Tanner?"

"Yes, Mrs. Chesney. An excellent meal."

"Thank you."

He rose to don his coat and hat. Voices from the kitchen met his ear.

"Martha, I've forgotten to bring up enough potatoes from the root cellar. I'll fetch them now."

Caleb grinned. She was a wily one. He stole out into the cool March evening and made his way to the root cellar behind the inn. She appeared out of the shadows, grabbed his hand, and led him to the structure. Lighting a candle, she descended the stairs.

"It will be cold down here," she warned.

"I guess we'll have to stand close to warm each other up." He chuckled as he followed her.

Once inside, He took her in his arms. Her lips, cool from the brisk air, warmed quickly. They were soft and started a fire inside him. His big hands easily circled her small waist. She softened against him, her arms winding around his neck.

Caleb ran his hands up and down her back. Desire grew inside him. Love mixed with lust in his veins. No matter how cold it was, his blood burned hot. With her willing in his arms, he could have easily seduced her there on the dirt floor.

He swiped his tongue over the seam of her lips, and she opened for him. He explored her mouth. The moist warmth and her tongue reaching for his drove him wild with passion. Aching to touch her in the places only a husband touches a wife, he mustered all the self-control he had. Sensing he'd come to the end of his rope, he stepped away.

"I have to stop."

"You do?"

"Or I will lose myself. And do something we'll both regret. I want you too much."

"And I want you."

"But we must wait."

"Yes. Besides, I don't propose to lose myself to you in such a dark, damp, and frigid place."

He laughed. "I'd much prefer a room with a blazing fire and a soft feather bed." He ran his thumb down her cheek.

"I think you're all the blazing fire I'd need." She chuckled. "Let me see. I came down here to get something, didn't I?"

"To get kissed by me."

She laughed. "I told Martha I'd bring something. What was it?" She sidled up to Caleb, resting her palms on his hard chest.

"Potatoes?"

"Oh, yes. Potatoes."

Caleb took a handful and passed them to her.

"They're cold." She stuffed them in the pockets of her apron. Once again, she approached him. "Please, my sweet man, wait. A bit longer."

He brought her hand to his lips. "You are worth waiting for."

She sighed, then turned toward the door. Holding the candle, she led the way out. Caleb embraced her once more, then turned toward his home.

"I see Charity was right. What were you two doing in the root cellar?" The Reverend Bloodgoode raised himself up to his full height of five foot seven inches.

"None of your business, Reverend. Now I bid you a good night," Caleb replied.

"Rush away you may, Mrs. Chesney. But God sees all. And He knows what you were doing in there, even if I don't. Of course I can imagine."

"Shut up, Ebenezer." Caleb fisted his hand at his side.

"Violence, Mr. Tanner? You surprise me."

"I'll do more than that if you don't keep quiet and leave us alone."

Ebenezer made a hasty getaway. When Caleb turned around, Abigail was gone.

Chapter Nineteen

March 15

M Ann Fitch supervised her servants setting out supper on the sideboard. Shuffling dishes around a bit until she was satisfied, she took her seat and rang the small silver bell at her place.

Belle, the house maid entered the dining room. "Yes, ma'am."

"Tell Mr. Fitch and Benjamin supper is ready."

Within five minutes the men joined her. Elijah filled his plate. "Cold turkey? Ah, my favorite. You bagged a fine bird, Ben."

"We have your favorite cheese, cheddar," Ann said.

"Excellent. Might have come from the British, but it's the best."

"And Giselle's brioche bread," Ann remarked.

The men loaded their plates with the tempting fare. Elijah took two thick slabs of bread and covered them generously with butter.

"Well, Ben. Seems the girl you're interested in comes from a good family after all. Your mother tells me her mother is a Wolcott. The Wolcotts of Danbury are very distinguished." Elijah took a bite of bread.

"I don't care about her family."

"Well, I do. I'm not leaving this business to some poor farm girl and her squealing brats."

"Our children will not be squealing brats!"

"Elijah! Ben! Let's not discuss this now."

"I see you still haven't fired Josiah Quint." Ben took a bite of cheese.

"And I don't intend to. He's a hard worker. Strong with an axe."

"So you say. Don't you have enough men?"

"Some won't make it through the season. I need Quint."

"I don't believe it." Ben sliced a piece of turkey.

"Why don't you get out there? About time you learned the business. Best way is from the ground up."

Horrified, Ann put down her fork. "You don't mean Benjamin should sleep in the bunkhouse?"

"Why not?"

"Really, Elijah." Ann buttered a slice of bread and put it on her husband's plate.

"You think I can't do it? I can do anything Josiah Quint can do. And do it better!" Ben's lips set in a firm frown.

"Why don't you show me?"

Benjamin pushed away from the table. He wiped his mouth with a napkin. "I will!" He stormed out of the room.

"Oh, Elijah! What have you done? I don't want our son out there with an axe."

"It'll do him good. Let him get a taste of how other people live. Let him work for a living the way my men do. Make a man out of him. And he'll stop simpering around after that girl."

"He's not simpering. She's a nice girl. Her mother helped me out at the Harvest Festival."

"Oh, you mean the fiasco about the pie?"

Ann's eyes widened. "You know?"

"Really, Ann. You should learn to cook one of these days." Elijah shook his head, smiled at his wife, wiped his mouth with his napkin, and pushed to his feet. "I didn't marry you because you were the best cook in Danbury. Just the best looking!" He chuckled.

Ann blushed. "Oh, Elijah."

"Let's see how our boy does swinging an axe, eh?" He left the room.

Ann hurried to the window. She spied Benjamin striding across the lawn. She chewed a nail. *Nothing good can come from this. Nothing good at all.*

Donning her coat, she stopped at the front door.

"Belle, tell Mr. Palmer to bring the carriage around immediately."

"Yes, Madam."

On the short ride into town, Ann Fitch worked out what she needed to do.

"Let me off at the blacksmith shop."

The carriage stopped, and Mr. Palmer helped her down. She hurried inside.

"Mrs. Fitch!" Caleb stopped hammering, put his tool down and wiped his hands on his apron. "It's a pleasure, ma'am." He gave a short bow.

"Thank you. I have a favor to ask."

"A favor? From me?" Caleb wiped his hands on his apron.

"You see, my husband has done something terribly foolish. He's dared Benjamin to work side-by-side with his men. Benjamin doesn't know anything about logging. He's never used a two-headed axe before. I'm so afraid he's going to get hurt, maybe even killed."

"How can I help?"

"You know everything there is to know about axes."

Caleb chuckled. "You flatter me, Mrs. Fitch."

"I want you to teach Benjamin how to use a double-headed axe." She clasped her hands together.

"Wouldn't it be easier to simply keep him from the logging camp?"

"He's as stubborn as his father. He's determined to show him he can do it." She tightened the tie on her coat.

"Well, then." Caleb cocked his head sideways.

"Please, Mr. Tanner. I'm begging you. I'll pay you anything you ask."

Caleb's eyebrows rose. "Anything?"

"Just name it."

"Okay. I want you to order some blue silk for a dress for Mrs. Chesney."

"For Martha?" She raised her eyebrows.

"No, for Mrs. Abigail Chesney."

"Done. When can you start?" She fidgeted.

"Today. I have more two-headed axes to deliver anyway."

"Thank you. Thank you so much. You have relieved this mother's mind." She smiled.

"I can teach, but it doesn't mean he'll get the hang of it."

"Benjamin's no fool. He's smart. He'll get it. If he wants to." She put out her hand and he shook it. Returning to the street, she was greeted by Mr. Palmer, who held the door of her carriage open. She settled inside. Her mind at ease, she could turn her attention to other tasks, like picking the right shade of blue for Mrs. Chesney's silk.

SAM RETURNED FROM DELIVERING a new pot to a customer. "Was that Mrs. Fitch's carriage?"

"It was."

"What was she doing here?"

"Nothing. Sam, sit down."

The young man settled on a stool, his gaze connected with Caleb's.

"Did I do something wrong?"

"No, son."

"I'm not your son."

"Sorry. You're right. And regarding my marriage to your mother..."

"You're not marrying my mother." Sam rose from his seat, but Caleb's strong hand on his shoulder, eased him down.

"I am. She wants to marry me and I her."

"She doesn't need you. She's got me." The boy's face clouded.

"She needs a partner, Sam. You're a great help to your mother, but she needs more."

"I can take care of her."

"You do a fine job, but you'll get married and move on. Someday you'll have a wife and children of your own."

"So, you can marry her then."

"I don't need your permission to marry her. You understand?" Caleb rested his foot on a low stool and leaned on his knee.

"Yes, you do."

"No, I don't. And she knows it. You're making it hard for her to find happiness."

"She's plenty happy."

"She will be with me once we're married. I love your mother very much. And I will do everything in my power to make her happy."

"Stop saying that!"

"You can't stop this. You'd do her a favor if you'd stop fighting her."

"You mean I'd be doing you a favor."

Caleb shook his head. "You don't understand, do you?"

"Oh, I understand. I know what you want to do to my mother."

Caleb sensed heat climbing to his cheeks. He needed to remember Sam was no child, but almost a full-fledged man in his own right. Caleb guessed Sam knew something about relations between a man and a woman.

"So this is what all the fuss is about?"

"Damn right. I'm no fool. I may be sixteen, but I know about these things."

Caleb laughed. "Oh? And what exactly do you know?"

Now it was Sam's turn to blush. "Enough."

"So you understand a man's need for a woman?"

The boy nodded.

"Well, this may surprise you, but a woman has a need for a man, too."

"No, no. I don't think so. It's all about the man."

Caleb laughed again, louder this time. "Not exactly. But you'll find out someday. If you pick the right woman."

"Don't you be tellin' me my mother has...has...those feelings for you."

"It's none of your business. Let's say she had those feelings for your father."

"That's different." Confusion clouded Sam's face.

"Why?"

"Because it is."

"It isn't, Sam. Trust me. If women didn't have those feelings, too, humans wouldn't be here anymore."

"Men force them."

"No! Never. Don't you ever force a woman!" Caleb shot up to his full height.

"I wouldn't. Saying it's what I heard."

"You heard wrong. You pick the right woman and there won't be any forcing."

Sam put his hands over his ears. Caleb gently pulled one down.

"Look, I didn't want to have this conversation with you. But you're so stubborn. Let's forget it. The wedding will go ahead, like Martha said, when the wildflowers bloom. I hope you can settle yourself to it and wish your mother happiness."

Sam bolted from the shop. Caleb sighed and shrugged. He loaded the axes for delivery in his wagon and mounted. Might as well deliver today and give Benjamin Fitch his first lesson in how to handle a two-headed axe.

As he rode to the Fitches' he thought back on what he could have said instead of what he did. Perhaps the discussion about the marriage bed should not have taken place. He shook his head. It seemed to have made everything worse, but Sam would not have relented no matter what Caleb said.

He sighed. Seemed like they would have to marry without Sam's consent or approval. Though it was the last thing he wanted, he refused to change his plans. He and Abby needed each other. Sam would have to face it sooner or later.

He pulled up outside the office and dropped off the axes then proceeded to the house. The servant who opened the door told Caleb to meet Benjamin out by the woodshed.

"My mother's forcing me to do this. I can handle an axe."

"Double-headed are different."

"Two heads. So what?"

"Not only two heads. Different purposes of each. Give it a try, Ben. If you really want to be a logger, you'll have to know how to use this and use it right."

"True. Okay."

Caleb handed an axe to Benjamin. "First. Hold it like this."

Chapter Twenty

M *arch 30*
The early spring sun warmed the air and melted the snow. The Delaware River soaked the riverbanks higher and higher, rising to meet the logs, soon to be passengers, floating down the water to Philadelphia. The swollen waterway created swift rapids, taking control of logs and debris from an early spring storm and sending them downstream faster and faster.

Fitch's logs had backed up on account of the storm. As soon as they'd wolfed down breakfast, the men gathered on the small dock where supplies were stored. The extra-long oars were stacked, ready to use to guide the logs and keep them in the center of the river, where they traveled faster and more efficiently. Fitch instructed them to control the logs, to keep them from bumping up on shore.

Long, narrow boards and nails were piled on one side. They were used to join several logs together at one end. Leather straps lay in a heap. The loggers used them to loosely bind the back end of the logs so they wouldn't split apart but could still ride with the current. Men rode these shifting rafts.

The water pooled at the eddy, making it possible to load logs on the river and then direct them to the center, where the current kicked in.

Ann Fitch stood at the tall windows in the magnificent dining room. She wrapped her shawl tighter around her to protect herself from a cool breeze from the hallway.

She trained her gaze on Lars, who directed the men. She loved watching the loggers work. Some so masterful and brave; they readily hopped on a huge log and manned the oar. Every season she prayed no one would fall in the water and drown or get crushed. So far, they had lost only a half dozen men over the years.

Watching her son approaching the river, she bit her lip. Why hadn't she put a stop to Elijah's foolish plan? Caleb had reported Benjamin had mastered the two-headed axe. She made Elijah swear not to let Benjamin ride the logs down the river. Still, her son was headstrong. He'd made up his mind whatever Josiah could do, he could do.

Josiah had words with Ben. Unable to hear what was going on, Ann rushed for the stairs. There needed to be one cool-headed person overseeing these two, and Elijah was nowhere to be seen. *Probably off tending to some stupid detail while his son was on the verge of a fight.* She huffed into her coat and burst out of the house. Fisting her skirt in each hand, she lifted it high enough to be able to run. She flew down to the shoreline and got there as things were heating up.

"Ann! What are you doing here?" Elijah stepped out of the bunkhouse.

"Are you paying attention? Your son and Josiah are having words."

Elijah turned in time to see the young men stand nose to nose.

"Your father doesn't want you ridin' logs," Josiah said.

"I can do anything you can do." Benjamin raised his chin.

"I didn't say you couldn't do it. Your father said you couldn't do it. So you ain't doin' it."

"Oh yeah?"

"Yeah. Go inside and play with your toys. This is men's work." Josiah puffed out his chest.

"Men's work? You're an ignorant farm boy. What do you know about logging?"

"'Bout as much as you."

Ann tugged on Elijah's sleeve. "Stop them. Stop them!"

"Nothing'll come of it. Hey, look! There's Caleb. Looks like he and Sam have the rest of those axes." Elijah waved.

As he and Sam unloaded the wagon, loud voices drew Ann's attention. Angry words had escalated to pushing and shoving.

"Stop!" Lars thundered. But the boys paid him no mind. "Get back!"

Josiah and Benjamin had inched closer and closer to the water's edge. Large logs were loaded into the river, hitting with a mighty splash, soaking anyone within a few feet. The recent storm had turned the dirt to mud. The water showered on the riverbank by the logs weakened the bank and made it slippery.

Ann hollered to her son. "Ben! Look out!"

But the sound of the logs hitting water and the ensuing argument drowned out her voice. She ran to Elijah.

"Do something! Do something!" She grabbed his forearm.

He turned to face the boys, who had skirted dangerously close to the edge. Caleb and Sam had stopped to watch.

"You think you're so smart?"

"Smarter than you."

As word traveled to town, a crowd had formed. Panic seized Sam as he watched his friends back up, oblivious to the drop-off right behind them. He ran full speed to save them. But he got there, right as the argument had come to blows. Josiah landed a punch on Benjamin's nose. Blood spurted forth. Ben yowled and swung at Josiah. The blow glanced off his shoulder, knocking him off balance.

Sam got there in time to pull Josiah away. Benjamin, blinded by pain, lashed out. Sam ducked, but the blow hit Josiah square in the chest, sending him over the side. As he screamed, Benjamin and Sam both reached out. They grabbed Josiah's hands. Ben yanked his rival up where he could grip the embankment. Not realizing Sam was off balance, Josiah jerked his hand from Sam's to haul himself up on land.

Sam flew into the water!

ANN FITCH SCREAMED. Caleb yanked his boots off, stripped off his pants and shirt. Bare-chested wearing only his drawers and the white scarf tied several times around his neck, he dove into the icy water.

Abigail Chesney pushed through the crowd. As Sam fell, she gasped and ran to the edge. She watched Caleb dive in. Her heart pounded double time as she covered her mouth with her hand.

Ann Fitch joined her. "Caleb will save him."

All she could think of was her heroic husband who had given his life to save their children. Would Caleb die saving Sam? The thought horrified her.

"No, no. Caleb! Sam! No, no! This can't be happening again. No." Hyperventilating, she couldn't breathe. She collapsed in a dead faint.

WHEN HIS HEAD BROKE the water, he looked frantically for Sam. Arms flailing, head bobbing above then sinking below the surface, he was in front of Caleb. The sting from the frigid water made Caleb's legs sluggish for a second. Then he sprang into action.

Charged with rescuing the boy who stood in the way of his happiness rankled Caleb for a split second only. Abby needed Sam, which was enough. He lifted one arm out of the water, then the other, and kicked his legs, the way his father had taught him.

The current carried Sam along. Slowly Caleb drew nearer to the young man. Pushing to beat the speed of the current, he stroked hard. Stopping for a second, he untied and unwrapped his long, white scarf. As he drew nearer to Sam, he called out.

"Sam! Grab the end! Tie it to your wrist!"

When Sam turned his head, Caleb saw the fear in his eyes. But Sam did what he was told. Caleb fastened his end to his own wrist. He yanked Sam closer. As they rode down the river, Caleb ducked underwater and came up behind Sam. Grabbing the neck of the boy's wet shirt in his fist, he pulled Sam up, so his head was above water.

The river carried them along at a good clip. Caleb turned on his side and tried to balance Sam on his hip. But the water was choppy, and he slipped this way and that. Caleb gathered more of the shirt in his hand, thus enabling him to steady the boy as the river took them along.

"Relax, Sam! Don't fight me. Don't grab me! Lie back."

Caleb did a sidestroke as he rode the river's current. He kept moving to keep his legs from going numb in the frigid water. He lifted his head to look ahead. They faced rapids quickly drawing near. They might be smashed against the rocks breaking the water there. Glancing behind, he saw a huge log bounding their way. They were sandwiched between two deadly prospects.

"Holy Christmas!" Caleb veered to his left, inching closer to shore. If he could grab a branch overhanging the river, maybe he could save them from getting crushed by the log. It was big and moving faster than they were.

He spied one overhanging the water. "Reach up, Sam! Grab this branch!"

He did, but it slipped through his hand, cutting the boy's palm. The log picked up speed, closing in, aimed right at them. Frantic, Caleb searched for a break in the shoreline. He saw it, up ahead. There was an inlet of some kind, but could they make it before the log smashed them into the rocks? They had to get there first. It kept bearing down on them, closing the distance between them. The cold sapped Caleb's strength. He grew weaker. Forcing panic down inside, he mustered all his strength and concentrated on swimming to the inlet.

He hooked his arm around Sam's chest and kicked his feet with his last ounce of strength. He put his head down, face in the water, and gave everything he had. He propelled them into the inlet only moments before the log, tossed up and down by the river, bounced past them. Caleb let out a breath. Raising his head, he stopped to tread water for a moment and figure out what to do.

A flat rock jutted out into the river just ahead of them. He swam to it, slowly as his legs had tired. Grasping the outcropping with his free hand, he watched the last of the big log zoom past, bobbing in the powerful current. Sam had passed out. Keeping his grip on Sam's shirt, Caleb dragged himself up on the rock first, then fished Sam out of the water.

Shouting from the shore drew his eye. A crowd had run down the riverbank to where Caleb and Sam were. Caleb saw the riverbed. He judged the water to be shallow enough to wade to shore. He jumped in then lifted Sam in his arms. Barely able to touch bottom, he walked slowly through the icy water, keeping Sam's head above the surface.

On the shore, people waited with blankets. Daniel Rhodes and Elijah Fitch loaded Caleb and Sam into the wagon, wrapped them up, and drove to the inn. Sam had not recovered consciousness. Once they arrived, Martha met them.

"Let's go. I got kettles on. Bring Sam here," she said, indicating a room on the first floor. "Sit in the dining room. By the fire. Sarah, hot tea for the man."

Barely able to speak because his teeth chattered so hard, he asked, "Where's Abby?"

ABIGAIL OPENED HER eyes. "Where am I?"

"In my house. You fainted." Ann Fitch sat by her side.

Sitting up, she removed the cloth on her forehead. "Where's Caleb? What happened to Sam? Is he alive?"

"Yes. Caleb got them to shore. Elijah and Daniel Rhodes took them to the inn."

"I must go." She pushed to her feet.

Ann turned to a servant standing by the door. "Fetch Mr. Palmer and have him bring my carriage around immediately."

"Yes, ma'am."

They were helped into the carriage, which fairly flew on its way to the inn. Abby jumped down and raced inside.

"Where's Sam?"

"Daniel's with him," Martha said.

Daniel Rhodes did the doctoring for the town as Fitch's Eddy did not have a permanent physician. Elijah stood in the doorway. She entered softly. As she knelt by Sam's bed, he opened his eyes. Blankets were piled on top of the boy, and the bed warmer had been shoved underneath the mattress. She stroked her son's face.

"Sam! Are you all right?"

"I reckon." The boy gave a small smile.

"He's got some damage from the cold, Mrs. Chesney, but it doesn't look too bad. I don't think he's going to lose any limbs or toes."

She shot a grateful look at Daniel.

"Mama, Caleb saved me."

"He did?"

"He managed to get Sam to shore, Mrs. Chesney," Elijah put in.

"Where is he?"

"In the dining room," Martha said.

"The boy needs rest, and warmth," Daniel said, rising. "I think he'll be all right."

"Thank you," she said, grasping his hand with both of hers. She pushed to her feet and hurried into the dining room.

Caleb sat close to the fire, his palms raised to the heat. A blanket tossed over his shoulders had been pulled as close as possible. His legs, bare from the knee down, were exposed to the roaring fire. The wool blanket covered his back but left most of his chest exposed. Water still dripped from his hair down his neck.

When she saw him from behind, her heart sped up. Her breath caught in her throat, and her eyes watered. As she ran to him, he turned.

"Abby, you're all right? Elijah told me you fainted." He pushed to his feet.

"Me? I'm fine. You, you, I just can't..." she broke down sobbing.

Caleb drew her to him, closing his arms around her slender frame. She sobbed into his chest, winding her arms around him, pressing her cheek to his pecs. Caleb stroked her hair, then kissed her head.

"Is Sam all right?"

Too choked up to speak, she nodded.

"Good. I'm glad."

Caleb eased down on a bench and lifted her onto his lap. He held her tight and rubbed her back. She clung to him, crying until she was spent

"It was a miracle we weren't crushed by the log." Caleb shook his head.

"What log?" She sat up straight.

"You didn't see it?"

"No."

Caleb set to explaining to her what had happened. Horrified yet fascinated, she listened.

"You could have been killed. I was worried you'd die like George did."

"Were you?" He gazed into her eyes. "So, you do love me?"

"More than I realized."

"Then we can tell folks you'll marry me when the wildflowers bloom?"

"Oh, yes. Yes, I'll marry you. Whenever you say."

A huge grin washed over Caleb's face. He kissed her.

Elijah Fitch entered the room. "Thought you might need these." He tossed the clothes Caleb had been wearing onto a chair.

"Thank you."

"Mighty fine job. Saving Sam Chesney the way you did, Tanner. Mighty fine."

"He's going to be my son soon."

"I heard. I talked to the Missus. We want you to have your wedding at our house."

"What?" Abby faced him.

Ann Fitch joined her husband. "We want to throw the wedding for you. At our home. Invite the whole town."

"Mighty kind of you. When the wildflowers bloom, they'll be ready." Martha Chesney leaned against the archway to the dining room.

HUNG BY THE FIRE TO dry, his clothes were finally fit to wear again, so Caleb dressed. Martha entered, carrying a plate of food.

"How's Sam?" He gobbled up the cheese, meat, and bread.

"I think he's going to be all right. Thank you for saving my grandson." Martha sat at the table with the blacksmith.

"Do you think he'll see me?"

Martha smiled. "Yes."

Caleb gulped down two more cups of tea before heading for Sam's room. Perched in the doorway, he watched Sam sleep. Still chilled, the blacksmith rubbed his hands together. He stared at the young man's pale face. "Will he live?"

Daniel Rhodes packed up his medical tools in a black satchel. "I think he's going to be all right. You can go in. I expect he'll wake soon."

"Thank you." He shook hands with Mr. Rhodes.

"Fine job, Mr. Tanner. Jumping in after the boy."

Caleb pulled a chair close to the bed. Sam looked innocent bundled under five wool blankets, fast asleep. He wondered if the young man might change his opinion of him now. Had the rescue made a difference? He took the boy's hand. His eyes fluttered open only for a second, but his hand squeezed Caleb's fingers gently.

Although often annoyed by Sam's hostility, when he had pulled him from the river, Caleb's heart squeezed. He didn't realize he'd developed an affection for Abby's son. He prayed Sam would recover. Perhaps he'd learned what it was like to be a real father?

AN HOUR LATER, A WEARY Abigail climbed the stairs. As she made her way through bushel baskets of apples, she tripped over a package on the floor. Bending down, she lifted the rectangular bundle, wrapped in plain cloth and tied with a thin leather strap.

"George," she whispered. She unwrapped it to reveal the snow-white silk fabric he had bought for her as a surprise. It seemed like ten years ago, not ten months. Sinking down on the floor, the shiny fabric in her lap, she brushed away tears on her cheek. What she had thought would be perfect for a wedding dress for Sarah someday, she could use now for her own wedding.

Pain seared through her as memories of him flitted through her mind. Would he object to providing material for her dress to wear when marrying another man? Guilt and sadness weighed her down. She raised her hand to her eyes, wiping away the wetness.

"I know what you're thinking." A female voice broke into her thoughts. It was Martha, leaning against the door jamb. "No, George wouldn't object to you using it for your wedding dress. He was smart. He'd want you to be taken care of, not to be alone. And he'd approve of Caleb. The man who saved his son. Go ahead, dear. Sew something wonderful. Make him proud."

She rose to hug her mother-in-law. "Thank you, Martha. I will."

Abby tucked the fabric under her arm and followed Martha down the stairs. Out of Martha's hearing, Abby raised her eyes to the heavens and whispered, "Thank you, George."

Epilogue

Caleb lifted Abby down from his wagon. He took her hand as they strolled to his home. She looked at the sky, still bright with sunlight in the late afternoon. She lifted her flowing white silk wedding gown above the grass and dirt as she accompanied him.

"The wedding was beautiful. The Fitches have a lovely home."

He nodded and kept walking. They stopped at a small table and two chairs set up on the grass. He ducked inside for a moment and came out with a small bottle and two tiny glasses.

"A toast?" He filled the glasses and took the seat next to his new wife.

Abby reached up to pluck the wildflowers from her hair. He put his hand over hers.

"Don't. Leave them. They're so pretty. Wildflowers become you."

He cupped her cheek before leaning down to kiss her. Her gaze connected with his. She saw true love shining in his eyes. Raising her glass, she spoke.

"To our new life." She drank the brandy.

"To our new life." He lifted his glass in the air, then downed the contents in one gulp.

Rising, he offered his hand. Abby stood, linked her fingers with his, and joined her new husband, finishing one journey to begin another.

THE END

About the Authors

Jean Joachim is an award-winning, USA Today best-selling romance author whose books have hit the Amazon Top 100 list in the U.S. and abroad since 2012. She writes sports romance, small town romance, big city romance, and romantic suspense.

Jean has over 60 books in ebook, print and audio. She writes fulltime, never far from her secret stash of black licorice. An avid bird and dog lover, she has a fondness for chickadees and pugs. A music lover, especially classical, she's married, has two grown sons and lives in New York City. She'd love to hear from you, email her at: sunnydaysbook@gmail.com

Find her books on her website: http://www.jeanjoachimbooks.com

A life-long student of American history, Michael Magness holds degrees in history and law from Case Western Reserve University in Cleveland, Ohio. History is his passion. Retired from business, he's an avid reader, married, father of three grown children and has one granddaughter. Michael lives with his wife Karen and his cat Sami in Brooklyn, New York. He spends his summers in Sullivan County, where Fitch's Eddy might have been so many years ago. This is Michael's first collaboration with Jean Joachim.

Coming soon,

Sarah's Dilemma

The Catskills Saga, book 2

Sam's Decision

The Catskills Saga, book 3

Other Books by Jean C. Joachim

PINE GROVE SERIES
UNPREDICTABLE LOVE
BREAK MY HEART
RENOVATING THE BILLIONAIRE
YOU BELONG TO ME
JUST ONE KISS
REWRITE THE STARS
SOME KIND OF WONDERFUL
ECHOES OF THE HEART
HEATHER & MIKE: THE ONE THAT GOT AWAY
SANDY & RAFE: SECOND PLACE HEART
LIZ & NICK: NO REGRETS
PAIGE & BILL: ONE FINE DAY
ANTHOLOGY
HOCKEY
THE FINAL SLAPSHOT
BOTTOM OF THE NINTH
DAN ALEXANDER, PITCHER
MATT JACKSON, CATCHER
JAKE LAWRENCE, THIRD BASEMAN
NAT OWEN, FIRST BASE
BOBBY HERNANDEZ, SECOND BASE
SKIP QUINCY, SHORT STOP
EXTRA INNINGS
FIRST & TEN SERIES

GRIFF MONTGOMERY, QUARTERBACK
BUDDY CARRUTHERS, WIDE RECEIVER
PETE SEBASTIAN, COACH
DEVON DRAKE, CORNERBACK
SLY "BULLHORN" BRODSKY, OFFENSIVE LINE
AL "TRUNK" MAHONEY, DEFENSIVE LINE
HARLEY BRENNAN, RUNNING BACK
OVERTIME, THE FINAL TOUCHDOWN
A KING'S CHRISTMAS
THE MANHATTAN DINNER CLUB
RESCUE MY HEART
SEDUCING HIS HEART
SHINE YOUR LOVE ON ME
TO LOVE OR NOT TO LOVE
HOLLYWOOD HEARTS SERIES
IF I LOVED YOU
RED CARPET ROMANCE
MEMORIES OF LOVE
MOVIE LOVERS
LOVE'S LAST CHANCE
LOVERS & LIARS
His Leading Lady (Series Starter)
NOW AND FOREVER SERIES
NOW AND FOREVER 1, A LOVE STORY
NOW AND FOREVER 2, THE BOOK OF DANNY
NOW AND FOREVER 3, BLIND LOVE
NOW AND FOREVER 4, THE RENOVATED HEART
NOW AND FOREVER 5, LOVE'S JOURNEY
NOW AND FOREVER, CALLIE'S STORY (prequel)
MOONLIGHT SERIES
SUNNY DAYS, MOONLIT NIGHTS
APRIL'S KISS IN THE MOONLIGHT

UNDER THE MIDNIGHT MOON
MOONLIGHT & ROSES (prequel)
LOST & FOUND SERIES
LOVE, LOST AND FOUND
DANGEROUS LOVE, LOST AND FOUND
NEW YORK NIGHTS NOVELS
THE MARRIAGE LIST
THE LOVE LIST
THE DATING LIST
STAND ALONE NOVELS
UNFORGETTABLE
SHORT STORIES
SWEET LOVE REMEMBERED
HOLIDAY HEARTS
CHAMPAGNE FOR CHRISTMAS
CHRISTMAS DUET
HANUKKAH HEARTS
SANTA'S SURPRISE
THE FINAL SLAPSHOT
THE HOUSE-SITTER'S CHRISTMAS
THE HOUSE-SITTER'S COUNTRY CHRISTMAS
TUFFER'S CHRISTMAS WISH
HANUKKAH HEARTS COLLECTION

Made in the USA
Middletown, DE
09 December 2020

27050000R00150